THE CORPSE IN THE CELLAR

A 1930s MURDER MYSTERY

THE CORPSE IN THE CELLAR

A 1930s MURDER MYSTERY

Kel Richards

Marylebone House

Originally published in Australia in 2013
as *C.S. Lewis and the Body in the Basement*
by Strand Publishing

First published in Great Britain in 2015

Marylebone House
36 Causton Street
London SW1P 4ST
www.marylebonehousebooks.co.uk

British Library Cataloguing-in-Publication Data
A catalogue record for this book is available from the British Library

ISBN 978–1–910674–17–8
eBook ISBN 978–1–910674–18–5

Manufacture managed by Jellyfish
First printed in Great Britain by CPI
Subsequently digitally printed in Great Britain

eBook by Midland Typesetters, Australia

Produced on paper from sustainable forests

THE TIME: The summer of 1933; Trinity Term has just ended at Oxford University.

THE PLACE: Somewhere in Cambridgeshire, not far from the County of Midsomer.

ONE

~

'Jack! Your wallet's fallen into the fire!' I shouted as I leaped forward and grabbed a pair of fire tongs. 'I don't know how long it's been there,' I grunted as I fished in among the burning logs and pulled out the black and crisp leather remains.

'How did it fall into the fire?' muttered Warnie, who through this wallet-rescuing rush had not shifted from his position leaning against the end of the mantelpiece. 'The last time I saw it,' he said, 'was when I paid for our tea.'

The teapot, surrounded by cups and saucers, still sat on a small table near the fireplace. We'd ordered the tea while the pub prepared our breakfast. And Warnie had used his brother's wallet to pay for the tea.

Warnie looked like a goggle-eyed goldfish swimming around its bowl looking for a way out. 'And then I sat the wallet on the mantelpiece,' he said in a dazed sort of way.

'Perhaps not the safest place for it, old chap,' said Jack gently.

'Oh . . . oh, yes . . . see what you mean,' Warnie mumbled as he took a sip from the large tea cup in his hand. 'Ah, sorry about that, Jack.'

Warnie now looked both stunned and wary—like a cat that's just been hit by a half-brick and thinks another might be on the way.

Jack said nothing but nudged the still smouldering wallet with the toe of his boot a bit further away from the flames.

The pub was *The Cricketers' Arms* in the village of Plumwood. It was the first stop on our walking holiday. We'd chosen it as our starting point so that I could call into Plumwood Hall, the country home of Sir William Dyer, whose library I had undertaken to catalogue.

The day before I'd met the owner of Plumwood Hall for the first time. He turned out to be a thin man with a face like an untrustworthy monkey—the sort of monkey other monkeys would never lend money to. However, on this occasion he was offering to fork over some of the folding stuff, albeit a modest amount, so we had shaken hands on an agreement: me in my capacity as an unemployed recent graduate of Oxford University, and Sir William as the vastly wealthy manufacturer of *Dyer's Digestive Biscuits* who had recently purchased the ancestral home of an impoverished baronet, including its large, and largely mysterious, library.

The wallet had now cooled enough to be touched and Jack picked it up. The leather was charred black, and when he opened it he found the notes it contained reduced to ashes.

'Oh dear me,' said Warnie, setting down his tea cup with a nervous clatter as if feeling the second half-brick hit. 'Oh dear . . . Oh dear . . . that was all the money for our holiday, wasn't it?' he muttered, looking embarrassed.

'All in notes,' Jack confirmed, 'no coins.' In the gloomy tone that Jack adopted for all things financial he added, 'Bankruptcy looms.' Then seeing his brother's woebegotten face he added, 'Cheer up, old chap. These things happen.'

'But how will we pay for things?' Warnie asked. 'I'm not carrying any money.'

'I can pay for our accommodation here,' I volunteered, 'and for breakfast.'

'Very kind of you, young Morris,' said Jack. 'And I'll call into the nearest branch of the Capital and Counties Bank and make a withdrawal from my savings account.'

'Where is the nearest branch of . . . whatever bank you said?' I asked.

'In Market Plumpton,' Jack said, 'a comfortable two hours walk from here.' I was about to ask how he knew, but he anticipated my question by continuing, 'I was in this district last year—on a walking holiday with Tollers and Dyson. I called into the Market Plumpton branch then.'

'Your breakfast is ready, gentlemen,' said the publican, walking into the room from the back parlour. 'I've served it up in the snug . . . if you'll follow me.'

Our unhappy adventure with Jack's wallet had happened in the front bar parlour of *The Cricketers' Arms*, so we now followed our host, one Alfred Rose by name, out to the small back private bar called the snug. There we found a table set for three, and three full English breakfasts already served and waiting.

'This'll cheer us up at any rate,' grunted Warnie as he settled himself in his seat. 'Eggs, bacon, sausages, toast—even some black pudding. That's what I call a proper breakfast.'

And for the next few minutes we were fully occupied breaking our fast.

When mine host Alfred Rose returned, he was carrying a fresh pot of tea. The publican had a white, puffy face—rather like a lump of dough that had been sat on the windowsill to rise and was now about ready for the oven. It always felt slightly surprising when the puffy dough opened a mouth, smiled broadly and began to speak.

'And what are your plans for the day, gentlemen?' he asked in the hearty voice, and with the broad grin, of the professional publican.

'We're walking to Market Plumpton,' I replied.

'Well, don't follow the road,' Alfred suggested. 'There's a much more direct walking path over the hills and along the ridge top. Much more pleasant walking too,' he added. 'I'll give you directions for finding the path when you're ready to leave.'

He poured out fresh cups of tea for all of us, and then said, 'But I thought you were heading north today. Why Market Plumpton?'

'We have to call in to the bank,' Jack explained as he finished the last of his egg and toast. 'There's a branch of the Capital and Counties Bank in Market Plumpton.'

The publican stopped pouring the tea and an earnest look came over his face, rather like a black cloud passing over the face of the sun. Shaking his head sadly he said, 'Rather you than me, gentlemen.'

'Why?' I asked. 'What on earth can be wrong with a bank? Or is it Market Plumpton itself you object to?'

'No, no, it's not the town. Lovely little market town it is. No, it's the bank. That building has a dark history.'

'What sort of dark history?' asked Warnie, his words muffled by a mouthful of bacon.

'Murder,' hissed Alfred Rose as if whispering a dreadful secret in the manner of a stage villain in an overacted melodrama. 'Murder—and a ghost.'

He was clearly dying to tell us the story so Jack invited him to do so.

The landlord set down the teapot, seated himself in a spare chair and leaned forward, his elbows on the table, his puffy face now flushed with colour and his small, black eyes shining like currants in the dough.

'That bank is in a building that was once an old Georgian terrace house. Built as a gentleman's residence it was,' he began with the relish of a storyteller savouring a well-loved tale. 'Some eighty or so years ago the owner was a certain Sir Rafael Black, a wool merchant. An awful man he was, a violent drunkard, rapidly working his way through his family fortune. His poor young wife, Lady Pamela, was terrified of him. He was a brutal man. Well, they do say that she took comfort in the arms of a handsome young footman.'

'Do they say what this young footman's name was?' I asked. Having an interest in folklore, I wanted to see how much detail was included in this particular tale.

'They say his Christian name was Boris, but I've never heard of any surname being mentioned. Anyway, Sir Rafael discovered the dalliance between Lady Pamela and this young Boris. He had been drinking heavily all day, as was his wont, and he now fell into a drunken rage. The terrified footman sought refuge in the cellar of the house. Sir Rafael raged around the house waving a cavalry sword and searching for young Boris. Now this sword, or so they say, was a razor sharp sabre, so Boris did well to keep out of the way. But eventually Sir Rafael made his way down to the cellar, and there he found Boris.'

'And this is where the murder comes in?' said Warnie, taking up another slice of hot buttered toast and spooning on marmalade as if the world was about to run out of the stuff and he had to get his share while he could.

'Exactly, sir. With Lady Pamela standing on the stairs and screaming for him to stop, Sir Rafael butchered poor Boris with that wickedly sharp sabre. Then seeing the dead body lying there in front of him seemed to sober him up. He realised what he'd done, and the consequences he'd face if caught. He forced his wife, trembling and sobbing with fear, to help him dig a hole in the cellar floor and bury the body.'

'Nasty business,' I remarked, pouring another cup of tea.

The publican nodded in agreement. 'From that day on Lady Pamela would wake in the middle of the night with violent, screaming nightmares. In due course she was dispatched to her relatives in Scotland to recover her sanity. With his wife gone, and perhaps from guilt over what he'd done, Sir Rafael descended even further into drink. Well, gentlemen, exactly one year after the night of the murder, one year to the very day, Sir Rafael was well into his cups when he dispatched his butler to the cellar to fetch yet another bottle of brandy. As the butler went down those cellar steps with a candle in his hand, he swears he saw a ghost—the ghost of the murdered man—and it was pointing at the floor. The terrified butler dropped the bottle of brandy he was carrying. It smashed loudly, and the brandy ran down the cellar stairs. Sir Rafael heard the sound and bawled murderous threats against the butler for "wasting good liquor". Then he dismissed the man from his service on the spot, with no notice and no good character.'

Alfred Rose drew a deep breath and continued, 'Of course this meant that the butler had no further loyalty to Sir Rafael. If anything, the very reverse. So the next morning he went in secret to the town magistrates and told them what he'd seen in the cellar: the ghost of the missing footman, pointing at the floor. The magistrates ordered the cellar floor dug up. What they found was the remains of the murdered footman, and the cavalry sword with Sir Rafael's coat of arms on the hilt buried beside him. Sir Rafael Black was charged with the murder and hanged.'

Jack smiled knowingly and asked, 'But that wasn't the end of the matter, was it, Alfred?'

'Indeed not, sir. From that day to this the ghost has reappeared once every year, on the anniversary of the murder. When the building was taken over by the bank, the old coal hole into the cellar was closed up, and the strongroom, the vault, was built into the back part of the basement—but that didn't stop the ghost. Over the years quite a few bank tellers or clerks who've gone down into that cellar on the anniversary of the murder have rushed back out again, their faces as white as a sheet, saying they'd seen the ghost.'

Alfred shook his head and added, 'I take the bus into Tadminster to do my banking. I'd never walk into that bank, gentlemen—never.'

'Jolly entertaining story,' chuckled Warnie. 'I must remember that—tell it to the chaps in the mess when I go back to barracks. But tell me this, landlord: surely this bank building you're so nervous about is perfectly safe for 364 days of the year? If the story is just as you tell it, the ghost will lie silently in its grave, or wherever it is ghosts lie, and only pop out on the one day each year.'

'That's the problem, isn't it?' gushed Alfred Rose, leaning forward over the table. 'Once a place is haunted . . . well, you never can tell. Best to keep away, that's what I say.'

'Tell us more about this annual "haunting day", Mr Rose,' I said. 'When exactly is the anniversary of this murder? When is the ghost due to make its annual appearance?'

'Well, as it happens, sir,' the publican replied, after clearing his throat, hesitating for a moment and glancing wildly around the room, as if looking for a way to avoid what was coming next, 'as it happens . . . it's today.'

TWO

~

As we slipped our rucksacks onto our backs in the warm morning sunshine outside *The Cricketers' Arms*, I said to Jack and Warnie, 'A colourful piece of local folklore, but not all that original.'

'You're saying it didn't happen?' asked Warnie.

'Something happened,' I replied. 'But a grim murder is fertile ground for growing colourful imaginary flowers.'

'If you say so,' Warnie muttered, half to himself. 'But I've heard some rum stories in the army—dashed rum. Now, which way did the landlord say we should head to find this walking track?'

'Down this road out of the village,' said Jack, pointing with the stick he always carried on a rambling holiday, 'then across a farmer's field and through a wood to the crown of the hill.'

The morning sun was as warm as a teapot and as yellow as butter as we started out. White clouds like inverted snowy hilltops drifted lazily across the sky, as if they were finding the morning so pleasant they were in no hurry to go anywhere. A gentle breeze followed us down the lane, politely offering to cool us if we found the walk too warming.

The first few minutes were spent in silence as we looked for the landmarks Alfred Rose had told us to watch for. Then, just beyond the last cottage at the end of the village, we saw the stile that would take us over a fence and into the field beyond.

My two companions were the Lewis brothers: Warren, known as Warnie, a major in the British Army, and my old university tutor C. S. Lewis, known since childhood to all his friends as Jack. It was Jack's suggestion that I join them on this holiday, and that we start at the site of my job interview with Sir William Dyer by spending our first night in the village of Plumwood.

Jack was dressed as he always was: an old grey Harris Tweed jacket with leather patches in the elbows; trousers of thickish grey flannel, uncreased and very out at the knees; sturdy brown walking boots; and an old grey felt hat. With his ruddy, cheerful face he looked like a farmer who'd be happy to stop for a chat about the weather and price of sheep.

When he was walking in the country, Jack always carried a stout ash stick. I was never sure whether this solid implement was just a walking stick to lean on over rough ground or also a weapon to beat off possible attackers. Jack was the mildest of men, but his stick looked to me more like an Irish cudgel than an aid to walking.

Even when dressed in mufti Warnie managed to make his tweeds as neat as a uniform, and kept his handkerchief in the cuff of his jacket, in the military fashion. As an impoverished student I was wearing my baggy flannels and an old sleeveless pullover. And, having shared digs with students who were often careless of other people's property, my haversack had my name, 'Tom Morris', carefully stencilled down one side.

Across the field we walked ankle-deep through lush green grass scattered here and there with buttercups greeting the morning sun. On the far side of the field a small herd of cows had their heads down, eating their breakfast, studiously ignoring our presence. 'Ramblers,' they seemed to be thinking, 'another lot of ramblers—can't see the point in all this walking.' And they kept on eating.

The rhythmic action of those bovine jaws matched our steady walking pace—which freed my mind to do some rambling of its own. I don't know if you've had my experience where walking seems to stimulate thinking: the steady rhythm of the feet seems to set the synapses firing. Under this stimulation I decided to tackle my former tutor about a book he had just published.

'I've read *Pilgrim's Regress*, Jack,' I said. 'Most enjoyable.'

'Ah, but did you understand it?' he asked with glee. 'The thing about allegory is that either you provide a key, in which case there's no point in writing allegory, or you don't and run the risk of being misunderstood, or of simply baffling the reader.'

'The point you were making,' I said, rising to his bait, 'was that if thinking and feeling are kept in balance—that is, if we don't become dry-as-dust intellectuals on the one hand or get sucked into a swamp of self-indulgent feelings on the other—then we will end up in religion. That is where the balanced life, taken to its proper conclusion, leads.'

'Well done, young Morris,' he chortled. 'You still know how to read a text. And how did you weigh up my conclusion?'

'I found it very narrow-minded,' I replied with a sly grin, deliberately appealing to Jack's fighting spirit, knowing there was nothing he liked better than a broadside attack.

Jack chuckled with delight at the prospect of a lively debate. 'Well, the right path is often like that. Indeed, it's often like the path we're on right now—quite narrow. That doesn't make it the wrong path; it just makes it a narrow one.'

'Now Jack,' I protested, 'you know perfectly well I'm not the least bit religious. I don't have a spiritual bone in my body. And your implication that anyone who's not religious has missed the whole point of life and is on entirely the wrong track . . . well, even you must admit that's decidedly narrow-minded and exclusive.'

'So your mind is closed on that subject?' His great, booming voice carried a lilt of laughter.

'No, the boot is on entirely the other foot. It's you who have the closed mind. Your Christian exclusivism—for that's what it is—is preposterous. More than that, it's offensive.'

'Go on, young Morris, go on. Lecture me on the subject. In what way am I being both offensive and preposterous at the same time?'

'By insisting that there is one true, proper goal at the end of every life's journey, a goal that some find and others miss out on. In a world as diverse and complex as this, that simply cannot be true. Everyone's journey through life is different.'

'So you object to the claim that there's a universal truth that can be found and felt and thought about rationally?'

'That's it!' I cried. 'That's exactly it. It's that expression "a universal truth" I find offensive.'

By now we'd reached the end of the field. Warnie unlatched the gate and we all trooped through. When I, as the last, went to walk on, Jack hurried back to close and latch the gate.

'Must be considerate to the farmers whose fields we walk through,' muttered Warnie as he once again took the lead. The path now led us through a sparse woodland of scattered trees and small bushes on a steadily increasing upward incline.

Jack paused to light his pipe, puffing great blue clouds of smoke around his head, and then resumed our debate.

'You're annoyed,' he said between puffs, 'by what you see as my claim to have discovered where real truth and purpose and satisfaction can be found.'

'That's it,' I gasped, stumbling over a knotted tree root. 'It's the claim that one way of understanding the world is right and all the other ways are wrong that's simply preposterous. Truth cannot be unique and exclusive in that way.'

'Oh, but it can. If I say there's only one Statue of Liberty in New York Harbour, I am making a very narrow truth claim, but I'm quite right for there is only one. And if I say there's only one correct way of doing the eight times table, again I'm right. If you attempt to do calculations using the eight times table and you arbitrarily change some of the numbers to suit your tastes, you'll get your sums wrong.'

Whether Lewis was right or wrong he could always argue well. I had found these rapid logical strides of his frustrating when he was my tutor, mainly because I could never quite keep up. There had been moments in our discussions of medieval literature when I felt I was slogging through a valley while he was leaping from peak to peak. Now he was doing it again.

'Hang on a bit,' I complained. 'Slow down there. I think that was a bit tricky.'

Jack hooted with laughter. 'The hand was quicker than the eye, was it?'

I concentrated for a moment and then said, 'It was the comparisons that were wrong. The Statue of Liberty and the eight times table are very precise, specific things. What is not, and cannot be, neat and precise like that is the way we look at the world, what the Germans call our world view, our philosophy of life, our framework through which we interpret the world . . . what's their word?'

'*Weltanschauung*,' supplied Jack. 'But we don't need a German word. We know perfectly well what we're talking about in plain English. And we're not talking about technical or academic philosophy here; we're simply talking about how you look at life—what you think it's all about, where you think you're going and what you think matters. In that sense everyone has a world view, from professors to plumbers to pastry cooks.'

'Yes,' I agreed hesitantly. 'And sometimes we want to stand back and ask ourselves if our way of looking at the world is right—'

'Or whether it's wrong,' Jack leaped in. 'So, you see, a world view can be either right or wrong. And I am proposing that there's one way of looking at the world that sees it rightly while all the others see it slightly out of focus or distorted in some way.'

We came out of the wood and ahead of us was a grass-covered slope up to the crown of a hill. As the path became steeper, we ceased talking until we reached the high point. Here we stopped to catch our breath.

Laid out before us were the rolling green hills and valleys of England. High hedges marked where the roads cut through the valleys and wound around the hills. In the distant fields were tiny animals that looked like miniatures that had spilled out of a child's toy Noah's Ark. The occasional car or truck or motorbike on those winding country roads looked like the toy tin cars I played with on the nursery floor as a child.

Below us, but still some distance away, was the small market town that was our destination. It was laid out like a collection of wooden blocks from a toy box, painted to look like buildings. Snaking around it was a silvery river fed by streams from the low hills beyond the town. Crossing the river on an iron bridge and plunging into the town was a ruler-straight railway line. A train was crossing the bridge as we looked—half a dozen carriages pulled by a small locomotive that puffed grey smoke and white steam into the morning air.

Between the foot of the hill below us and the town was a patchwork of farms and fields. In one of those fields a tractor was pulling a plough, leaving a feathery cloud of brown dust trailing behind it. Immediately in front of us was a ridge of high land we could follow to the outskirts of the town.

'Now, Jack,' I said, turning around to find his ruddy farmer's face only a few feet away, 'this business of you claiming that Christianity is exclusively true and every other view of the world is wrong—'

'Is that what I'm saying?' he asked with a teasing tone in his voice.

'Yes. Therefore—'

'And how does that differ from anyone else's point of view?'

'It's being exclusive. Narrow.'

'And it's exactly the same claim that everyone makes. You, for instance, young Morris, have a world view I take it?'

'Yes, I've thought things through and I am now a convinced atheist.'

'As I once was. My book, as you discovered for yourself, is the story of my journey from atheism, to philosophical idealism, to theism, to Christianity told as an allegory. And the reason you currently hold to atheism, Morris, old chap, is because you believe atheism to be true.'

'Of course,' I jumped in to reply quickly. 'If it wasn't true there wouldn't be any reason to believe it.'

'And that,' said Jack, pausing to relight his pipe, 'is exactly the same for everyone. Every serious way of looking at the world and thinking about the world is believed to be true. All claims to truth are exclusive claims. So the problem with Christianity is not whether it's guilty of exclusivism or not, but whether it's true.'

THREE

~

The streets of Market Plumpton had not been laid out for motor cars. Much of the town appeared to be Elizabethan, judging from the appearance of the oldest buildings, and seemed to have been designed for a fat cow to be walked through the streets—but only one fat cow at a time, and not very fat either.

The local landowner who commissioned the building of the place, centuries before, can't have been too happy at the time. 'But this is not what it looked like on the plans!' he would have protested. 'The streets looked much wider.'

'Ah well, your lordship,' the builder would have explained. 'There was a problem with the supplies—something to do with too much rain in the clay pits of Cornwall. And then, of course, the Street Pavers' Guild withdrew from negotiations. You know how it is. We just had to make do.'

And his lordship would probably have responded with a round collection of Elizabethan abuse: 'thou bolting-hutch of beastliness, thou swollen parcel of dropsies, thou huge bombard of sack, thou stuffed cloak-bag of guts' and so on. They had a lovely line in invective in those days. But the result was the series of narrow streets though which we now walked.

As we made our way towards the centre of the small town, Warnie remarked, 'There's no way two cars could pass in a street like this.' And he shook his head at the sad lack of foresight, or cheapskate cost-cutting, on the part of the town's medieval forefathers.

As if to make his point, at that moment an Austin Seven drove down the street and we three had to step hastily onto the narrow footpath and flatten ourselves against the wall of the nearest terrace house. The small car occupied the entire road width.

At the end of the street we stepped out into the town square. It was paved from side to side with ancient, well-worn cobblestones. On three of its sides were shops and offices, and on the fourth was the town church standing in its churchyard. This was built from blocks of warm, honey-coloured stone, and beside it was a free-standing bell tower.

Jack gazed around and said, 'Over there. That's the place.'

We walked in the direction he indicated. It was clear that this was the building Alfred Rose had told us about: a Georgian gentleman's terrace house now converted to bank offices.

We climbed the three steps up from the street and entered through the open front door. To one side was an impressive staircase leading to the upper levels, while immediately in front of us was an area obviously designed for customers: straight-backed chairs against the walls and under the front window a desk littered with blank bank forms. Facing the window was a counter that divided the staff from the customers.

There was the usual hushed and sacred silence so often found in a bank, telling us we had stepped into the modern world's most holy place: the Temple of Mammon. And, as always in a bank, the moment I stepped through the front door I felt as if I was invading their privacy.

The bank was empty except for two staff members. In the teller's cage behind the counter was a large, beefy young man, looking more like a farmhand than an office worker. According to the gold-lettered sign on the counter in front of him he was 'Franklin Grimm, Teller'. Behind him, in the small office area, a young woman tapped in a desultory way at a typewriter.

'Good morning,' said Jack, stepping up to the counter and whipping off his hat. 'I'd like to make a withdrawal please.'

'Certainly, sir,' said the teller in a cold voice that suggested he was never in favour of money being taken out of the bank. 'Do you have an account with us?'

'Not with this branch,' Jack explained, 'with your Oxford branch, but I do have my passbook with me.' As he spoke he pulled off his rucksack and fished in its depths. After a moment of fumbling he produced a small, blue-covered booklet which he handed to the teller.

Franklin Grimm opened this and perused its contents with a look of deep suspicion on his face. The lengthy silence that followed was broken only by the quiet clattering of the typewriter.

'So your account is actually with the Oxford branch of the bank then, sir?' was the question that finally emerged from the sceptical teller. He had finally deduced this astonishing fact from Jack's reference to Oxford and from the word "Oxford" appearing in large letters on the front of the passbook.

'Correct.'

'Do you have any identification on you, sir?'

'What sort of identification?'

'A passport, driver's licence, anything of that sort.'

'Do I need something of that sort?' asked Jack with a note of surprise in his voice.

'Well, sir,' said Franklin Grimm with a coldly superior sneer, 'how can I be certain that you are indeed the person whose name appears in the front of this passbook?'

'What nonsense!' snorted Warnie. 'This is definitely Jack. Tom Morris here and I can both swear to it. I'm his brother—known him all his life.'

'So,' continued the teller, 'you're assuring me that this man is your friend and brother Jack?'

'Exactly!' said Warnie, blowing out his cheeks in indignation.

'Well, that does present me with a problem, sir,' said Grimm, 'since the name in the front of this book is not Jack Lewis, or even John Lewis, but Clive Staples Lewis.'

'Yes!' insisted Warnie, becoming quite heated. 'That's him.'

'Clive Staples Lewis is also Jack Lewis?'

'Yes . . . well . . .' Warnie suddenly saw the problem. 'When he was quite a small child he told the family that he didn't like his name and wanted to be called Jack. And he has been ever since.'

Another silence followed this explanation with the teller slowly turning over the pages of the passbook. Finally he looked up and said to Jack, 'Do you have any paperwork at all, sir, in the name of C. S. Lewis?'

'Not on me, no,' Jack admitted. 'All I have in my rucksack, apart from that passbook, is clean clothing and my sponge bag. And in my pockets . . .'

With these words he patted his pockets and produced the contents. 'Just my pipe and tobacco pouch and a couple of books.' Jack set on the counter two small volumes: the Oxford World Classics edition of *Palgrave's Golden Treasury* in its blue cloth binding, and a compact Bible, printed in small type on what used to be called rice paper.

'Hang on,' I volunteered, and digging into my jacket pocket I produced the book I was carrying: *The Pilgrim's Regress* by C. S. Lewis. I waved it in Jack's direction and said, 'That's him, you see—the author.'

'I see,' said Franklin Grimm very slowly. 'So you have a book written by this C. S. Lewis and a savings bank passbook belonging to the same man, but no other identification?'

'I was here last year,' Jack boomed, becoming slightly annoyed by this farrago of nonsense, 'when I was passing through on another walking holiday. On that occasion I dealt with the manager. He may well recognise me. If, that is, the same man is still the manager here.'

'Mr Ravenswood has been here for six years, sir,' said the teller.

'That's the man,' Jack said with delight. 'I remember the name—Ravenswood. Just wheel him out of his office, my good man. I'm sure he'll recognise me.'

The teller turned and said to the young woman at the typewriter, 'Is Mr Ravenswood in his office, Ruth?'

'No, Mr Grimm,' she replied. 'He's down in the cellar doing the quarterly maintenance.'

The teller turned back to us and said with a smarmy smile, 'Perhaps you'd care to wait until Mr Ravenswood is available?'

'Take me down to him in the cellar,' said Jack in that great voice of his that could fill an Oxford lecture hall. 'He just needs to take a glance at me and authorise the withdrawal, that's all.'

Franklin Grimm suddenly looked undecided. Clearly he felt keenly the superiority of the bank officer over the mere customer, but Jack carried so much authority in his manner and his voice that the teller was now uncertain how far he could take this.

He reached his decision, coming down on the side of safety. 'If you'd step through this counter flap, sir, I'll take you down to Mr Ravenswood in the cellar.'

As he spoke he stepped out of his teller's cage and raised the counter flap beside it.

Jack entered the office behind the counter and followed the teller towards a door in the far wall. Warnie and I glanced at each other and decided, pretty much simultaneously, not to be left behind. So we followed them.

The young woman looked up, startled by our entry into the sacred ground of the bank's office. She was too stunned to speak. She just sat there with her mouth open, looking like a cod in a fish shop window—a cod who was clearly waiting for either an explanation or an apology.

The door at the rear of the office opened onto a steep flight of steps that led down into a dimly lit cellar. In fact, the only light came from a single naked light globe dangling on the end of a piece of flex in the centre of the room.

'Mr Ravenswood? Sir?' called out Franklin Grimm. Facing us was a solid brick wall with a large steel vault door set into it. This was standing ajar, and, in response to the teller's call, a man emerged from the strongroom behind the steel door. He was a large, solidly built man with a puffy, red face. He was wearing a business shirt but no jacket and his tie was slightly askew. As he emerged he was wiping his hands on an oily rag.

'Yes, what is it, Grimm?' he growled. But before the teller could reply he saw the rest of us—Jack standing beside the teller and Warnie and me on the stairs.

'Who are these people? And what are they doing here? Did you bring them down into the cellar? That's against bank policy!'

This prompted Grimm to look over his shoulder and become aware of our presence. 'You two, go back upstairs!' he snapped. Warnie responded by leaning his elbow on the railing of the stairway, making it clear that he had no intention of moving. I felt the same: I was neither an employee nor a customer of the bank, and saw no reason to snap to attention and follow orders.

A look of frustration and helplessness swept over Grimm's face. He turned back to his manager and indicated Jack standing by his side. 'This man wishes to make a withdrawal from his passbook account, sir. But his account is with the Oxford branch and he has no identification. He says that you might recognise him from a visit last year.'

'Step into the light, if you please, sir,' said Ravenswood. Jack moved to stand immediately under the circle of yellow light thrown by the one light globe. 'I have seen your face before . . . you were with a party of hikers or ramblers . . . from Oxford, if I recall.'

'The name is Lewis,' said Jack. Then he turned to Grimm and asked, 'Is that sufficient identification?'

'Should I . . .' Grimm began to ask, but Ravenswood interrupted him to say, 'Yes, yes, yes, let him withdraw whatever he wishes against his passbook.'

While this was going on, Warnie was looking the staircase up and down. 'This is the place,' he said quietly to me.

'What place?' I asked.

'This must be where Lady Pamela stood, screaming, as she watched Sir Rafael Black butcher her boyfriend, Boris the footman.' Then pointing at the floor below us he added, 'That must be where the poor blighter was buried.'

Jack having obtained his authorisation, we all turned to troop back up the stairs. But before we could take our first step, the door above us was thrust open and a young man burst in. His explosive arrival set us on a path that was to lead to violence and murder.

FOUR

~

'Ravenswood!' shouted the young man, spotting the manager. 'You're the one! Don't turn around and go back into the strong-room. You'll answer to me!'

With these words he bounded down the stairs, pushing Warnie and me roughly to one side. Franklin Grimm stepped forward to block the newcomer's path. They were both beefy young men with the build of rugby backs.

'Mr Proudfoot!' said Grimm firmly. 'You're not allowed in the cellar.'

The two of them stood toe-to-toe for a moment, glaring at each other. 'I'm not leaving until I've spoken to Ravenswood, so either stand aside or I'll knock you aside,' growled the visitor.

'There's no need for violence,' said the manager. 'I'll speak to Mr Proudfoot alone. You take these other gentlemen back upstairs, Mr Grimm.'

The teller stepped out of the way of the angry young man and slowly, with backward glances over his shoulder, as if doubtful that he was doing the right thing, walked towards the foot of the stairs.

Angry young Mr Proudfoot advanced towards Ravenswood with both hands clenched into fists and his muscles tensed. The manager stood his ground.

'I'm not going to hit you, Ravenswood,' hissed Proudfoot through tightly clenched teeth. 'I'd like to thrash you until you're bleeding and broken, but . . . I'm not going to do that.'

He stopped speaking and breathed heavily, as if making a massive effort at self-control. He looked like a man who had a dozen angry bulldogs snarling inside his chest, and he was pulling hard on their leash to keep them under control. Those of us standing on the stairs were riveted by this drama and stood frozen where we were.

'If I gave in to my emotions,' Proudfoot continued, 'if I did what I feel like doing to you, I'd end up in a police court on an assault charge. And I'm not going to give you that satisfaction.'

There was another long, tense silence, and then Proudfoot resumed, 'You're going to be the one who ends up in the police court, Ravenswood—not me.'

The bank manager swallowed hard and then said, 'I have no idea what you're talking about.'

'You're a cool customer, I'll give you that,' growled Proudfoot with barely controlled fury. 'But you know you're a worm, a snake, something less than a human being. You're something disgusting that belongs in the gutter.'

As these words were spat out, Franklin Grimm started to move back down the stairs as if to intervene, but Jack laid a restraining hand on his arm and shook his head. I could see what Jack was thinking: namely that an intervention by a third party might only inflame an already volatile situation.

'All the way here I've been thinking about how you've got away with it,' Proudfoot said in a voice just above a whisper, 'and I think there must be evidence . . . evidence that could be found . . . a trail of some sort . . . oh, yes Ravenswood . . . I'm not going to hit you . . . but I want you to know that I'm going to the police . . . and to your head office . . . and to my solicitor

. . . and you will lose your job . . . your career . . . that's why I'm not thrashing you now . . . because I want *you* behind bars . . . not me.'

This speech came out in machine gun bursts of words, with breathy, panting gaps in between. Proudfoot was clearly having great difficulty controlling his violent emotions.

'Now look here, Proudfoot,' Ravenswood said. 'I have no idea what you're talking about—'

'Shut up! I won't listen to your lies! I'm not interested in what you say . . . so I suggest you say nothing.'

As he spoke these words Proudfoot raised his fists again, and Ravenswood responded by remaining silent while stepping back half a pace. A look of sheer terror flickered for the barest moment across the bank manager's stony face.

'Your world is about to come crashing down, Ravenswood,' said Proudfoot. 'The sky is about to fall on you. I just wanted the pleasure of coming here and looking you in the face while I told you that.'

With those words he turned and took a step towards the foot of the stairs. It looked as if he was about to leave. But then his self-control snapped.

He spun around; in two swift paces he rushed forward, seized Ravenswood by the shoulders and thrust him in through the open vault door. Then Proudfoot pushed the heavy door closed as easily as you or I would close the cover of a book. He quickly pushed the locking levers into place and spun the dials of the combination lock.

'There,' growled Proudfoot with satisfaction, 'let him sit in there for a while and think about his future.' Then he charged past us up the stairs, brushing us out of the way as he went.

The four of us stood in the cellar in stunned silence. We had witnessed a scene of high drama, but it was not at all clear what it was about.

When Franklin Grimm showed no signs of moving, Warnie muttered gently, 'You'd better let your boss out of the vault, young man.'

The teller blinked as if waking from a deep sleep and muttered in a stunned and hushed voice, 'I can't.'

'Can't?' asked Warnie.

'I don't have the combination.'

'Then who does?' I asked, with my usual flair for asking the obvious.

'The only person in this branch who knows the combination is Mr Ravenswood, and he's . . .' He gestured helplessly at the locked steel door. 'It's bank policy. Only the manager knows the combination of the vault.'

'Not a very sensible system,' said Jack. 'Surely there's someone else—'

'Not in this branch,' Grimm interrupted irritably. 'Bank policy, I tell you. I'll have to telephone to our regional office in Tadminster.'

'And they'll tell you the combination over the phone?' I asked.

'No,' said Grimm, shaking his head. 'Against bank policy. They'll have to send someone on the first train—one of the district managers who knows the combination for this branch.'

'But, my dear chap,' protested Warnie, 'your manager is—'

'I know! I know!' snapped Grimm. 'But the strongroom is large and there's plenty of air. And there's an electric light in there. Mr Ravenswood won't be happy, but he should be all right and perfectly safe until someone arrives to let him out.'

Then he waved us towards the stairs and bustled into activity. 'Come on, come on. We all need to get back upstairs. I need to make that phone call.'

'And we all know why,' muttered Warnie, almost under his breath, as we trooped back upstairs.

'Why?' I asked in a half-whispered question.

'Bank policy,' enunciated Warnie slowly, turning around to grin at me.

Back in the office Franklin Grimm grabbed the nearest telephone and dialled a number. When it was answered he asked for a Mr Johnson and rapidly explained the situation.

Putting down the phone and turning to us, he said, 'He'll catch the first train. Or at least one of the managers will. Should be here by the middle of the afternoon.'

We were all standing around the inner office, being watched with wide-eyed astonishment by the girl at the typewriter, who had heard Grimm's telephoned explanation of what had just happened.

'Ruth,' he said, 'you should never have let Proudfoot into the cellar.'

'I didn't,' the girl protested, tears welling in her eyes. 'Honestly, I didn't. He asked where Mr Ravenswood was, and I said downstairs, and he just pushed past me. I couldn't stop him.' She almost wailed these last words—like a cat whose tail had formed a sudden and unnervingly intimate relationship with a hobnailed boot.

'No, no, I'm sure you couldn't really have stopped him,' said Grimm after a long pause, patting the girl on the shoulder. 'No one will say it was your fault.'

The teller seemed to be, for the moment, unaware of the fact that Jack, Warnie and I were on the wrong side of the counter, lounging on bank desks immediately beside him, taking in all this human drama.

'Will Mr Ravenswood be all right?' asked the young woman in a tremulous voice.

'He'll be fine, Ruth,' said Grimm. 'It's a large strongroom. He won't run out of air. He's just . . . locked in, that's all.'

'While we're waiting,' said Jack in as jolly a tone as he could manage under the circumstances, 'would it be possible for me to make that withdrawal?'

Grimm looked blankly at Jack, who continued, 'Ravenswood did identify me, and he approved the withdrawal.'

'Ah, yes,' the teller admitted in a vague voice, rather like a man wandering out of a dense fog who is surprised to discover he is no longer alone. 'In fact, you gentlemen should leave the office. Just go through the flap to the customers' side of the counter please, and then I'll deal with your matter, Mr Lewis.'

We did as he asked. Grimm was still in something of a daze as he returned to his teller's cage, accepted Jack's passbook, made a withdrawal entry after first having discussed the required amount, and stamped the page. Then he counted out the notes and handed them over to Jack, who folded them into his pocket.

These routine actions seemed to help Franklin Grimm settle down and focus more clearly on the situation.

'What young Nicholas Proudfoot did probably amounts to assault,' he said, more as a question than a statement, and it was a question directed at us as the eyewitnesses.

'Oh yes, I should say so,' muttered Warnie.

Grimm turned around and told Ruth to call the police, inform them of what had happened and ask them to send an officer.

'And I must ask you three gentlemen to wait until the police arrive,' said Grimm. 'They may want to take statements from you.'

We agreed, and seated ourselves on the uncomfortable straight-backed chairs in the customers' waiting area.

A young man wearing a police uniform and hiding much of his face behind a moustache the size of an overgrown hedgerow arrived a few minutes later. Grimm quickly briefed him.

The policeman then introduced himself to us as Constable Dixon and pulled a small notebook out of his top pocket to take our statements. As he did so, Grimm said, 'I think I should get back down to the cellar, just in case there's anything I can do. Most probably there's not, but I should check.'

He disappeared through the doorway at the back of the office and hurried down the stairs into the dimly lit cellar, while we dealt with the dimly lit policeman who, slowly and patiently, took down our account of the events.

'What was that?' asked Jack in the middle of this note-taking.

'What was what, sir?' asked the constable. 'I heard nothing.'

'I heard a cry or a shout.'

'Are you sure, sir?'

'Jack has very acute hearing,' said Warnie.

'It seemed to come from the cellar,' said Jack. 'I think we should investigate.'

'I'm sure it's nothing, sir,' said Constable Dixon ponderously, 'but just to set your mind at rest, I'll take a look.'

We, of course, followed him through the door and down the stairs into the cellar. At first we could see nothing in that dim, yellow light. Then the constable saw the sprawled figure lying in the shadows. As he hurried across and knelt down beside the body, we followed and gathered around him.

It was clear what we were looking at: the size of the neck wound and the amount of blood made it obvious. It was the teller, Franklin Grimm, and he was dead.

FIVE

~

'Is he . . .?' asked the policeman.

Jack, who was kneeling closest, replied, 'I saw enough dead men in the trenches during the war. He's most certainly dead.'

Constable Dixon rose slowly to his feet and put his notebook back in his top pocket. 'I shall have to report this to my superiors,' he said in his slow, ponderous way.

'I should think that would be wise, old chap,' agreed Warnie.

'What happened down here?' I asked.

'Our friendly teller has been stabbed in the neck,' said Jack. 'And remembering the bit of first aid I picked up in the army, I should say the blow struck his carotid artery and he died instantly.'

'I'm sure you're right,' muttered Warnie quietly. 'I've seen shrapnel take chaps like that.'

'But who stabbed him?' I persisted. 'There's no one here. That's to say, there was no one in this cellar except Franklin Grimm. He was alone. So who stabbed him?'

'In such cases, sir,' said Constable Dixon politely, as if speaking to the slow child at the back of the classroom, 'we police officers usually find it's a matter of suicide. Very sad, of course, but then these things do happen.'

'Then where's the weapon?' Jack asked.

'We will find it in due course, sir,' replied Dixon.

'I doubt it,' Jack insisted. 'If Mr Grimm stabbed himself in the neck, and died almost instantly, the knife he used should be here—beside the body. But it's not. In fact, look around you. It's nowhere in sight.'

Constable Dixon scratched at his luxurious moustache, blinked rapidly and looked around. He started to say something and then stopped. Overcome by uncertainty, his mouth opened and closed several times but no sound came out of it.

Standing there in that dimly lit cellar, with a dead body at our feet and deep, gloomy shadows stretching away into blackness, the terrors of childhood seemed to come back with a rush. The darkness gathered itself into the monstrous shapes of nightmares and advanced towards us menacingly.

In broad sunlight the tale of murder and butchery this cellar had witnessed was a harmless folktale. But now, in the darkness, in the presence of death, the imagination played tricks, and shadows seemed to hide the pulsating menace of ghostly revenge. Quite suddenly Boris had ceased to be a funny name in an old tale, and had become, in my imagination, powerful phantom hands reaching out of the grave.

I shivered and tried to shake off the tricks my mind was playing on me.

Then I looked again at Constable Dixon, whose mouth was opening and closing as he gasped for air—like a man drowning in the deep end of the swimming pool hoping that someone would notice before he had to embarrass himself by crying out for help.

'I suggest, old chap,' said Warnie in a fatherly manner, 'that you make a quick search of this cellar before your superiors turn up and ask you where the weapon is.'

'Search?' asked the constable. 'Ah, yes. A search. Thank you, sir. Very good idea, sir.'

He unhitched an electric torch from his belt and turned on its powerful beam. He swept this around the small room. We saw a plain concrete floor, brick walls, the closed and locked vault door, a couple of broken office chairs—and nothing else. There was no knife, and there appeared to be nowhere a knife could be hidden.

'Well . . .' began the policeman cautiously, 'this is very strange. I don't understand . . .' Then he reached a decision. 'We all have to go back upstairs,' he said firmly. 'You gentlemen first, and I'll follow right behind you. Then I'm locking that door at the top of the stairs and calling Inspector Hyde. He'll know what to do.'

Back in the office Constable Dixon made his phone call. When he got to the part explaining that Franklin Grimm was dead, the office girl, sitting at the next desk, howled and burst into tears. When Dixon hung up the phone, he rather awkwardly tried to comfort the sobbing girl, reaching out a tentative hand to pat her shoulder and muttering, 'There, there.'

'Can I get you a glass of water . . . or something,' mumbled Warnie, feeling as uncomfortable as the rest of us in the face of the girl's distress.

She sniffed, dabbed at her eyes and nose with a pathetically small piece of lace handkerchief, and then whispered, 'No . . . no, thank you. I'll be all right in a moment.'

Within three minutes of the phone call Inspector Hyde was striding through the front door of the bank. He was a bustling, efficient, restless little man. Beside him was a taller, solidly built, stocky man, later introduced to us as Sergeant Donaldson.

'Where's the body, Dixon?' the inspector demanded, without a glance at us.

Constable Dixon unlocked the cellar door and led his senior officers down the stairs. We heard them moving about and speaking quietly, and when they returned ten minutes later the inspector was saying, 'Well, where is the weapon, Dixon? Answer me that?'

The constable had the good sense to remain silent. The inspector waved a hand at us, asking Dixon, 'Are these the witnesses you mentioned?'

'Yes, sir.'

'Gentlemen, I must ask you to wait here a little longer while we take additional statements. And I'd ask you not to leave Market Plumpton without my permission.' Jack, Warnie and I glanced at each other. Our prospects of a walking holiday were sinking fast.

'Now, young lady,' said the inspector, turning his attention to the tear-stained office girl. 'The bank is closed for the remainder of the day. You are to lock the front door.'

She blinked the tears from her eyes and said, 'But it's not closing time yet . . .'

'Nonsense!' snapped the inspector. 'There's been a serious crime committed here, and I am in command of the crime scene. You will lock up immediately.'

'Yes, sir,' she responded mildly, taking a large bunch of keys from a desk drawer and walking to the front door. A moment later it closed with a soft thud, shutting out the street sounds, and shutting us in with the bristling inspector. In response to a commanding gesture from his superior, Constable Dixon walked over and stood with his back to the closed front door. Clearly we were not going to be allowed to leave for a little while yet.

'Now, gentlemen,' said the inspector. 'I apologise for neglecting you so far. The name is Hyde. I am the inspector of police for this district. What can you tell me about this suspicious death?'

'In all probability, nothing more than your constable has already told you,' said Jack.

Sergeant Donaldson pulled out a notebook and pencil, and during the conversation that followed took copious notes. He began by taking down our names, addresses and occupations. There was a look of slight surprise on his face when he discovered that Jack was a Fellow of Magdalen College Oxford, that Warnie held a commission in the British Army, and that I was about to start work for Sir William Dyer at Plumwood Hall.

'Did any one of you go back down to the cellar?' asked Hyde.

We all looked at him and shook our heads.

'Jack was withdrawing money from his passbook account, and we stood beside him,' Warnie explained.

'In fact,' I added, 'the late Mr Grimm insisted that we three all stand on the customers' side of the counter, so none of us was even close to the door leading to the cellar steps.'

'So who could have gone through that door and down those steps?' asked the inspector quietly, putting the question more to himself than to us. Then he turned around to face the office girl.

'Miss,' he barked. She went pale and dabbed at her eyes with an already soaked handkerchief. 'You're Ruth Jarvis, aren't you? Todd Jarvis's daughter?'

'Yes, sir,' she replied in a voice little above a whisper.

'How long have you worked here?'

'Two years, sir.'

'Now, you were here in this office. Did you follow Mr Grimm down those steps into the cellar?'

Her only response was to break into a fresh round of howling.

'She couldn't have, inspector,' said Jack. 'We were facing the office and if she'd moved we would have noticed. She didn't leave her desk. In fact, I'm sure she didn't stop typing.'

'That's right,' sobbed Ruth Jarvis. 'I didn't stop typing. Not the whole time I didn't stop. You can see the work in my machine.'

Inspector Hyde actually walked through the counter flap and stood at her desk looking at the sheet of paper in the typewriter and the pile of completed sheets beside it. Then he spun around and faced us again.

'Well, if it wasn't Miss Jarvis, then who was it?' he demanded.

There was no answer to that question, so we didn't try to provide one. I saw the suspicious gleam in his eye and wondered if he thought he was looking at some secret society of Gentlemen Murderers. At least, that's what his narrowing gaze said to me. What did he imagine we were? The Oxford League of Assassins: mysterious murders committed to order on short notice—reasonable rates. Is that what he imagined? His suspicion of us couldn't have been clearer if he'd worn it as a broad phylactery on his forehead.

'Perhaps there's another way into the cellar,' mumbled Warnie after a long silence. 'Only thing I can think of.'

'And we thought of it too, Major Lewis. Some seventy or eighty years ago, when this was a private residence, there was a coal hole from the street into the cellar. But that was sealed up years ago. No, this door is the only way down and the only way out.'

'Well, no one went down,' I said, 'and certainly no one came out.'

'Does it make any sense to you, Donaldson?' the inspector snapped at his sergeant.

'There's some funny business going on here,' said the sergeant, 'but I don't know what it is.' As he spoke his forehead crinkled, like a junior clerk struggling with a tricky clue in a *Times* crossword.

'Have you made a more thorough search for the weapon?' Jack asked.

'Yes, yes, yes,' groaned the inspector. 'First thing we did. It's not a big cellar, and it's almost bare. Donaldson, Dixon and I went over it very carefully. The weapon that young Grimm stabbed himself with—if, that is, he did stab himself—has definitely disappeared.'

As he said the words 'stab himself' Ruth Jarvis howled again. Clearly this was going to drag on for some time, so I walked over to one of the straight-backed wooden chairs and sat down, stretching my legs out in front of me.

'Come along, inspector—this is getting us nowhere,' said Jack. 'The facts are the facts, and we can sit around talking about them until doomsday and they won't change.'

The inspector didn't like this and he responded by saying that we would be required as witnesses and were not to leave the town at least for the next few days. Then he looked at his watch and asked, 'How long has Ravenswood been locked in that strongroom now?'

'No more than half an hour,' I said. 'The teller told us there was plenty of air in the vault and the man with the combination should be here early this afternoon.'

'In fact, we should check that vault door. Donaldson, you come with me. Dixon you stay here and keep an eye on . . . these people.'

As they disappeared back into the cellar, Warnie muttered, 'I say, Jack. Does this mean that we're suspects or something?'

'It's not "something", it's definitely "suspects". After all, this is a small town and we're the outsiders,' Jack replied.

'I think it's quite offensive,' puffed Warnie. 'You're an Oxford don, I'm an officer in the British Army. It's outrageous that we should be treated as suspects.'

A few minutes later the inspector and his sergeant reappeared.

'Well?' asked Jack. 'What did you find?'

'That vault door is locked up as strong as a prison.' With these words Inspector Hyde ran his fingers through his thinning hair. 'Well, I'm beaten,' he muttered. 'This is too much for me. I'm going to phone the Chief Constable and get permission to call in Scotland Yard.'

SIX

~

The question then arose of what was to be done with us. The inspector decided that we should find ourselves some accommodation for the night and make ourselves available tomorrow for the man from Scotland Yard.

'Where were you planning to stay?' he asked.

'Not here,' said Jack firmly. 'Not in Market Plumpton.'

'Well, you're staying here now,' insisted the inspector, looking like a small, pugnacious rat trying to herd a crowd of larger and more important rats into a corner. 'In the light of what's happened, gentlemen, you'll have to revise your plans. Dixon, escort these men to *The Boar's Head*.'

'Yes, sir,' said the constable, unlocking and opening the front door of the bank and standing back to allow us through.

Behind us we could hear the inspector making his phone call to the Chief Constable. 'Colonel Weatherly? It's Inspector Hyde, sir . . . ah, we have a problem . . .'

But we heard no more, for Constable Dixon was saying, 'If you'll just follow me, gentlemen, I'll show you the way to *The Boar's Head*. You'll like it there, nicest little pub in town.'

We had stepped back out into the blazing sunshine of a warm midday and found ourselves blinking in the light. The nightmare behind us started to fade. In fact, as we walked into the sunshine I was finding it moment by moment more impossible to believe that there really was a dead body in the bank cellar—a body for which there was no possible, logical explanation. The warm sun made it all seem like a wild story from a cheap novel—the sort of detective novel Warnie loved to read. If Warnie had told me that exactly the same thing had happened in something called *The Secret Nine* or *The Purple Hand Strikes Again,* I would not have been the least bit surprised.

The constable led the way out of the town square, on the opposite side to the church, and around several corners until we reached the pub.

'There it is, gentlemen,' he said with the pride of a gardener showing off his prize pumpkin at a county fair. 'Frank Jones is the publican. Good chap. And his wife Annie is the best cook for miles around. I often have a bite to eat here myself.'

He then plunged through the open door of the bar parlour and introduced us to the man wiping glasses behind the bar. Dixon stood close beside us and watched carefully as each of us signed the register. Then Frank Jones summoned his wife to show us up to our rooms. Halfway up the stairs I stopped and looked back. The constable and the publican had their heads together in a whispered conversation.

Annie Jones showed us to three rather small, but neat and cheerful, rooms. I tossed my rucksack onto my bed then joined Jack in his room. Warnie did the same, dropping into the only armchair in the room with the words, 'This is a bit of a turn up for the books, eh? Here we are in the middle of a murder, what? Almost like being in the middle of a book actually. Sort of thing that Agatha Christie woman writes about. Rather like her books myself.' Then he chuckled and said, 'She always baffles me . . . always turns out to be the person I didn't expect. Jolly clever, eh?'

'Unfortunately,' said Jack, lighting his pipe, 'the role we have in this particular plot is far from ideal.'

'What do you mean?' said Warnie. 'I don't follow you, old chap.'

'I mean that in this particular story we are cast as the main suspects,' Jack replied with a merry twinkle in his eye.

'What? No. Surely not. But that's absurd,' spluttered Warnie.

'Well, think about it,' Jack continued. 'We are outsiders and strangers—in a small town suspicion is sure to fall on us first.'

'And did you see Constable Dixon whispering to the landlord as we came upstairs?' I asked.

'I did,' Jack said, 'and I'm certain the landlord was receiving his instructions. If we three "suspicious characters" should attempt to flee, I'm sure he's been ordered to telephone the police station immediately.'

Warnie began to make 'harrumphing' noises, but before his indignation could turn into words, Jack said, 'Don't worry about it, Warnie old chap. Our shoulders are broad enough to carry a bit of local suspicion for a few days.'

'And after all,' I added, 'we were the only people in the bank at the time Franklin Grimm died . . . apart from the office girl, and she's a little thing who surely could never have murdered a big chap like Grimm. Oh, and apart from the manager Ravenswood, who was locked behind the brick wall and thick steel door of the vault while the murder was happening. So you can understand them wanting to make sure of us.'

'It may seem understandable to you,' Warnie protested, 'but it seems like dashed impertinence to me!'

Jack laughed and said, 'Come on, let's see if we can get some lunch downstairs.'

Ten minutes later we were seated in the snug with a pint and a pork pie in front of each of us.

Warnie took a long sip from his glass of bitter, smacked his lips and said, 'That's what I call real ale.'

Jack was wolfing down his pork pie as rapidly as usual when I said, 'Now, it seems that we have time on our hands, so how about that debate we never quite finished on our walk this morning?' Jack nodded as he swallowed a mouthful. 'You proposed,' I continued, 'that there's one way of looking at the world that sees it right, while all the others see it slightly out of focus or distorted in some way.'

'Indeed,' Jack said, pausing before he took another bite. 'And I go further by giving that true way of seeing the world a name—Christianity.'

'And that's where you just can't be right,' I leaped in. 'You're making the mistake—the arrogant mistake, if you don't mind my saying so—of treating your world view, Christianity, as being somehow "more equal" than all the others. That just can't be the case. All world views are equal, and all should be regarded with respect.'

'In that case, young Morris,' Jack responded with his booming voice and his big, broad grim, 'you are respectfully wrong.'

'Hang it all, Jack, you must see that all these options are pretty much equal. All the major world religions—Christianity, Hinduism, Buddhism, Judaism, Islam and so on—are ancient and widespread. Each is held to be true by intelligent chaps. And atheism is much the same. There have been atheists since the dawn of time, and there are probably more today than ever. You see what I mean—all equal, all doing the same job of making sense of the world for someone, of providing a picture of what the world is like and how it works. So perhaps it's just a matter of what suits you.'

'So you're saying, are you, young Morris, that "equal" means "the same"?'

I sensed that I was walking into a trap here, but I couldn't say no because that was pretty much the point I was making. I just nodded.

'Nonsense!' laughed Jack as if I had just made some hilarious joke. 'Mind you,' he added more soberly, 'you're not the first to fall into that trap and you won't be the last. It's becoming more common for people to make the mistake of thinking that "equal" must mean "the same". Mrs Pankhurst, or at least her more radical suffragettes, made the mistake of thinking that women could only be equal to men if they were pretty much the same as men.'

'But surely—' I protested.

'Hear me out,' said Jack. 'The fact is that "equal" never means "the same"; it always means, and must mean, "equal but different". That's what the equals sign means in mathematics, and that's what the word means in ordinary language.'

'Rubbish!' I hooted back at my old tutor. 'Not only rubbish, but illogical rubbish. Equal means identical. To be equal is to be exactly the same.'

'Really?' asked Jack quietly with a gleam in his eye. And that gleam told me that my argument might be in trouble. 'I'm no mathematician, but even I know that in a mathematical formula both sides of the equals sign are not identical, are not exactly the same, but they *are* equal. To give you a simple example, and because I'm hopeless with numbers it will have to be very simple, I could write twenty multiplied by five on one side of the equals sign and the number one hundred on the other—and I'd be perfectly correct. Each side of the equals sign is equal to the other. But they're not the same, they're not identical. In fact, it would be pointless to write down that one hundred equals one hundred. The whole point of the notion of "equals" is that two things are unalike yet equal.'

'I'm no better at numbers than you are, Jack,' I protested. 'So forget mathematics. In fact, I suspect that once you move outside of mathematics you won't find a single example of "equal but different"—since that is an expression that makes no sense.'

'It makes every sense in the world, young Morris. Picture a set of scales, an old-fashioned set of balances, with a pound of lead on one tray balanced by a pound of wheat on the other. You can see that picture, can't you? On one side a bag containing a pound of wheat seeds and on the other a bar of lead. Both weigh one pound. The scales are perfectly balanced because they're equal. But they're certainly not alike: one is mineral, the other is organic, one can be planted and grow, the other can't, one can be turned into food, the other can't . . .'

'No need to go on—I see the point. But that's an aberration. In most cases "equal" means "identical". In human affairs, for instance—'

At which point Warnie interrupted to say, 'I can think of another example, old chap.'

Jack went back to finishing his pork pie and I turned to Warnie. 'Go on.'

'Two chaps I know in my regiment—Ted and Alf. Thoroughly nice chaps, both of them. As it happens they joined the army on the same day . . . I've heard them say it in the mess more than once. Both have the same rank—they're both majors, like me. And they both have the same length of service, and the same pay and benefits. Absolutely equal in every respect. But they're not interchangeable. Ted is an army surgeon and Alf is an army engineer. Isn't that Jack's point, old chap? Equal but different?'

Jack had finished his pork pie and was sweeping up some crumbs with his napkin. He chuckled and said, 'Warnie made my point better than I could. There would never be any reason to put an equals sign between two things, or people, that were identical. We only use the word "equal" to indicate that these two things or people that are different are of equal weight in the scheme of things.'

He paused to take a deep draught from his pint. 'So,' I said, gathering my thoughts, 'you're claiming that even if we say every way of looking at the world is to be given equal respect and consideration, we're not bound to think they're all the same or have the same explanatory value, hence "equal" doesn't mean they're all true.'

Jack set his glass back down on the table and said, 'Precisely. And the next step is that it can't be just a matter of what suits you. That's relativism, and relativism kills rationality—'

Before Jack could finish what he was about to say we were interrupted.

'I have it!' cried Warnie, his voice vibrating with discovery.

Jack and I both turned to look at him. 'Have what?' I asked.

'I know who murdered Franklin Grimm!'

We looked at him expectantly.

'It was Boris,' he said. 'You know, the ghost of the butchered footman. Today is the anniversary of his slaughter, so he was due to reappear. And he did—and murdered the bank teller.' Having delivered this pronouncement, Warnie sat back with a satisfied grin on his face.

SEVEN

~

A stunned silence followed Warnie's pronouncement. Jack and I both stared at him while Warnie finished off the last of his pint oblivious to our amazement.

'In other words,' Jack said to his brother, 'We're not caught up in an Agatha Christie murder story but in an M. R. James ghost story? Or a macabre tale by Edgar Allan Poe?'

'Well, look at the facts, old chap,' Warnie responded. 'Bank cellar sealed up tighter than a drum. No way in, no way out. Only one person in the cellar. That one person dies violently—and no weapon is found. I should think Edgar Allan Poe would be cracking his knuckles with delight and breaking out the good brandy to celebrate a plot like that.'

'The point is,' said Jack, 'it's not a story. It may be a plot, but it's a murderous plot that obeys the laws of physics, and the laws of logic.'

Before Warnie could respond I glanced through the window and interrupted to say, 'Look who's outside.' The others turned to peer through the small, diamond-shaped panes of the snug window. And they saw what I saw: Constable Dixon, lounging on the other side of the street, trying, without success, to look inconspicuous.

'Keeping a watchful eye on the chief suspects,' muttered Jack quietly.

'Treating us as if we're bally criminals,' muttered Warnie. 'Have a second pint, Jack?'

'Later,' Jack replied.

At that moment the phone in the front bar began to ring loudly. It rang for so long I was rising to answer it myself when a flustered Annie Jones, wearing an apron and carrying a tea towel in one hand, rushed in from somewhere in the back of the pub and picked it up. She listened for a moment and then went to the front door.

'Bill!' she called out to Constable Dixon on the other side of the street. 'Telephone for you.'

The constable flushed a bright pink at having his surveillance advertised in this way, but hurried across the road.

'Hello?' he said tentatively as he picked up the phone. He listened for a minute, punctuating his listening with the occasional muttered 'Yes, sir', then put the phone down with a final, 'Very good, sir.'

All of this we saw and heard through the open doorway between the snug and the front public bar. A moment later Constable Dixon was looming over us, saying, in his most official voice, 'Inspector Hyde has just telephoned, gentlemen. He requests your presence back at the bank premises please.'

'What now?' moaned Warnie, but we all dutifully rose and followed Dixon out onto the street and down the few short blocks to the bank. Here we found the street door still closed and a handwritten sign pinned on the door: 'Bank closed until further notice.' After a few firm and officious knocks by the constable the door was opened by Sergeant Donaldson, who waved us inside.

He ushered us into the customers' waiting area and told us to take a seat. Several minutes passed in dull silence, broken only by the loud ticking of the bank's office clock.

I turned to Jack and complained, 'This is like waiting at the dentist.'

He smiled grimly and said, 'And there's no promise the procedure will be painless when it happens.'

Then the front door opened again and Inspector Hyde bustled in, accompanied another man in a pin-striped business suit.

'Ah, you're here, you're here,' said Hyde, seeing us seated and waiting. 'Be with you in a moment, gentlemen.' Then he ushered his pin-striped visitor behind the counter and through the door leading to the cellar steps. Sergeant Donaldson went with them, leaving us to our own devices. We looked at each other, wondering what was going on.

'Well, I don't know about you,' said Warnie, rising from his seat and obviously still feeling keenly the insult of being a suspect, 'but I'm not waiting here like a shag on a rock.'

Jack also stood to his feet adding, 'Well said, Warnie. Let's see what they're up to.'

A moment later all three of us were through the door at the back of the bank office and standing at the head of the cellar stairs. Instinctively we moved quietly down them, not wishing to attract too much attention.

The pin-stripe-suited gentleman was standing in front of the vault door. He first felt the locking bars and checked the door. It was, he found, securely and fully closed and locked. Then he drew a piece of paper from his pocket and, consulting this from time to time, began manipulating the dials of the combination locks. There were two of these, one above the other. He operated each in turn, twisting them to the right and the left and bringing them to rest on a particular number with each turn. This operation took a couple of minutes.

When he was satisfied he had successfully executed the combination, he pulled on each of the two locking levers in turn. With a loud clunk each swung into the unlocked position. Helped by Sergeant Donaldson, he then pulled open the heavy steel door.

Ravenswood the bank manager stumbled out.

'Are you all right, sir?' asked Inspector Hyde.

Ravenswood looked dishevelled, flushed and slightly breathless. 'Thank you . . . thank you . . .' was all he could gasp at first. Then he saw the man in the pin-striped suit. 'Ah, Mr Johnson . . . you've come all the way from Tadminster?'

'Are you all right, old chap?' asked Mr Pin-stripe.

'Perfectly well, thank you, sir,' Ravenswood replied. 'I'm so sorry to have put you to all this trouble.'

'Not at all, not at all,' said Johnson soothingly.

Behind Ravenswood we could see into the bank's strongroom. It was lit by a single electric light globe. This revealed to the left of the door a stack of lockable safe deposit boxes, and to the right a number of locked metal tubs on trolleys, presumably containing the bank's cash deposits. Between these two arrays was a clear alleyway, and in this alley was a small wooden table containing an open ledger book, a pen and a pot of ink. Presumably this ledger was to sign-in and sign-out customers opening their safe deposit boxes. Under the table was a small tool box and beside it was a single wooden chair with a suit coat draped over the back of it.

'I feel so foolish,' Ravenswood was saying loudly, 'allowing something like this to happen . . . it was a customer . . . temporarily upset . . . problem over a loan . . . you know the sort of thing.'

'Think nothing of it,' said Johnson, patting him on the arm. 'These things happen. Unfortunately financial difficulties can make some of our customers somewhat fraught or even irrational. You can't hold yourself responsible for the emotional behaviour of one customer.'

'And I don't want the customer prosecuted,' said Ravenswood hastily, turning to Inspect Hyde. 'I take it that's why you're here?'

'Not entirely, sir . . .' Hyde began.

'Not good for the bank to be seen to prosecute a customer for a moment's bad judgement due to . . . well, as Mr Johnson said, financial distress,' Ravenswood continued, ignoring the policeman's interruption. 'So thank you for coming, inspector, but your presence is not really required.'

With these words he turned around and walked back into the strongroom. He fetched his suit coat from the back of the chair, turned off the electric light and walked back out again.

'Well, we can lock it again now, can't we?' he said to Johnson with a nervous smile. 'I really don't feel like going back in there for the rest of the day. I've seen quite enough of the inside of that vault just for the moment.'

Ravenswood was babbling nervously, and who could blame him, I thought, after being locked for hours inside his own bank's vault. He and Johnson pushed the heavy steel door closed once more, pressed the locking levers into place and spun the dials of the combination lock.

'There's more that's been going on here, Mr Ravenswood,' said Inspector Hyde, 'than just your being locked in the vault.'

'I've explained about that,' Ravenswood insisted. 'Young Nicholas Proudfoot was upset about his loan—a young man, afraid of losing his farm, you can understand his emotional stress . . .'

'That's not why I'm here,' said Hyde more firmly. Ravenswood looked at him blankly and blinked uncertainly. 'I'm afraid I have to tell you, sir,' continued the policeman, 'that your teller, young Mr Franklin Grimm, is dead.'

'Dead?'

'Yes, sir.'

'But how?'

'He was stabbed, sir.'

'Stabbed?'

'In the neck, sir. He appears to have died instantly.'

'But . . . I don't understand . . .'

'None of us quite understand just at the moment, sir—but that's why we're here. That's the matter we're looking into. Now, I'd like everyone to go back up to the office please. Sergeant Donaldson will be locking up the cellar for the time being, and he'll be hanging on to the key. This is now a crime scene.'

'You too, gentlemen,' he said noticing, at last, our presence hovering on the stairs. 'You shouldn't even be here,' he added irritably.

As I turned to go I looked down and saw that Grimm's body had been removed. Presumably the police surgeon had come in our absence, made his initial examination and removed the body.

Upstairs we scattered ourselves around the small office of the bank. We each found a chair or the edge of a desk to sit on while the inspector stood in the middle of the floor in the manner of a master of ceremonies. He cleared his throat and was about to begin when Ravenswood demanded some explanation of what had been happening in his bank while he was locked in the vault.

'What I have discovered so far,' replied the inspector, 'is that the first step that was taken following your unfortunate . . . ah . . . incarceration was a phone call to Mr Johnson here, or one of his colleagues, at the regional headquarters of the bank in Tadminster. In line with bank policy Mr Johnson declined to release the number of the combination lock over the phone, and instead took the first train here so that he could open the vault door himself.'

'Yes, yes,' urged Ravenswood, impatient at this slow giving-evidence-in-court police manner.

Inspector Hyde raised a hand as if asking him to wait and be patient, and then resumed. 'But before Mr Johnson could arrive, your teller, young Mr Franklin Grimm, seemed to decide that he should position himself in the cellar, on the unlikely chance that he could be of some use to you there. While he was in the cellar alone, and this door here—the only entrance leading to the cellar—was under constant observation by your office girl, Ruth Jarvis, and these three customers, Mr Grimm died from a stab wound.'

'But . . . but . . . I don't understand,' protested Ravenswood.

'Precisely, sir,' said Hyde. 'Just at this moment none of us understand exactly what happened. Or how. Or why. Or who could possibly have done what was done. There was, it appears, a faint cry heard coming from the vicinity of the cellar. When that sound was investigated, Mr Grimm's body was discovered with a single fatal knife wound to the neck. And the knife that did the damage was nowhere to be found.'

'What happened to it?' asked Mr Johnson, clearly gripped by Hyde's narrative.

'Ah,' said the policeman, 'that's the crux of the whole matter, sir. Either the knife was carried away by Mr Grimm's murderer, in which case no one can account for how he got into and out of the cellar; or else, if the wound was self-inflicted, the knife has somehow dissolved into thin air. Either way, what happened was totally impossible.'

EIGHT

~

In the long pause that followed Inspector Hyde's statement I heard Warnie whisper just behind me, 'It was the ghost.' Although I didn't believe him I felt that slight shiver down the spine that we describe as 'someone just walked over my grave'.

Ravenswood ran his fingers through his dark hair and muttered, 'This is awful, simply awful. What about poor Ruth? How has she taken it?'

'She's very distressed, sir, as you'll understand,' explained Hyde. 'So we sent her home. Sergeant Donaldson escorted her to her mother's house, and that's who's looking after her now.'

'Poor girl,' moaned Ravenswood. 'I believe she and Grimm were quite close—more than just work colleagues, if you understand my meaning. Whether there was actually an understanding between them or not I don't know. Perhaps matters hadn't got quite to that point. But they certainly saw each other outside the office.'

'Thank you for that, sir,' said the inspector. 'We'll talk to the young lady about that in due course. Now, did Mr Grimm have any enemies? Can you think of anyone who may have wanted him dead? Or who may have benefited from his death?'

Instead of answering, Ravenswood dropped heavily into an office chair and muttered, 'I just can't take all this in . . .' His voice trailed away.

Inspector Hyde's manner shifted from that of a police official to something more like that of a friend addressing a fellow member of his golf club—which he probably was, given how small the town was.

'Now, Edmund,' he said to Ravenswood, 'pull yourself together, old chap. We need your help if we're to make any progress in this dreadful business.'

'Yes . . . yes, of course,' the bank manager replied. 'I'll do whatever I can.'

'Ravenswood,' said Mr Johnson, from the distant corner where he was standing. 'Is there anything the bank can do? Would you like us to send in an acting manager for a few days while you get over the shock.'

'No,' replied Ravenswood quickly. 'That won't be necessary. I'm fine to carry on. I will need another teller until I can recruit and train someone local—if you have someone you can spare from head office?'

'I'll arrange something,' said Johnson. 'Leave it to me.'

'Gentlemen!' snapped Hyde. 'You can get back to the bank's business shortly, but for the moment there is a man dead, I have a detective from Scotland Yard arriving on tomorrow morning's train, and I need to have a report with sufficient detail that I can hand to him. So, if you don't mind, we'll get on.'

Johnson stepped back to his distant corner and said nothing while Ravenswood simply nodded.

'And let me remind you, in case you've forgotten, that I've closed this bank to the public. It's now a crime scene. It won't be reopened until our Scotland Yard colleagues are satisfied that they have fully investigated the scene of this tragedy. So let's have no more talk of bank business.'

Ravenswood and Johnson looked suitable chastened. Both nodded their understanding.

'Now, let me ask you again: can you think of anyone who may have wanted Mr Franklin Grimm dead or who may have benefited from his death?'

Edmund Ravenswood was silent for a moment and then said, 'Well, Grimm sometimes had an unfortunate manner, and he may have got people's backs up from time to time, but I can't imagine that was reason enough to kill him.'

Inspector Hyde suddenly swivelled around to face Jack, Warnie and me and snapped, 'And how well did you gentlemen know Mr Grimm?'

'Not at all,' said Jack firmly. 'We met him today for the first time.'

'But you, Mr Lewis,' continued Hyde, 'have been in Market Plumpton before. And you've had dealings at this bank before. That's correct, isn't it?'

'Only once before, last year. I was passing through on a walking holiday with two other friends and I called in here to withdraw some money. On that occasion I saw only Mr Ravenswood here.'

'Do you remember that?' Hyde asked, putting his question to the bank manager.

'I believe I do,' Ravenswood replied thoughtfully. 'This is not a busy branch, and I believe I do remember Mr Lewis's visit. If I recollect correctly, he called when Mr Grimm was on his lunch hour so I dealt with him myself.'

At this point Jack protested vigorously that we were mere visitors, passing through, that our role as eyewitnesses was a matter of chance, and that we really had no more to offer. Hyde bristled, but he reluctantly agreed that we could go back to the pub. As long, he said, as we made ourselves available to speak to the man from Scotland Yard tomorrow. So it was that we made our escape from the dark and gloomy bank building, with its high ceilings and dark timber walls, out into the fresh air and sunshine.

Back at *The Boar's Head*, Jack, Warnie and I ordered drinks and went out to the beer garden behind the pub. This was a grassed yard that sloped down from the back door to the rapidly flowing Plum River that circled half the town. Wooden tables and chairs were scattered across the lawn. We found a place in the warm sun not far from the towpath at the water's edge where we could sit down and stretch out our legs.

'This is looking like a pretty duff holiday,' grumbled Warnie.

Quite right, I thought, but if we can't walk at least we can talk.

'Now Jack,' I said, 'we were interrupted this morning when you made that outrageous claim that relativism kills reason. Surely you can't mean that?'

'I think the truth of that would be obvious even to a sea anemone of average intelligence. If everything is relative—if what is true from your point of view is not true from mine—then the whole category of truth simply ceases to exist and reason has no function. Unless there is a shared objective truth, there's nothing we can reason about together.'

'Cut it out, you two,' puffed Warnie. 'We have other problems—problems we ought to do something about.'

'Such as?' I asked.

'Well,' said Warnie, 'obviously we're suspects, and I have no confidence in the police to release us to resume our holiday any time soon. In all the detective novels I've read, the police are complete duffers and they need Lord Peter Wimsey or Hercule Poirot to step in and solve their mysteries for them. So we can't just leave this to the police.'

'What's the alternative?' I asked.

With glee Warnie replied, 'We step in and do something about it ourselves.'

At this point Frank Jones arrived with a tray bearing three pints of bitter. As he placed drinks on our table I asked, 'Do what, Warnie, old chap?'

'Well, Jack has twice the brains of any Scotland Yard fellow,' replied Warnie with brotherly loyalty. Although it was more than that, I knew: my old tutor had a brain the size of the Albert Hall.

'And you are suggesting that Jack do what exactly?' I asked.

'Solve the murder!' spluttered Warnie. 'Jack can solve this puzzle faster than anyone else, and get this shadow of suspicion off us, and get us released to resume our holiday.'

All of this the publican Frank Jones followed with great interest, so Jack turned to him and said, 'Mr Jones, would you like to pull up a chair and join our conversation?'

Jones glanced back at the kitchen window before he replied, 'Don't mind if I do. It's either this or peel potatoes, and I know which I'd prefer.'

'Now, Mr Jones,' Jack continued, in his hearty, friendly manner, 'what we need is local information, and a publican knows everything about a town. Will you help us?'

'It would be my pleasure, gentlemen,' replied a grinning Mr Jones, looking as happy as a rabbit offered a particularly large and enticing lettuce leaf. 'Although whoever killed Franklin Grimm should probably get a medal.'

'You didn't like him?' I asked.

'No one did,' the publican replied. 'Well, the young women of this town did.'

'And I take it,' said Jack, 'that as a result the men of the town didn't.'

'You have put it in a nutshell, Mr Lewis—in a nutshell. But that wasn't the only thing that caused resentment.'

Our silence encouraged him to continue. 'Well, he grew up on a farm, you see. And there he was, working in the bank—going to work each day in a suit and collar and tie. He really thought he was a cut above the rest of us. And everyone knows he only got the job because he's Ravenswood's brother-in-law.'

'Is he indeed?' said Jack. 'Now that's very interesting.'

'Oh, yes. It was Edith Ravenswood who badgered her husband into hiring Franklin. But he never really came to terms with the responsibilities of the job.'

'In what sense?'

'He used to make snide remarks, Mr Lewis, to this one or that about the state of their account. Well, that's confidential, isn't it? That's something that shouldn't be spoken about outside the bank. Highly improper, I considered it. He was a young man inclined to put on airs, and sneer at others. You can take it from me: there are quite a few in this town who won't shed a tear over the death of Franklin Grimm.'

'You mentioned his popularity with young women. Will any of them shed a tear?'

'That's a good point, Mr Lewis. Well spotted. He was devilishly good looking, and a big, strapping lad was Franklin. And he had a way with him. He could be charming when he wanted to be—when he thought it was in his interests. So he sort of hypnotised quite a few young women in this town. Not all of them were single neither—there were a few young married women who fell under his spell. Whether any of their husbands ever suspected or not I don't know. Of course, if one of them did, and took his revenge, well . . .'

He left the sentence hanging and tapped the side of his nose as he gave a knowing wink. Then he returned to the subject of the young women themselves, the victims of Mr Grimm's apparent ability to cast a spell.

'I'm not sure if they all knew just how many women he was friendly with at the same time. Some of them may have thought they were the only one.'

'And we know one of his young women was Ruth Jarvis,' muttered Jack thoughtfully, speaking more to himself than the rest of us.

'It all sounds terribly complicated and messy to me,' I said.

'There was a very hot-headed young man we saw earlier today,' Jack said, changing the subject. 'A young farmer named Nicholas Proudfoot. He burst into the bank and was shouting threats at the manager.'

'At Edmund Ravenswood?' said the publican. 'That does surprise me. I would have expected him to be after Franklin Grimm, not Mr Ravenswood.'

We nodded for him to continue. 'Well, Nick Proudfoot has a pretty young wife—very pretty, if you ask me. Her name's Amelia, and she's as beautiful as one of them pin-up girls. You know how people talk in small towns: well, the talk is she might have an admirer. And if she has surely it'd Grimm, the local Lothario—the local man about town, as it were.'

'What Proudfoot said in his angry outburst in the bank seemed to have more to do with a loan,' Jack suggested. 'Does that make any sense to you, Mr Jones?'

'I know the Proudfoots had to mortgage their farm a year or two back. And since then the seasons have been bad, so he may have been struggling with payments. But that's not the bank's problem. I can't quite see why he'd be shouting at Mr Ravenswood.'

'Perhaps we should ask,' said Jack. 'Can you give us directions to Nicholas Proudfoot's farm?'

'No problem.' And with these words Frank Jones dug a scrap of paper out of his pocket and began scribbling a rough map.

Then came a flood of instructions that involved marking where we were with an X and explaining how many left- and right-hand turns we had to take.

When he'd finished his explanation, he added, 'But will Bill Dixon be happy about you leaving town, even if it's only to walk out to a local farm?'

'Ah, that's a thought,' murmured Warnie. 'If he sees us going he might try to stop us.'

'Well,' said Jack with a gleam in his eye, 'we must see about that.'

NINE

~

We took our half empty pints of bitter through into the front bar and looked out of the window. Sure enough, Constable Dixon was settled in his observation post on the opposite side of the street.

'They seem to be serious about our being suspects,' groaned Warnie.

However, Dixon did not appear to be a happy policeman. As we watched, a gust of breeze pulled at the policeman's jacket and made him grab his helmet. I wanted to hum a few bars of 'A Policeman's Lot Is Not a Happy One'—but seeing Warnie's grumpy face I thought better of it.

The weather seemed to have picked up something of Warnie's mood. The sunny, smiling face of the morning had disappeared and been replaced by gloomy, grumpy clouds. It was as if the weather had said, 'That's your lot! No more Mr Sunny from me today!' We stood at the window of the public bar watching the late afternoon breeze slowly gathering strength, picking up leaves and scraps of paper and pushing them over the cobbles.

'Now, this investigation of our own that we've thought of conducting,' said Jack quietly.

'That I thought of!' blustered Warnie with a laugh. 'I suggested it first.'

'I speak, of course, of the investigation proposed by the senior officer in our ranks,' Jack responded with a grin.

'A jolly good idea too,' I added. 'The sooner this mysterious tragedy is investigated and solved, the sooner we can have a real holiday.'

'Hear, hear,' said Warnie, raising his glass in a toast.

'To this I add a further proposal,' Jack resumed, 'that we begin tomorrow morning—when the wind has died down, the sun is back out, and there just might not be a policeman on watch. Come on, let's take our drinks into the snug.'

We did, and to our great delight we found a log fire blazing in the small fireplace. Glancing through the diamond-paned window, I saw that Constable Dixon was now beating his arms against his sides and stepping back into a doorway to avoid the worst of the wind.

With a poker I pushed around the cheerfully glowing logs in the fire. Not that I really know anything about fires, but it was burning so well I thought it deserved a bit of encouragement. I returned the poker to its rack and fell with a sigh into a seat in the ingle nook.

'Now, Warnie,' I said with a cheeky grin, 'don't go balancing anything on the mantelpiece above the fireplace.'

Warnie went pink. He huffed and puffed a bit, and then murmured, 'I still feel a bit stupid about that.'

Jack leaned over and patted his knee saying, 'Nonsense, old chap! You've got to stop thinking about it.'

Warnie shook his head sadly, grumbled under his breath into his beer, and wandered over to the grey, twilit window to commiserate with the miserable weather outside.

'Now, Jack,' I said, 'this business of your saying that Christianity is true in a way that no other world view or religion is true—it just won't wash. This claim to exclusivity that you

Christians make is both muddled nonsense and offensive nonsense.'

Jack leaned back in his armchair and took his pipe from his jacket pocket. 'I can see, young Morris,' he replied, 'that you've come out of your corner with your fists up ready to battle this one out. So let's hear your argument.'

'I grant you that there is objective, knowable truth in lots of areas of life—there's only one Statue of Liberty in New York Harbour and so on. But belief systems are different. They're more like poetry than arithmetic. They're more like music than geometry. Having a preference for one set of beliefs over another is like having a preference for Beethoven over Bach.'

'So it's really just a matter of taste and preference? It's aesthetic rather than logic?'

'Yes, something like that. Belief systems are based on the visions and philosophy and experiences of their founders. Buddha had certain experiences and ideas and founded Buddhism. Mohammad had certain other experiences and ideas and founded Islam. Rudolf Steiner had different experiences and ideas and founded Anthroposophy, which your friend Barfield keeps banging on about.'

Jack laughed heartily, but said nothing, so I continued, 'And the same could be said of Confucius and all the rest. You can't say one set of those experiences, those ideas, was in some sense "right" and the others "wrong". It makes more sense to say that these are different poetic visions of the same large, difficult-to-see truth.'

'So in your view they're all just different roads up the same mountain?'

I thought for a moment about this suggestion and then said, 'Yes, that's a good way to put it. That paints a mental image for me. When you say that, I picture a mountain the way a child would draw one—simple and conical. And winding around that mountain is an interconnecting set of roads, tracks and pathways. Some of them zigzag up the slope; others cling precariously to the steep sides. Some are broad and well-travelled; others are narrower, less well known and less often found. But what matters is getting to the top, not which road you take to get there.'

'And what you are claiming is that you are superior to all of these different "visions", as you call them?'

'No . . . no,' I said hesitantly. 'That can't be right. I'm certainly not intending to say that sort of thing at all. I'm not claiming any sort of superiority.'

'Oh, but you are!' Jack pounced, like a batsman seeing a loose ball coming down the wicket towards him just begging to be whacked to the boundary. 'You're claiming to see the whole mountain, and to see the many different paths leading to the top, while everyone else is on their own narrow path, blind to the bigger picture that you see. You are claiming access—based, presumably, on your reason, your rationality, your intelligence and your education—to a universal truth, a bigger truth, that devout Christians, Jews, Hindus, Buddhists, Muslims, Mormons, even Anthroposophists, and all the rest are missing.'

'Now, hang on a moment,' I said as I gathered my thoughts. 'It may well be the fact that a secular mind—an atheist mind, if you prefer—using reason alone, or reason supported by good information, may well be able see a greater truth than any ancient belief system. Particularly in the light of the dawning scientific age all around us.'

'So what you're now saying is not that all the great world religions are equality right, but that they're equally wrong—and that only your scientific atheism is right. Am I understanding you correctly?'

I felt backed into a corner. I felt like a slightly dazed lamb pushed up against the side of a pen by an experienced sheep dog. This conversation had begun with me accusing Lewis of arrogantly trumpeting Christianity's exclusive access to the truth. Now he had somehow reversed the charge and was accusing me, as a secular rationalist, of making that same offensive claim of sole access to the truth.

I wasn't quite sure how the tables had been turned, and I thought it was time I pinned him down to some firm answers on his own position.

'My turn to ask the questions,' I said as I drained the last of my pint of bitter.

'Fire away, young Morris,' said Jack with a cheerful grin. Lewis was what my grandfather would have called a 'bonny fighter'—someone who relished a good scrap over serious ideas.

'Are you saying there's no truth in any belief system other than Christianity?' That question, I thought, would put him on the spot.

'I would make the assumption,' Jack replied with energy, 'that any belief that has enjoyed wide currency over many centuries must contain some truth. Such a belief system must have some pieces of the jigsaw puzzle of life. In a similar way, your secular atheism—now held so enthusiastically by some intelligent and thoughtful people—must contain some truth: some pieces of the jigsaw puzzle.'

'Then what we need to do is to put all our pieces of the jigsaw puzzle together!' I cried triumphantly, gleefully seizing on this new metaphor. 'Which is what I think I was saying at the start of this conversation.'

'However,' said Jack, holding up a finger and urging me to be patient, 'what if it's the case that each of these world views contains some genuine and some false pieces of the puzzle?

How then do you sort out which pieces to include and which pieces to discard?'

I didn't have an immediate answer. Jack continued, 'What if your own popular "scientism" contains some truthful bits (about how the physical world works, for example) and some false bits (such as the claim that there is *nothing but* the physical world, meaning that categories such as "mental" and "aesthetic" and "spiritual" are imaginary)? A mixture, you see, of true and false.'

Jack gave me a moment's silence to mull this over. Warnie had completely lost interest in our discussion and had pulled a pack of grimy old cards from his pocket and begun to play solitaire.

Jack resumed, 'Is it not possible that this is the case—that many world views, including your own, might be a muddled mixture of bits of truth and bits of falsehood? How do we sort out the true and helpful bits from the false and mistaken bits in order to put the jigsaw puzzle together?'

It was happening again! I had started asking questions, and within a minute I was being put on the spot and asked to come up with answers. Well, I wasn't falling for it this time. This was one of those occasions when the best answer to a question is a question.

'So what's your answer to that question?' I asked. 'How would you sort out the pieces of the puzzle? How would you know which to discard and which to keep?'

'My answer is that we use what we always use with a difficult jigsaw puzzle: the picture on the top of the box. That will show us the whole picture and how everything fits together—or is meant to fit together. And Christianity is "the picture on the top of the box". When an atheist is converted to Christianity, as I was, what he finds is not that he's lost everything he once believed but that it now fits into a larger picture—the picture towards which it had been pointing all the time. And the same is true for Christian converts from a Hindu or Buddhist or whatever background. Jesus does not come to destroy but to fulfil.'

'You know what I think?' said Warnie as he scooped up his cards. Jack and I both looked in his direction. 'I think it's time for dinner.'

And it was. Warnie had picked up the delicious aromas drifting out of the kitchen of *The Boar's Head*. Ten minutes later we were feasting on roast beef and potatoes with Yorkshire pudding. This occupied our full attention for some little time.

As Warnie sopped up the last of his gravy with a piece of bread, he said, 'Now let's talk about a mystery really worth puzzling over.'

'Meaning?' I asked as I poured a second cup of tea out of the large, old-fashioned floral teapot in the middle of the table.

'Meaning the mystery of who killed Franklin Grimm, and why, and how.'

'I think we have to leave the how to one side for the moment,' Jack suggested, lighting his pipe. As always he had finished his meal while Warnie and I were still ploughing through our roast beef.

'In the end,' Jack continued, taking a few puffs and sending clouds of blue smoke into the air of the snug, 'in the end either knowing *who* will answer the question of *how* they did it, or discovering *how* will tell us *who* did it.'

'Whodunit,' I corrected. When both Jack and Warnie raised their eyebrows I explained, 'Well, that's how they say it on the back jackets of all the detective novels. It's always "whodunit".'

'No need to lapse into grammatical absurdity, young Morris,' Jack responded in his most tutor-like manner. 'Since the scene of the crime is occupied by the police and not accessible to us, we leave aside the question of *how*—at least for the moment—and focus on *whom*.'

'And that means . . .?' prompted Warnie.

'That means that tomorrow morning we escape from police surveillance and make our way out of town to interview the volatile Mr Nicholas Proudfoot.'

'Hear, hear,' Warnie applauded. 'In the meantime, how about another pint of bitter?'

TEN

The next morning after breakfast we took our cups of tea through into the front bar and looked out of the window. Sure enough, Constable Dixon had once again taken up his post on the opposite side of the street.

'Has he been there all night?' groaned Warnie.

'Perhaps another constable did the night shift,' Jack suggested. 'Either that or Inspector Hyde decided we were unlikely to do a midnight flit.'

'How do we get past him?' I asked.

Jack grinned and replied, 'We don't. We take him with us—at least for a while. Finish your tea, and then follow me.'

With those words he stepped out into the street, waved at the policeman and said loudly, 'Good morning, Constable Dixon. We're just going for a little stroll around your town. Do a bit of sight-seeing. Care to accompany us?'

Dixon shuffled his feet uncomfortably. He looked as guilty as a cat caught crouching over the remains of the fish you'd been planning to eat for dinner. Caught in the act, a cat will usually raise one eyebrow as if to say, 'Fish? What fish? Oh, *that* fish. I hadn't noticed it before. I wonder who left it here.'

All of those emotions and attempts at looking innocent

flitted over the policeman's face one after another like the changing traffic lights at an intersection.

For a while he opened and closed his mouth soundlessly as he struggled to find something to say. Eventually he touched his helmet and said, 'Good morning, sir' as he ostentatiously turned his back on us and stared off into the far distance. Or at least as far as the other end of the street.

Jack waved us on and the three of us headed up the street towards the town square.

'Does that mean he's not following us after all?' asked Warnie.

'Oh, he's following us all right,' replied Jack. 'If you glance over your shoulder from time to time you'll see what I mean.'

For the next ten minutes Jack led us on a merry chase. Instead of heading directly towards the town square, he back-tracked and wove in and out of the narrow streets of the oldest part of Market Plumpton. And from time to time I looked over my shoulder—usually just in time to see a flash of blue police uniform darting behind a lamp post. Unfortunately, a lamp post was never quite enough to hide the rather bulky shape that was Constable Dixon.

'Rather nice lamp posts, aren't they?' said Jack with a wicked grin, seeing the same bootless manoeuvre. 'Rather handsome old cast iron affairs. I take it they began life as gas lamps and have since been converted to hold electric lights.'

He patted the next lamp post we walked past, saying in a loud voice, 'Very nice piece of late Victorian industrial design. There are hints of the William Morris arts and crafts influence in that wrought iron. You know what I think I'd like to see? I'd rather like to see a lamp post like this transported into a different environment—perhaps into a woodland setting somewhere, perhaps a woodland under a blanket of snow. That would create a very nice image, don't you think? That's the sort of mental picture that starts the imagination ticking over.'

Jack kept prattling whimsically like this as we walked, sometimes striding rapidly ahead and sometimes dawdling so that poor Constable Dixon on our trail never knew whether he was about to lose us or bump into us.

At last we came out into the town square and began a slow stroll around the shopfronts, just as if we were the idle tourists we were pretending to be. As we made our way towards the church on the far side of the square, I glanced back to see that Constable Dixon had taken up his post in front of a millinery shop. As I looked back he turned his attention to the shop window and appeared to become deeply engrossed in ladies' hats.

'So what's the plan, Jack?' hissed Warnie in a theatrical whisper.

'We shall do what any tourist would do. It's a very old church—we'll take a look around.' And as we walked through the lychgate into the churchyard, Jack said in a loud voice, 'Very old. The main part of the building might be Norman.'

We made our way to the free-standing bell tower and made a slow circuit around it. There was a wooden door on one side, but when Warnie tested it, it proved to be locked. I hurried to the corner of the tower and looked around it in time to see Constable Dixon striding rapidly across the square in some panic, apparently fearing he might have lost us. As he was looking desperately left and right, Jack stepped out from the behind the tower and gave him a cheerful wave. He responded with an embarrassed nod, and then ostentatiously turned his back on us and began to swing his truncheon rhythmically like a constable walking his beat.

We ambled slowly across the churchyard, stopping to

comment on the oldest of the headstones on our way to the church door.

'Look at this one,' said Warnie. 'I rather like this.'

I stood beside him and looked down at the epitaph on the old, weathered headstone: 'WE ALL HAVE A DEBT TO NATURE DUE. I'VE PAID MINE AND SO MUST YOU.'

'A bit grim,' I said.

'True, nonetheless,' Warnie chuckled. 'And here—this one's an even more awful omen: "Grim death took me without any warning. I was well at night, and dead in the morning." Does that come from the man's family, do you think? Or did some stonemason with a sense of humour suggest it?'

Then we noticed that Jack was not with us—he had disappeared inside the church and we hurried to follow.

It was a nice little church interior, although very plain, apart from some whimsical carvings on the lectern. Jack walked the length of the aisle and then turned and said, 'Warnie, take a look out of the window and tell me what our friendly policeman is doing.'

As Warnie edged along the pews to a window, I muttered, 'This is like a scene from a Ben Travers farce.'

Warnie sidled up slowly to a window so that he could see out without being seen, and then said in a low voice, 'He's in the churchyard now. He has his hands in his pockets. He has his back to the church. And he appears to be whistling.'

'Excellent,' said Jack. 'This is our chance. Let's see if the vestry door is unlocked.'

It was. And we left the church on the far side of the building, away from the churchyard. Ahead of us was a narrow lane that ran between the back fences of two rows of terrace houses. We three trotted up this as quickly as we could.

Several minutes of rapid walking brought us almost to the edge of town. Jack fished Frank Jones' scribbled map out of his pocket and looked at it for a moment.

'It appears that we keep going this way for the next block,' he said, 'then turn left and that should put us on the northern road out of town.'

A few minutes later we were walking down a narrow country road between high hedgerows, and still going quite quickly—aiming to put as much distance between ourselves and a possibly pursuing Constable Dixon as we could.

When we reached a low rise, I looked back down the hill towards the town. I could see a lot of winding country road from that height, but no policeman—it was deserted.

'We seem to have lost our faithful constable,' I said. 'Now, what direction do we head in?'

'Not entirely certain,' Jack admitted. 'Warnie, you know more about maps than I do—take a look at this.'

Jack handed over the scrap of paper that was our guide and Warnie studied it for a minute. 'Hmmm, I'm not sure, old chap. I'm used to army maps, not sketch maps like this.' He glanced up at the sky and then said, 'I wish Mr Jones had seen fit to indicate which way was north on his little map.'

'Here, let me have a look,' I said. Warnie happily handed it over. At first it looked like just a series of squiggly lines wandering across the page. I tried turning it upside down and then sideways. I held it at arm's length and squinted at it as if trying to bring a blurred picture into focus. Then I turned it back so that the X that marked the position of *The Boar's Head* was at the bottom. That was when it seemed to start making sense to me.

'I think I can see where we are now,' I said uncertainly. 'Or where we might be. See this curving line here?' I pointed at the paper. 'Well, I think that's the road we're on. Ahead of us should be a crossroads, and that's where we turn right.'

Jack and Warnie looked over my shoulder, and then Jack told me to lead on. We walked for perhaps another quarter of a mile and came to a fork in the road. This appeared not to be marked on Frank Jones' map, so we took a chance on the left-hand fork. A hundred yards further on I became convinced we were heading in the wrong direction and persuaded the others to go back and take the other road.

When Warnie grumbled I said, 'Well, we're supposed to be on a walking holiday, and at least right now we're walking!'

Back at the intersection where I thought we'd gone wrong we headed up the right hand fork instead of the left. A hundred yards later we came to the crossroads, with the ancient oak tree Frank Jones had told us about on the corner.

'Well done, young Morris,' said Jack, slapping me on the back. 'You've got us back on track. Now we head right from here, don't we?'

The map said we should, and so we did. Half an hour of brisk walking brought us to a farm gate. Hanging from the roadside letterbox next to the gate was the name 'Proudfoot'. And just behind some trees we could make out the farmhouse.

'Well,' said Jack as he unlatched the gate, 'let's go and see what young Nicholas Proudfoot has to say for himself.'

We walked through and relatched the gate behind us. We hadn't gone far down the farm track when a chorus of dogs began yapping to alert the inhabitants to our arrival, and alert us to the fact that we were stepping on territory that was rightly theirs under the Canine Real Property Act.

Soon the farm dogs were dancing around our feet, telling us that they knew we were strangers and intended to keep an eye on us. Warnie, who has a way with dogs, stopped to talk to them. Soon he was scratching their backs and had become their new best friend.

There was no sign of life at the old stone farmhouse. Its weathered walls were covered with moss and lichen. There was complete silence in the yard in front of the house—apart from the panting, yapping dogs—and the place looked deserted.

Jack knocked on the front door. The sound seemed to echo throughout the house, and for a long time there was no response.

'There's no one here,' muttered Warnie.

'No, I definitely heard a sound,' Jack said, and he knocked again. Eventually footsteps could be heard, and the door was opened halfway. The face we saw was that of a young woman with dark eyes and dark hair. In other circumstances she would have been strikingly beautiful, but the most striking thing about her that morning were her eyes—red and swollen from crying.

'Good morning,' said Jack in his softest and most affable manner. 'Mrs Proudfoot, isn't it?' She nodded blankly. 'My name is Jack Lewis; this is my brother Warren and our friend Tom Morris. We just happened to be in the bank yesterday when your husband visited Mr Ravenswood, and we wondered if we could have a word with him please.'

Her only response was to collapse in the doorway in a dead faint.

ELEVEN

~

There was a moment of awkward embarrassment as three single males looked at a fragile young woman lying unconscious at their feet. Jack cupped his hands to his mouth and called out loudly, 'Hello! Hello! Anyone there?' We waited but there was no response, so Warnie scooped the unconscious young woman up in his arms and carried her inside.

The front door of the farmhouse opened onto a hallway. This hall ran straight through the middle of the cottage, exactly bisecting it. It was what I believe is called in the country a 'shotgun cottage', meaning you could fire a shotgun through the front door and it would go straight out the back door.

The first door on the right proved to be a small sitting room, filled with over-stuffed armchairs and a lounge. Warnie laid her on the lounge. Then we stopped and looked at each other. The farmhouse was ominously quiet except for the loud ticking of a cabinet clock in the hall. Amelia Proudfoot lay on the lounge as unmoving as if she were in a coma. But at least she was still breathing—we could see that.

I followed Jack's example and stepped into the hallway and called, 'Hello? Anyone about?' Then I went back out through the front door and called again. The sound of my voice died away in the distance with no response. I came back to the small front parlour, looked at the others and shrugged my shoulders.

Warnie looked down at the young woman, then he looked helplessly at Jack and said, 'What do we do now?'

'Morris,' said Jack to me, 'find the kitchen and put on the kettle. This young lady needs a cup of strong, sweet tea.'

I returned to the narrow hallway and explored. The kitchen was the last door on the right. Inside I found an Aga cooker with its fire burning, so I filled a kettle from a jug of water beside the sink and put it on a hotplate. Then I stoked up the wood fire in the Aga and hunted around for a teapot and the tea caddy. I found both in a side dresser, along with cups and saucers. When the kettle boiled, I made enough tea for the four of us, put the teapot, cups, saucers, a bowl of sugar and a jug of milk on a tray, and carried it back into the front room.

Young Mrs Proudfoot was just starting to move and groan as I re-entered the room. Her eyes flickered open and she suddenly pushed herself bolt upright with a look of terror on her face.

'Please don't be anxious, Mrs Proudfoot,' Jack said soothingly. 'We're the visitors who knocked on your door just before you fainted. I hope you don't mind—we've brought you inside and made you a cup of tea.'

She opened her mouth to say something, but the words wouldn't come. She was still a little shaky and reached a trembling hand out to the arm of the lounge to steady herself.

'Will tea be all right?' asked Warnie. 'If you like I can hunt around for something stronger—a little brandy perhaps?'

She shook her head. 'Tea's fine, thank you,' she half-whispered in a weak voice.

'We do apologise for barging into your house like this,' said Jack, 'but when you collapsed and no one else seemed to be around, we thought we should do something.'

She nodded and tried to smile.

'If you'd rather we leave, we will,' Jack offered.

She saw the tray and the crockery I had brought in from the kitchen, shook her head and said softly, 'No . . . no . . . It's all right. Help yourselves to tea.'

We did. Then we seated ourselves in the old armchairs, sank back into their cavernous embrace, and sipped on our tea in silence for a few minutes. Eventually the colour began to return to the young woman's face, and she spoke again.

'You said you wanted my husband, I think?'

'Yes,' Jack responded, 'but I take it he's not around.'

'He's taken the pony trap,' she said, and then added, a little uncertainly, 'He's gone into town, I think . . .'

Whatever train of thought our question provoked seemed to have an effect on her. She lowered her eyelids and her face lost all its colour and went quite pale again. We sipped our tea in silence for a minute while she regained her composure.

'Perhaps we can ask you, Mrs Proudfoot,' Jack said after taking another sip of tea, 'do you know why your husband was so angry with the bank manager, Mr Ravenswood, yesterday?'

'What did he say?' she asked anxiously.

'Not a lot,' Warnie said. 'He was so angry he didn't make a lot of sense. It was quite remarkable really, the way he seemed to be restraining himself. There was clearly a lot of anger there, but he seemed to be bottling it up. All I can really remember is his promising that Mr Ravenswood would end up behind bars. Or something like that anyway. Then, of course, he pushed Mr Ravenswood into the bank vault. Officially I suppose that counts as assault. Not that the police seem very interested in that—they're more preoccupied with the murder.'

'Murder?' said Mrs Proudfoot in alarm.

'Ah, haven't you heard?' Warnie continued. 'That teller chappie, Franklin Grimm, has been murdered. Nasty business. Brutal stab wound.'

Oddly she seemed relieved by this news, as if she had expected him to name a different victim. She sank back into the cushions on the lounge, thoughtfully drinking her tea.

'So what was your husband so angry about?' Jack pursued.

She blinked and looked at him. She had been so deeply lost in thought that she hadn't heard his question, so he repeated it. But still she didn't reply immediately. She gazed off into the distance and it seemed to me that thoughts were rushing through her head as she tried to puzzle out what had happened—and to decide whether it had any connection with her husband's problems.

Jack repeated his question a third time.

There was another long silence before she replied, 'There's a loan. We have a loan. It's a mortgage on this farm. If we default we lose the farm . . .' Her voice trailed away.

'But there must be more,' Jack prompted.

'I really don't want to talk about it,' said young Mrs Proudfoot firmly.

'Do you mind if I ask you about Franklin Grimm?' I said.

She turned towards me. She said nothing, but she was clearly waiting for a question, so I continued, 'It was a fairly brutal murder, as Warnie said, so can you think of anyone who . . . well, hated him enough, I suppose, to violently kill him?'

Another prolonged silence ensued, broken only by the ticking of the old-fashioned cabinet clock in the hallway. Mrs Proudfoot stared down into her tea for a long time, then she said slowly, 'Well, there's Ted, I suppose.'

Jack encouraged her to explain, and she said, 'He's Nick's older brother. He's not a happy man. In fact, he's a bitter man.

For a start he resented Nick inheriting this farm. As the oldest in the family he thought it should have gone to him. But he was—well, shiftless is what they say, isn't it? And he drank a fair bit when he was younger. So when their father died, it was Nick who helped his mother run the place. And when she died she left it to Nick. All Ted got was the small amount of money she had in her bank account. It was all very awkward. Nick had the farm but not the money he needed to fix things up around here, and Ted had the money but no intention of putting any of it into the farm.'

She stopped to drink some more tea.

'But where does Franklin Grimm come into it?' I asked.

'I was coming to that,' she resumed. 'Ted was already an angry, bitter young man and then this other business happened. Ted had a girlfriend, Julie Miller—a nice girl. She could have straightened him out, I think. But she never got the chance. Franklin Grimm had a sort of way with girls, and he set his cap at Julie. I think she got swept off her feet by the attention and the charm. It had happened to other girls before her, but I think she believed Franklin Grimm was going to be all hers. He wasn't, of course. Horrible man. His own pleasure was all he cared about.'

She paused again and sipped her tea. It was clear there was more to the story, so we waited.

'Then Julie disappeared,' young Mrs Proudfoot resumed after a long silence. 'She left town. No one in Market Plumpton seemed to know where she'd gone. For months we heard nothing. Then, eventually, word came through. Julie's parents were dead, but her aunt and uncle were worried so they asked the police to make some enquiries. They found Julie had died during childbirth. Alone. In a cheap London bed-sit. The baby died too. Well, Ted was distraught, and he made all kinds of threats against Franklin. He was certain it was Franklin Grimm who'd got her in the family way. And it must have been. She wasn't seeing anyone else at the time. Ted got very drunk, night after night. And when he was drunk he always threatened to kill Franklin. But when he sobered up he never did anything about it.'

She put her cup and saucer down on the small polished table in front of her. It was clear that the story was over and she intended to tell us no more.

'Where might we find Ted,' Jack asked, 'if we wanted a word with him?'

'He's a farmhand these days, working on the Farnon place,' she said.

'Far from here?'

'I'm afraid so. You need to cross the river and walk around to the east of the town to reach it.'

'And was Franklin Grimm,' I asked, 'ever particularly friendly with your husband—or with you?'

She understood the implication in my question and snapped out a sharp reply. 'Certainly not! He was an odious man and we had nothing to do with him. Either of us.'

In the awkward silence that followed we finished our tea and placed the cups and saucers back on the tray.

Jack stood up and said, 'We really should take up no more of your time, Mrs Proudfoot.'

'If you're feeling fully recovered, that is?' Warnie said.

'Yes, thank you. And thank you for bringing me inside. And for the tea.'

The dismissal was clear, so we said our goodbyes and walked back out into the farmyard. We heard the front door close and lock behind us. Then we heard a bolt slide into place.

Jack gestured at the door and said, 'Clearly she has no intention of answering any more questions.'

'So what now?' asked Warnie.

'Back to town, I think,' Jack said.

So we made our way back to the road and began to retrace our footsteps.

We hadn't gone far when we rounded a corner and saw, coming towards us, a puffed and red-faced Constable Dixon. He was wiping his forehead with a large white handkerchief and at first he didn't see us. When he did, he gulped and stared saucer-eyed at us. Clearly he could no longer pretend not to be following us. This caused so much cogitation it was almost possible to hear the gearwheels spinning inside his head.

'Morning,' he puffed as we drew level with him. Then he took off his helmet, scratched his head and said, 'It'll save me a lot of trouble if you gentlemen would be kind enough to tell where you've been and where you're going now.'

Warnie drew himself up to his full height and blew out his cheeks. 'I'm not sure it's any of your business, old chap.'

'Come on,' said Jack sympathetically, 'we don't want to get our friendly local policeman into trouble with his superiors.' Then he turned to Dixon and said, 'We've been visiting the Proudfoot farm—trying to find out what caused the scene at the bank yesterday morning.'

Constable Dixon pulled out his small notebook and pencil and dutifully wrote this down. 'And where might you be going now, sir?' he asked politely.

'Back to town,' said Jack with a hearty laugh. 'Come and walk with us, constable.'

The policeman smiled and said, 'With pleasure, sir. But not the way you came—that's the long way. I'll show you a shorter route.'

'Lead on, Constable Dixon—we're in your hands!'

TWELVE

As we started out I asked Constable Dixon how he managed to find us.

'I tracked you, sir,' he said, tapping the side of his nose, 'like a Red Indian in those James Fennimore Cooper books I used to read when I was a lad—footsteps in the damp soil, that sort of thing. Besides which, starting from the church there are not many roads out of town, so it wasn't really all that hard. I just started in the general direction and looked for any little signs that you might have passed this way.'

He paused to mop his brow again with his large white handkerchief and then complained, 'It was not a nice thing that you gentlemen did back there—sneaking out of the vestry door of the church and giving me the slip.'

'Not a nice thing?' grunted Warnie. 'I like that.' Then he turned to me and said, 'The hide of the man: he treats us like criminals and then complains when we behave like the perfectly innocent gentlemen we are! Not nice indeed!'

He huffed and puffed and harrumphed for the next minute or two but finally settled down. And Constable Dixon appeared to have decided that it was wise not to say any more on the subject.

When we had walked a hundred yards further on, the policeman pointed to a side road, little more than a cart track, and said, 'This way is shorter, more direct—it leads down to the stream, and then we can follow the towpath back into town. And if you don't mind my asking—what have your amateur investigations turned up so far? If it's not a secret, that is. Inspector Hyde is bound to ask me, and . . .'

'We don't want to get you into trouble,' Jack laughed heartily. 'In the absence of Nicholas Proudfoot we ended up interviewing his wife. She was either not willing or not able to explain whatever lay behind what her husband Nicholas did at the bank yesterday—that volcanically angry performance of his. She talked vaguely about a problem with a loan, and I can't see how that can have anything to do with the murder. At least, not at the moment I can't.'

The policeman thought about this for a while, then he asked, 'Just now I accused you gentlemen of conducting your own amateur investigations. Now you speak of "interviewing" Mrs Proudfoot. Does this mean you really are playing at being Sherlock Holmes? If you don't mind my asking, that is.'

'Exactly!' hooted Warnie. 'Not leaving it up to some chappie from Scotland Yard. If you'd read as many detective novels as I have, you'd know those Scotland Yard chaps never know what's going on. Always has to be someone to tell them!'

'So you're sort of investigating for yourselves . . .' It was more a comment than a question from Constable Dixon. 'Just like those stories in the *Strand Magazine*? Although personally I prefer the Sexton Blake stories myself.'

Jack laughed again and said, 'Something like that. Although perhaps not quite as energetic as Mr Holmes or some of the others.'

'My brother,' said Warnie as he slapped Jack on the back, 'could run rings around Sherlock Holmes for sheer brain power. And he will too.'

'I'm not sure the officers from Scotland Yard will be happy about that,' moaned Dixon. His face crinkled up like a worried toad—a toad who's just been told his mother-in-law is coming to visit and may be staying some time.

We plodded on in silence while the policeman slowly digested all this. Then the foliage surrounding the cart track we were on opened out as we came to the banks of a fast-flowing stream. Following one side of the bank was a narrow walking path, and down this Constable Dixon led us in single file.

Eventually, having digested what we had told him, he turned around to ask another question. 'And what did Amelia Proudfoot actually tell you? If you don't mind my asking, that is.'

'Ask whatever you wish, constable,' said Jack. 'And the answer is, as I tried to explain, that she told us precious little. We wanted to understand the source of her husband's explosive anger displayed in the bank yesterday, and she was clearly most reluctant to tell us anything. In fact, her reluctance seemed to suggest that she feels she has something to hide—either concerning herself or her husband—that she doesn't want the wider world to know.'

'Ah, yes,' Dixon nodded sagely, 'I'm sure you're right, sir. If you don't mind my mentioning this to the officers from Scotland Yard?'

'Tell them whatever you wish, constable,' Jack replied. 'We just want this matter dealt with as swiftly as possible so we can be on our way. When are the experts from the Yard due to arrive?'

'They should be in Market Plumpton by now, sir. They were due on the morning train.'

Then he asked us why we had taken such a long road out to the Proudfoot farm. Warnie explained that we were following a sketch map provided by the publican, Frank Jones, adding, 'And we . . . humph . . . found the map a little . . . a little . . .'

'A little vague and imprecise,' I said. 'In short, we may have got just a little bit lost for a moment there.' As I spoke I dug into my coat pocket and pulled out Frank Jones's map. When I handed this over to Dixon, he found himself wrestling with its meaning as much as we had done. He turned it upside down and sideways.

'It's just a lot of squiggles,' said the constable, nodding as if now understanding something that had baffled him. 'I'm not surprised you had difficulty finding the right road.'

The stream curved around a bend ahead of us, and as we rounded the curve we saw a bridge crossing the water—an old stone bridge. Drawing closer we saw that it connected two other cart tracks on either side of the stream, and standing on one side of the bridge was a pony trap. The pony in the harness was calming chewing on the thick grass on the river bank, but of the owner or driver of the cart there was no sign.

'I recognise that,' said Constable Dixon. 'That's Nick Proudfoot's pony trap. Now why would he leave it standing here and walk off? And where's he gone to?'

We all four walked out to the centre of the old stone bridge, with the policeman swivelling his head in all directions looking for the missing man.

'He can't be far away,' said the constable. 'He hasn't tied up the horse or anything. The pony might just wander off, taking the cart with him once he's finished his feed. Why would anyone do that?'

We followed the policeman's example, turning around and scouring the landscape with our eyes. For several minutes the only sound was the roaring rush of the fast-flowing stream beneath the bridge. This was yet another puzzle to add to the growing list of puzzles that Market Plumpton was presenting us with.

'I wonder if that's your answer,' said Jack at last, pointing to a dark shape in the water at the next bend in the stream. It was being bounced by the strong currents but appeared to be caught in a tangle of tree roots.

Warnie was the first to move. He crossed the bridge and pushed through the thick undergrowth on the opposite bank towards the dark shape in the water. The rest of us followed as quickly as we could.

'It's a body,' Warnie called out from ahead of us. He clambered down the bank, balanced precariously on two large, round stones and grabbed hold of the figure's arms. Then he backed up the bank, pulling the body with him as he came. He dropped it in the long grass and turned it over. We hurried to his side.

The face had been battered and bruised against the stones on the bed of the stream, so the man's identity was not immediately obvious to us. But it was to Constable Dixon. 'It's Nick Proudfoot,' he gasped.

As soon as he said the name I recognised the man who had burst into the bank the day before. The face looked quite different—behind the scratches and bruises it had the calm of death—but it was the same face.

'Well . . . well . . .' puffed the policeman, looking around anxiously as he tried to work out what to do next. 'Well . . . this is a turn up for the books. Well . . . steps need to be taken here. Something needs to be done.' Probably for the first time in his career the local constable was wrestling with a problem larger than failure to abate a smoking chimney or dropping litter in a public place. And clearly he was out of his depth.

Jack intervened to say, 'Someone needs to go into town immediately to inform your superiors, constable. But someone needs to stay with the body as well.'

'Yes, yes, quite right, sir,' huffed Constable Dixon, pulling himself together. 'So, I'll go into town . . . no, that's not right. I can hardly leave you gentlemen here with the body—on your own, so to speak, without an official keeping an eye on you . . . and on the body . . .' His voice trailed away.

'What you mean,' said Jack, with an amused gleam in his eye, 'is that we're suspects in this murder too.'

'Well . . . well . . .' blustered the policeman, 'it might not be murder. But still, I am in charge of the scene of this . . . this tragedy, and I can hardly leave.'

'Would you like all three of us to go into town and inform Inspector Hyde?' asked Jack, a teasing note in his voice.

'All three of you?' Constable Dixon seemed to have sudden and alarming visions of all three of us taking flight and absconding, not something he would enjoy having to explain to his inspector. 'Ah, perhaps not . . .'

'I suggest,' said Jack helpfully, 'that young Morris here—being the youngest among us—would make fastest progress. So why don't you send Morris into town? Just give him directions to reach the police station and he can alert them. Warnie and I will wait here with you, to keep an eye on the body and perhaps to have a look around while we're waiting for reinforcements to arrive. What do you think?'

It took the constable a minute or two of silent thought to work out just exactly what he did think. But in the end he decided that Jack's proposal was the only practical one.

He gave me directions. 'Just follow this towpath. You'll get to the main road bridge into town—it leads to the high street. Follow that to the town square. The police station's just off the square.'

I double checked his directions and then set off at a jog. I knew I couldn't sprint all the way to town, but I thought I could keep up a fairly steady pace.

To conserve my energy and my breath I varied my pace between a fast walk and a slightly faster trot. As I ran I looked at the stream that was my constant companion. It was, I noticed, quite deep as well as fast flowing, and I wondered how Nicholas Proudfoot had died. Had he drowned? Or had he been dead before he hit the water? And why had Jack talked about 'this murder'? Couldn't it just have been an accident? What made him think this was a second murder? He must have had a reason, I was sure, but I couldn't immediately see what that reason was.

And if he was right, if this was another murder, how did it connect to the first—the murder of Franklin Grimm? It seemed to me that we were wading into deep, murky, mysterious waters.

THIRTEEN

~

Constable Dixon's directions had been clear and helpful, and within half an hour I was back at the edge of the town. I found that the towpath led me directly to the footpath over the road bridge. I followed this to the high street, and in turn followed the high street until it opened into the town square, where we had set out that morning.

Around the corner, where the high street joined the square, I found the blue sign that identified the police station. I sprinted up the steps, and just inside the dark brick walls was a counter that separated the public from the policemen.

Behind this, seated at a desk, was the same Sergeant Donaldson we had seen at work the day before as Inspector Hyde's silent assistant. This Donaldson was a solid, stodgy man who appeared to have been assembled out of some sort of suet. And when he moved, which he did rather ponderously, it appeared that the suet had not entirely set.

'Ah, it's you!' he said, leaning forward on his desk. 'The detectives from Scotland Yard have been looking for you. Where are the other two?'

'Still with the body,' I replied.

'I'll go and tell Inspector Hyde you're here,' he said turning towards a back office. 'The Scotland Yard men are with him now—' He came to a sudden halt as my words sank in. He turned back towards me, trembling like a jelly in a high wind. His eyes were staring, like windows with the shutters suddenly thrown open. 'Still with the what?' he asked.

'The body.'

'Which body? Whose body?'

'Nicholas Proudfoot. We found him dead in that stream to the north of the town—if you know the one I mean.'

'Yes, yes, it's a tributary of the Plum River. He has to cross it when he comes into town from his farm. You found him in the water, you say?'

'Yes.'

'Just wait there. Stand there. Don't move.' And he rushed off in an urgent wobble into the back office. Less than a minute later he was back, followed by three men. One of them was Inspector Hyde who had questioned us the day before; the other two I didn't recognise.

'You're Morris, aren't you?' said Hyde, striding up to the counter in his busy, bustling manner, looking every inch (and he didn't have many inches) the small man with the Napoleon complex.

'Tom Morris, yes.'

'And you say you've found Nicholas Proudfoot's body?'

'Well, *we* have—myself, my friends, Jack and Warren Lewis, and Constable Dixon.'

'Dixon was with you?

I nodded and said, 'He's still there—keeping an eye on the body, along with my friends.'

Hyde turned to talk to the other two, then he decided he first should introduce them to me—or, more likely, me to them. The taller of the two was identified as Inspector Crispin and the shorter, stockier individual as Sergeant Merrivale.

'Is the police car in the yard?' Hyde asked Sergeant Donaldson.

'Yes, sir.'

'We'll take that. It'll only seat four, so you can follow on your bicycle, Donaldson. In fact, if you take the towpath and we take the road you should get there almost as quickly as we do. But before you do, telephone Dr Haydock. I want him to come out and inspect the body before we move it.'

The police car did seat four—but only just. It was a small, black Ford Popular. Hyde and Crispin sat in the front seat while I squeezed into the back alongside the somewhat bulky form of Sergeant Merrivale. It was like sitting beside a bag of large, lumpy potatoes—potatoes that remained entirely silent throughout the journey, and seemed to concentrate entirely on spreading out and occupying as much of the back seat as possible.

For the last part of the journey we needed to hang on to whatever we could as the small car bumped and bounced over the unsealed cart track that led from the road to the river.

After ten minutes of this we arrived at the old stone bridge that crossed the stream. Seeing the car appear out of a cloud of dust, Constable Dixon rushed towards us with the look of a man delighted to hand over his responsibility to somebody more senior. Dixon led the others to where the body lay on the embankment and stood back.

The tall man, Inspector Crispin, was immaculately dressed and quietly observant. He spoke little, but when he did it was with authority. He looked and sounded more like a school master than my idea of a Scotland Yard detective. At any moment I half expected him to turn to one of the uniformed men and say, 'You there, the boy at the back of the room—are you paying attention?'

The other policeman from London, Sergeant Merrivale, was very respectful to the taller man, like an army sergeant in the presence of his colonel.

These two, Crispin and Merrivale, crouched over the body, emptying the pockets and examining the wounds. Then Sergeant Merrivale went back to the police car and returned with photographic equipment. He took pictures of the corpse and the surrounding area from every angle, then returned the equipment to the boot of the car.

While this was going on, a breathless and red-faced Sergeant Donaldson arrived, cycling up the towpath and oozing exhaustion from every pore. In a puffed voice, gasping for air, he reported to Inspector Hyde, who turned to Crispin and said, 'Anything my men can do, sir?'

'Search the area,' said the Scotland Yard man. 'Both banks and in the water as well. You men should look for anything that strikes you as being out of place. And for bloodstains or signs of violence anywhere in this general vicinity.'

Donaldson and Dixon set off to carry out this assignment. Jack, Warnie and I had been standing well back, watching proceedings, but now Jack stepped forward and said, 'You might like to take a look at the top of the stonework in the middle of that bridge.'

Inspector Crispin said nothing but asked a question by raising his eyebrows.

'There are fresh scratch marks—could be the scene of a fight, a struggle or some act of violence.'

'Show me,' said Crispin. With Jack in the lead we all trooped back to the old stone bridge. In the centre of the arch we stopped where Jack indicated a number of broad scratch marks across one of the large stones. They appeared to be newly made. The dark green moss that covered the stones had been scraped off, revealing the honey-coloured sandstone underneath.

'Fresh all right,' Crispin agreed, and set Merrivale the task of retrieving his equipment and photographing these marks.

Jack, I noticed, had lost interest in the scratch marks and was staring intently at the thick branches of the willow tree that hung over the bridge. I was about to ask what was so interesting about the tree when I was stopped by a shout that came almost from our feet. We all hurried to the side of the bridge and looked down.

Constable Dixon had waded into the water almost up to his waist and was struggling to stay upright in the fast-flowing current.

'There's something here, sir,' he was shouting, 'but it's hard to reach.'

'Help him, Donaldson,' shouted Inspector Hyde impatiently. 'He's wet—you might as well get wet too. Wade in and help him.'

Sergeant Donaldson took off his jacket, dropped it on the bank and waded into the cold rushing stream. It took them the next ten minutes, with the aid of a broken tree branch, to fetch out the object Constable Dixon had found. When they finally struggled with it up the bank, it turned out to be an old brown leather suitcase.

Inspector Crispin joined the dripping wet local policemen and said, 'Open it. Show me what's inside.'

I felt sorry for our old friend Constable Dixon, whose cold fingers had to fumble with the catches for some time before he got them open. When he did so he flung back the lid to reveal—a suitcase full of large stones.

Dixon straightened up and shook himself like a wet dog—a very disappointed wet dog that had just returned to its favourite hiding place in the garden to discover all its buried bones were missing.

We all stepped back from the fine spray of water coming off the shaking policeman as Inspector Hyde exclaimed, 'Rocks! Who in his right mind would throw a good leather suitcase full of rocks into the water? It makes no sense. And Dixon—stop that at once! You're making the rest of us as wet as you are!'

'Sorry, sir,' mumbled Dixon, suddenly feeling as unloved as the same wet dog at a family picnic.

Crispin smiled slowly as he said, 'Rocks—nothing but rocks. And that makes it interesting, doesn't it?' Then he leaned forward to examine a small piece of frayed rope attached to the handle of the suitcase.

Clearly Inspector Hyde could find nothing even remotely interesting in a soaking wet suitcase full of rocks, but he made no objection when Crispin ordered the find to be put in the boot of the police car. The two sergeants, Donaldson and Merrivale, between them carried the heavy bag to the car and put it in the boot beside the photographic equipment case.

At this point a loud, rattling petrol engine announced the arrival of the police surgeon, Dr Haydock, in an Austin Seven. He was a cheerful, hearty man who kept addressing the corpse as if it were still alive.

'Let's see where you've been hurt, shall we?' he said to the dead man as he rolled the body over. 'Dear me, you're not in good shape, are you? What have you been up to, Nick Proudfoot? How did you manage to do this?'

He fingered the wounds on the front and back of Nicholas Proudfoot's head just as gently as he would have done with a patient in his surgery.

'Those blows,' said Inspector Crispin, crouching down beside the doctor, 'are they pre-mortem or post-mortem?'

'Hard to tell until I get him on the slab and do a proper examination. The water has washed away most of the blood that would otherwise have indicated which wounds bled freely and which didn't.'

'Could *any* of them have been delivered before death?'

'The one on the back of the head, possibly. But don't hold me to that. I'll do the post-mortem as soon as possible.'

'Any idea whether he died from the blows or from drowning?' asked the Scotland Yard man.

Dr Haydock shook his head sadly, as if dealing with a recalcitrant patient who was not listening to his instructions.

'After the post-mortem, inspector,' he said, 'and not before. I need to open him up to see if there's water in the lungs or not. But I can tell you one thing immediately: Nicholas Proudfoot was my patient and I happen to know that he couldn't swim. So as soon as he went into this cold, fast-flowing water, with no one here to rescue him, he was a dead man.'

This drew a grunt from Crispin, who rose to his feet scratching his chin thoughtfully.

'Now inspector, my dear chap,' said Warnie, bustling forward, 'surely you don't need us around any longer? Morris and my brother and I are supposed to be on a walking holiday. Inspector Hyde took our statements: surely we can be on our way? What do you say, eh?'

'I'm sorry, Major Lewis,' replied Crispin, 'but not just yet. In fact, I'm calling a meeting at the bank this afternoon to ask all of the principal witnesses to go over their evidence with me at the scene of the crime. Let's say two o'clock, shall we?'

Warnie's round expressionless face hid his disappointment as he muttered, 'Ah well, if you say so . . . two o'clock then.'

FOURTEEN

~

Then there arose the question of how we were all to get back to town. Inspector Hyde banned Dixon and Donaldson, both still soaking wet, from riding in the police car and told them they had to walk—or, in Donaldson's case, ride his bicycle—back into Market Plumpton. Jack, Warnie and I clearly wouldn't fit in the car with the three policemen so we announced that we too would walk back to town.

We set off down the towpath beside the stream, leaving Dixon and Donaldson waiting for a vehicle to come to pick up the body, and Inspector Hyde making plans to go and break the news to young Mrs Proudfoot at the farm on the drive back to town.

The late morning sunshine was warm and the breeze gentle. The weather seemed to be saying, 'You've had enough grim news for one day, I'll try to cheer you up.'

But the weather was failing to work its magic on Warnie. 'Nice day for walking,' he grumbled. 'Should be walking. Should be off on our holiday. Shouldn't be stuck here to answer the same fool questions over and over again.'

'Think of it as an adventure,' said Jack, slapping his brother on his back. 'You must admit the murder of young Mr Grimm is most mysterious and intriguing, and I would have thought, for a passionate reader of detective novels such as yourself, dashed interesting.'

'Well, yes, I suppose so,' grunted Warnie, a slightly surprised expression on his face. 'Hadn't thought of it quite like that. I do love a good mystery.'

We were walking in single file, as we had to do down that narrow towpath, with Warnie in the lead, followed by Jack with me bringing up the rear.

I had had quite enough of violent death in the last two days, and I wanted to throw the switch to some other topic entirely. So I picked up on Warnie's words and said, 'I also love a good mystery, Jack—and I find it quite mysterious that an intelligent man such as yourself keeps insisting that only Christianity can see the truth about life in this world.'

'I have you puzzled, have I, young Morris?' Jack replied, looking over his shoulder with a cheerful grin on his face.

'That's the word! Puzzled. No one—and no one way of looking at the world—can see the whole story and the whole truth. That's how scholarship works: each researcher contributes a bit of the picture. Remember our discussion of the jigsaw puzzle? Well, if life's a puzzle, and we each do our bit of puzzling things out, we each have a bit to contribute.'

'But we need some standard to evaluate each contribution,' said Jack. 'Some way of knowing whether an idea is a part of the truth or a pointless blind alley leading us in the wrong direction, or even a flat-out falsehood. Hence my claim that Christianity, in the jigsaw puzzle image, is the "picture on the lid of the box" that the puzzle comes in—the picture that shows us what we're aiming at with all our ideas and discoveries.'

'See, that's what puzzles me,' I said. 'That seems like a remarkably arrogant claim to make. You were once an atheist, so you know there are other ways of looking at the world.' I was groping for the words to express the vague notion floating somewhere at the back of my brain. But my brain was not helping me find it. It seemed to think it had had quite enough shocks for one day and was putting its feet up somewhere in a dimly lit corner of my cerebellum and having a little doze.

'Look,' I said, 'your mention of a "blind alley" made me think of something that might explain what I'm getting at.'

Jack said nothing, but I saw his head nod as he waited for me to go on.

'You've heard the story—we all have—of the four blind men and the elephant.'

'I've heard it,' said Warnie from his position in the lead. 'Chappie who'd served in India told it to me. Very clever, I thought. Very interesting.'

'Remind us,' said Jack.

'Well, in the story there are these four blind men—' Warnie began.

'No,' Jack said, 'I want to hear how young Morris explains it and what he thinks it means.'

'Oh, all right then,' mumbled Warnie, slightly miffed.

'The story I heard,' I said, 'went like this. Four blind men were walking down a road and came upon an elephant. They had never encountered an elephant before, nor had the concept of an elephant been explained to them. So they gathered around this animal and each of them grabbed hold of a different part of the beast. Then they argued about what they'd encountered. One blind man was feeling the elephant's ear and said he'd found a large leaf from a palm tree—the sort of large, flat leaf used as a fan. The second blind man had the tail and said he'd found a rope. The third had the elephant's trunk and said he'd found a hose. And the fourth ran his hands over one of the elephant's legs and said he'd found a large tree trunk.'

I paused at that point, so Jack asked, 'And what do you think the story—or fable, or parable, or whatever you call it—teaches us?'

'That none of us has an exclusive and complete grasp of the truth. Not one of us can get hold of all of the truth. Each one of us can comprehend only part of the whole, so we have to pool our knowledge—and even then our understanding is likely to be partial and incomplete.'

'But your conclusion doesn't fit,' Jack said. 'It's not a reasonable conclusion to draw from the story.'

'Hang on,' I protested. 'I'm not drawing some strange or eccentric conclusion. The moral I see in that story is the moral most people see. In fact, it's the whole point of the story.'

'Well, in that case,' Jack insisted, 'the story doesn't support the moral.'

I was now completely confused so I said nothing, and Jack continued, 'There's one person in your story who *does* see the whole picture—who understands all the parts and how they fit together and what they mean.'

This baffled me. 'Who?' I asked genuinely puzzled by his remark.

'The storyteller,' said Jack with a hearty laugh.

He let this sink in and then continued, 'The only reason the story has any meaning or any point at all is that it's told by a storyteller who *knows* the object is an elephant—to an audience that knows the object is an elephant. Clearly the storyteller is not blind and can see that it's an elephant being groped by the four sightless men. The storyteller is clearly familiar with elephants and knows the animal for what it is. If there had been no sighted storyteller at the encounter, there would be no story.'

We all had to duck as we passed under a low-hanging tree branch, then Jack went on, 'If you told that story to blind men who knew nothing of elephants, the story would mean nothing. It only has meaning because a sighted storyteller who is familiar with what elephants really are is telling us the story and drawing the moral. Without the storyteller who sees the bigger picture, the story is meaningless. And the same is true of life. In the story the four blind men are meant to represent each of us—individuals groping towards the truth. And perhaps that's not a bad picture of how each of us copes on our journey through life. But in that case, who does the storyteller represent? Who is it who sees the bigger picture and understands what the bigger picture means?'

He stopped while we pushed through some bushes that almost overgrew the narrow towpath, and then he resumed, 'Even the most intelligent and well-informed men I know have limitations. In fact, being human involves having limitations. So what we all need is the equivalent of the "sighted storyteller" to give us the big picture and make sense of it all, to tell us the meaning and the purpose. We all have some of the clues—for instance, our in-built moral sense, our sense of right and wrong, is a clue to the meaning of the universe.'

'But you say we need help to see the bigger picture?'

'The real arrogance is in those human beings who insist they know enough, who refuse to be told, who refuse to submit to the direction of a greater intelligence than theirs.'

We rounded a bend at this point and the town came into view. 'Nearly there,' said Warnie.

Jack stopped for a moment and turned around to face me. 'Imagine your blind men examining an unfamiliar building. They each feel different parts of it and disagree about how those parts fit together, what they mean and what they're for. Then the architect of the building arrives. He tells them about the design—what it looks like, its purpose and what its function is.

It would be stubbornly arrogant of those blind men to refuse to listen, wouldn't it?'

Well, yes, of course it would, but I wasn't going to admit that out loud—so Jack continued.

'The testable claim of Christianity is that God is the architect in my little fable, and the "sighted storyteller" in yours. We all fight against that—I know I did. But eventually I gave in and admitted that God was God and that I wasn't. God closed in on me. I suddenly felt as if I was Hamlet and had made the startling discovery that I was in a play by someone called Shakespeare, and that the Author wanted to meet me.'

By now we had reached the River Plum and were mounting the footpath to the main bridge across the river. Jack walked silently for some minutes and then said, 'It was really quite an uncomfortable encounter when I realised I had to face God.' Then after another pause he added, 'But, of course, reality is often uncomfortable.'

From the bridge we walked up the high street, then turned into the narrow streets in the older part of town that led to the pub. We arrived at *The Boar's Head* in time for lunch.

'Welcome back from your morning walk, gentlemen,' said Frank Jones with his professional publican's heartiness. 'Interesting morning?'

'You could say that,' Warnie chuckled. 'But I'd call it a famishing morning. Lunch about?'

'It's a nice day, gentlemen,' said the publican, 'so why don't you take a seat at a table out in the beer garden and I'll bring it out to you?'

Five minutes later he arrived with a plate loaded with slices of cold roast beef, bread, pickles and a nice piece of cheddar. He also brought us three pints of bitter. For some minutes we were too busy concentrating on our welcome meal to talk much.

Then Warnie leaned back in his chair, took a sip from his pint, wiped the foam from his moustache and said, 'Odd thing. One of the detective novels I brought with me—been reading it at night in bed—is called *It Walks by Night* by a chappie named John Dickson Carr. Reminds me a bit of our mystery—our "corpse in the cellar of the bank", as those detective writer chappies would call it.'

He took another sip of his beer and continued, 'Anyway, in this book a chap is beheaded, in a closed room, when he's on his own, with the doors under observation and the window forty feet off the ground. Jolly puzzling. Just like our bank chappie. And there's this suspected villain who claims he has the powers of a werewolf. Rather like the ghost in our bank cellar, I thought.'

'And so,' said Jack with a grin, 'how did it all work out at the end of the book? Supernatural powers? Or deadly human ingenuity?'

'Well, I haven't actually got to the end yet,' Warnie mumbled into his beer. 'Let you know when I do.'

Just then Constable Dixon advanced across the lawn towards us.

'You look much better than the last time we saw you,' I said. 'Much less like a drowned fish and much more like a policeman.'

'Well, I did have to change into a fresh uniform, sir,' he muttered, then he drew himself to his full height and said, 'I have been sent to fetch you. Inspector Crispin from Scotland Yard is waiting for you at the bank.'

FIFTEEN

~

On the front door of the bank the now slightly tattered cardboard notice was flapping in the wind, still making its announcement to the citizens of Market Plumpton: 'Closed until further notice.' Dixon had a key. He let us in and relatched the door behind us.

When we went from the entrance lobby into the bank office, we discovered a group already gathered and apparently waiting for us.

Inspector Crispin came forward, saying, 'Thank you for coming. Now everyone is here and we can begin.'

I looked around and saw Sergeant Merrivale looming quietly in the background and Constable Dixon guarding the front door. Seated at one of the desks, looking red-eyed and miserable, was Ruth Jarvis, the bank's clerical officer we'd met the day before. Standing side by side were the manager, Edmund Ravenswood, and an unfamiliar woman. As Inspector Crispin went around making the introductions, we discovered that she was Edith Ravenswood, the manager's wife. She was also the sister of the dead man, Franklin Grimm.

'In a moment,' said Crispin, 'I'll try, with your help, to reconstruct a timetable of the events of yesterday. But before I do, we should consider the possibility that Franklin Grimm committed suicide. The absence of any sort of weapon would then be the puzzle we'd need to solve. So, psychologically, is it possible that Franklin Grimm killed himself?'

Put bluntly like this, the idea provoked a sob of anguish and another wave of silent tears from Ruth Jarvis.

'Mr Ravenswood, let's begin with you,' Crispin continued. 'Did you see any signs of depression or anxiety or stress in Mr Grimm at all?'

'No, you're way off beam there, inspector,' growled Ravenswood firmly. 'He was a cocky young chap, was Grimm. Full of himself and his own importance and his plans for making money. I never saw him in a dark mood, not once. Never a moment of self-doubt. If anything, far too full of himself.'

'Sounds as though you didn't like him very much,' the Scotland Yard inspector responded.

'He did his job, that's all I care about. Given my preference I might have hired a quieter chap. But Edith wanted me to give him a job, so I did—as a favour to her. And, as I say, he was efficient enough.'

'Yes, he was your brother, wasn't he, Mrs Ravenswood?'

Edith Ravenswood was dry eyed, but she was pale and clearly shaken by what had happened. In response to the inspector's question, she only nodded.

'Younger than you, or older?'

'Three years younger.'

'Why did you ask your husband to give him a job here in the bank?'

'He was too good for farm work,' she said quietly. 'Too clever. Too ambitious. And he always did well at school. I was sure he'd suit the bank, and it would get him into a professional job.'

'Was he happy here?' I was surprised by Inspector Crispin's question—it was one that would never have occurred to me.

'Happy enough,' Edith Ravenswood replied cautiously. 'He would have left sooner or later. Very ambitious, as I said.'

'So what about the possibility of his taking his own life?'

'Never.' She was very certain about that. 'Franklin was full of . . . hope. Yes, hope and confidence about his future. It would have been completely out of character for Franklin to commit suicide.'

'Miss Jarvis, I understand Mr Grimm was your friend as well as your colleague here at the bank, is that correct?' The inspector's question seemed to catch Ruth Jarvis by surprise.

'Well . . . we went out together.'

'Nothing more than that? I'm told that over the past few months you and Mr Grimm were almost constant companions.'

'Yes, I suppose so.'

'So how serious was this relationship? Had he proposed to you?'

'No,' she replied quickly. 'Franklin wasn't interested in marriage. Not just yet, anyway.'

'And you were?'

There was a long silence. The clock on the bank wall ticked loudly and every eye was fixed on Ruth Jarvis. Finally she nodded, then buried her head in her hands.

Inspector Crispin pulled up a chair, sat down beside her and said, in a quiet, comforting voice, 'Come along, Miss Jarvis. Whatever the truth is will come out sooner or later. You might as well tell me now.'

When she didn't respond immediately, he added softly, 'And it might help us to catch Mr Grimm's killer.'

There was another even longer silence, then finally she said, in a voice so small it was almost a whisper, 'I'm going to have his baby.' With these words she broke down again and shook with silent sobs, her face in her hands.

'Mrs Ravenswood,' said Crispin, 'would you be so kind as to fetch a glass of water for Miss Jarvis please?'

'She needs something stronger than that,' snorted Edmund Ravenswood. 'This young woman needs a brandy.'

'Water will do for the moment,' the policeman insisted. 'Mrs Ravenswood?'

The manager's wife bustled away and returned a few moments later with a glass of water that she handed to Ruth Jarvis, who accepted it with trembling fingers. She sipped the water and started to settle down and pull herself together.

'Feeling a little better?' asked Crispin gently.

Ruth Jarvis nodded.

'Did Mr Grimm know you're pregnant?'

Again she nodded.

'Did he suggest—or did you suggest for that matter—that he should marry you?'

Slowly and haltingly she explained that when he said nothing about marriage, after learning of the pregnancy, she raised the topic. But he was firmly against it. He hinted that she should get rid of the baby while it was still early in the pregnancy. When she insisted that she could never do that—she would have the child—he said he would 'do the right thing'.

'And what did he mean by that?' Crispin asked.

'He talked about money,' sniffed Ruth, dabbing her eyes with a soaking wet handkerchief. 'He said he'd pay for the baby's support.'

'A very difficult time for you,' Crispin said sympathetically. 'Now, let me bring you back to the question I need answered: could Franklin Grimm have committed suicide.'

'Never,' replied Ruth firmly. 'He kept telling me that he had big plans, and he wouldn't be staying in Market Plumpton for the rest of his life.'

'Did he tell you what those plans were?'

'No.'

'Or hint?'

'No.'

Inspector Crispin stood up and paced thoughtfully around the office. 'Well,' he said at length, 'if the consensus is that suicide is so very unlikely—and Mr Grimm certainly never left a suicide note—we must consider murder.' He turned to face us and said, 'Gentlemen, what time did you arrive at the bank yesterday morning?'

'Shortly after ten o'clock,' said Jack. 'Perhaps a quarter past—no later.'

'And what happened then—exactly?'

'Exactly? Well, Morris and my brother stood in the customer area while I approached the teller's cage and asked the teller—'

'Mr Grimm?'

'As you say, Mr Grimm—asked him to make a cash withdrawal from my savings account passbook. He asked for identification. Having none, I suggested the manager, Mr Ravenswood here, might be able to identify me. Miss Jarvis told us that Mr Ravenswood was in the cellar, and Mr Grimm opened the flap in the counter and invited me to follow him.'

'Meanwhile,' said Crispin, looking up at me, 'you two did what?'

'Well, we followed, of course,' volunteered Warnie. 'No point in us hanging around like a shag on a rock. Or two shags on a rock, I suppose. Or perhaps like two shags on two rocks. Anyway, we followed Jack and the other chappie down the stairs.'

'You had no particular reason for doing this?'

'Didn't think about it really,' mumbled Warnie. 'Bit boring standing around waiting, so we followed, if you see what I mean.'

'And this would have been about twenty past ten I take it?'

'About that,' Jack agreed.

'Now, Mr Ravenswood: you saw Mr Grimm and these gentlemen enter the cellar?'

'I was in the strongroom, and as I walked out of the vault door, Grimm and Mr Lewis here were just approaching. I remembered Mr Lewis and identified him. Then I noticed these other two standing at the foot of the cellar stairs. I told Grimm in plain terms that they shouldn't be there. Until I pointed it out I don't think he'd noticed that they followed him.'

'Then?'

'Well, then Nicholas Proudfoot came charging in. Like a bull in a china shop.'

'This is the young farmer who died this morning?'

'Yes, I was told about his death. Tragic. Awful business.'

'So, Mr Ravenswood, what was he so angry about? I've been told he was shouting incoherently. But it can't have been entirely incoherent to you since you were the target of his remarks. What was it all about?'

'Well, to be honest, there was some problem with the loan I'd advanced to him against a mortgage on his farm. He'd borrowed to buy new equipment, and to improve the fencing and hedging and generally bring the place up to date—it was pretty run down. Then the weather turned nasty for most of a season, and then farm gate prices for produce dropped. So he was in a bit of difficulty.'

'Had he missed payments?'

'Yes, more than one—and another payment was due. I told him two days ago, quite bluntly, that I had to foreclose on the mortgage. He didn't like it at all. He blamed me, but I said it was out of my hands—rules of the bank, that sort of thing. In fact, now that he's dead, the machinery's already begun to turn and the bank's foreclosing on the mortgage immediately.'

Edith Ravenswood spoke up and said, 'Oh Edmund! That's

terribly unfair on poor Amelia Proudfoot—a widow one day and the farm gone the next.'

Ravenswood shrugged his shoulders, 'If it was only one payment that had been missed . . . but it's out of my hands.'

Inspector Crispin intervened to ask, 'And that's what his anger was all about?'

'As far as I could understand it, yes,' replied the banker. 'As you said, he was almost incoherent.'

'And then?'

'Well, just as I thought he was going to leave, he pushed me into the strongroom and closed the vault door. Took me completely by surprise—right off guard, so to speak.'

'And you gentlemen saw this?' Crispin asked, turning back to us three.

We nodded. 'It was just as Mr Ravenswood described,' Jack said. 'As soon as it happened—as soon as the vault door was slammed closed and the combination locks turned—the young man charged up the steps and out of the cellar.'

'Leaving you three and Mr Grimm. So, what steps did you take?'

Warnie said, 'Well, that Grimm fellow tried the vault door, but it was definitely locked shut. Wouldn't budge. So we came upstairs. Grimm insisted that he didn't have the combination and he'd have to call the bank's regional office.'

'That's right,' said Ravenswood. 'Bank policy. In a small branch such as this only the manager has the combination.'

'And you were locked inside the vault?'

'Exactly. I was locked inside the vault.'

'Was there enough air for you to breathe? Were you in the dark, or is there a light?'

'Oh, there's an electric light all right. That wasn't a problem. And a chair for me to sit on—the chair we have there for bank customers when they're accessing their safe deposit boxes. And it's a large strongroom, so I would have had hours before the air began to get stale.'

'So then,' the Scotland Yard man continued, 'you three were back up here in the office with Mr Grimm?'

'Yes, sir,' Ruth Jarvis volunteered. 'I saw them come back up, and Mr Grimm told me what had happened and then rang Tadminster and asked them to send over one of the managers who had the combination. Then Franklin thought he should go back downstairs again.'

'Why?' said Inspector Crispin. 'That's not at all clear to me.'

'He was flustered,' said Ruth. 'I think he thought he should be closer to Mr Ravenswood, just in case he might be able to do something to help. There's a small air vent in the concrete wall of the strongroom—perhaps he wanted to make sure it was open.'

'So he took off back downstairs. What then?'

Jack took up the story. 'Before he left he'd issued me with the cash I'd requested and stamped my passbook. But he'd also reported the matter to the police, so Constable Dixon over there had arrived to take our statements. He was doing that when I heard a faint cry from downstairs.'

'Did the rest of you hear it?' asked Crispin, casting a glance around the room.

'No, not a peep,' said Warnie, 'but then Jack has unusually acute hearing.'

'This would have been when—about half past ten?'

'About that.'

Crispin nodded and went on, 'So you then went downstairs and found the dead body?'

We nodded.

'Then if you'll accompany me, we'll all go downstairs now,' said the policeman, 'to the scene of the crime.'

SIXTEEN

~

It turned out that the silent Sergeant Merrivale had the key to the basement door. He turned it in the lock and stood to one side while the rest of us followed Inspector Crispin in single file down the narrow wooden staircase into the bank's cellar.

Perhaps it was just my imagination, but it felt cold and damp down there. And with only a single light bulb there was a dim, yellow, almost ghostly light that faded away into black shadows in the distant corners. The cellar smelled in equal proportions of mildew, mice and mortgages.

'Timing to begin with,' said Crispin, once we'd assembled at the foot of the stairs. 'You've suggested it was twenty past ten, or something like that, when you came down here. So Nicholas Proudfoot must have burst in, when? Twenty-five past?'

'At the very latest,' Jack said.

'Mrs Ravenswood: where were you at twenty-five past ten yesterday morning?'

'Me? Oh, just upstairs, in our flat. Doing some mending.'

'Was anyone with you?'

'No, I was alone.'

'Show me where you three gentlemen were standing,' said Crispin, turning to us. Warnie and I shuffled back until we were just at the foot of the stairs. Jack took a pace forward towards the vault door, which I noticed was once again securely closed and locked.

'And Mr Grimm was where?'

'Immediately in front of where I'm standing,' Jack said, 'or perhaps just to one side.'

'That's more like it,' said Ravenswood. 'If I remember correctly he was standing almost beside you—and I was here, where I am now, immediately in front of the vault door.'

'Then Mr Proudfoot appeared.'

We nodded.

'Did anyone try to stop him?'

'Afraid not,' Warnie admitted. 'We were like stunned fish in the fishmonger's window. Couldn't believe what we were seeing and hearing. Didn't move, I'm afraid.'

'Did you move, Mr Ravenswood?' asked the Scotland Yard man.

'Well, I suppose,' the bank manager admitted, 'I must have backed away a few steps. He was so wild I didn't know what he was going to do next—so I backed away a little. That's how I came to be standing in the open doorway to the vault.'

'At the end of his tirade Mr Proudfoot pushed you in through the vault doorway?'

'That's correct. Caught me right off balance. I staggered backwards, and before I could do anything to stop him he'd swung the door closed on me.'

'And then he pushed down the locking levers and spun those dial things there,' said Warnie, pointing at the combination locks.

'How did he know how to do that?' asked the Scotland Yard man.

'His late mother had a safe deposit box in the strongroom,' Ravenswood explained. 'It contained her will and the deeds to the farm and so on. Young Nicolas was usually with her when she came to the bank. He'd seen me operate the locking mechanism a number of times.'

'So then you were locked in,' continued Inspector Crispin, who was pacing up and down by this time.

'Securely.'

'And you couldn't get out?'

'That's a top of the range vault door, with a double combination lock,' said Ravenswood. 'The whole thing is made from heavy duty tempered steel. The vault itself is double brick on the outside with steel cladding on the inside walls.'

'You definitely couldn't get out?'

With a dry, cynical laugh Ravenswood said, 'Not unless I was Houdini!'

Crispin turned to us and said, 'Did Grimm test the locks? Did he try to open the door?'

'Several times,' I said. 'It was definitely securely closed and locked.'

'How many other ways are there into this cellar?'

'None,' said the bank manager firmly. 'None at all.'

'But when this was a private residence I'm told that part of this cellar held coal—so there must be a coal hole somewhere?'

Ravenswood led us all over to a far corner and pointed to a metal plate in the ceiling of the cellar. This, he explained, had once been the coal chute but it was bolted closed, and had been bolted closed for many years. Sergeant Merrivale pulled out a powerful electric torch, climbed up on a box and examined the plate.

'Heavily bolted,' he said to Crispin. 'And the bolts are rusted over. This hasn't been opened for years.'

'So that just leaves—' began the inspector.

'The door at the top of that flight of stairs,' said Ravenswood, finishing his sentence for him.

'Do you agree, Merrivale?' said Crispin, turning to his sergeant.

'There are no concealed doors, or panels, or entrances to secret tunnels—nothing of that sort, sir. I've looked. These walls and floor are solid rock, and that strongroom wall is double brick with a layer of concrete lined with steel on the inside.'

We all looked slowly around the damp stone cellar with its heavy wall dividing the strongroom half from the part where we stood. The total impossibility of the murder of Franklin Grimm loomed before us like some ghostly phantom.

Inspector Crispin pulled a long blue envelope out of his top coat pocket. From this he extracted a single sheet of paper.

'The police surgeon's report,' he explained. 'Dr Haydock says that Mr Grimm was killed by a single blow to the neck that severed the carotid artery and penetrated his wind pipe. It was a narrow blade that tore the skin roughly on penetration.'

Ruth Jarvis began to sob again and Edith Ravenswood went over to put an arm around her shoulders.

'Narrow blade, eh?' said Warnie. 'Knew a chap in my regiment once who had a knife like that—a stiletto he called it. Said it was Italian. Said lots of Italians carried them.'

'Dixon, are you there?' called out Crispin.

Dixon's voice came from the dark at the top of the stairs acknowledging his presence.

'Are there any Italians in Market Plumpton?'

'No, sir.'

'Or in the district?'

'Not that I know of, sir.'

'When we get back to the station, you should check on that.'

'Yes, sir.'

Inspector Crispin paced back and forth in silence for a minute or two, then he turned to his sergeant and asked, 'How carefully has this place been searched?'

'Very,' replied Merrivale. 'The local force searched it

yesterday, and then I went over it again myself at lunchtime today.'

'You've done your own search?'

'Yes, sir.'

'And you found no entrance except that staircase?'

'Correct, sir.'

'And no trace of a weapon?'

'None, sir. Mind you,' Merrivale continued, 'the weapon was obviously small and might have been concealed and carried away.'

'Yes, there is that.' Inspector Crispin resumed his pacing.

'Do you need us any longer?' asked Jack.

The policeman sighed heavily and said there was probably nothing more to be accomplished for the time being, but that we were not to leave the district without his permission.

'In that case,' suggested Warnie, rubbing his hands together, 'back to the pub for a drink.'

Outside the bank we discovered that black clouds had rolled across a copper-coloured sky and were getting to grips with each other like rugby players packing down in a scrum. A fine, misty rain had begun to fall. We turned up our coat collars and hurried back to *The Boar's Head*. As we stepped into the welcome warmth of a blazing fire, I made some cynical remark about this being an English summer.

'You have nothing to complain about, young Morris,' said Jack with a grin as we pulled up chairs about the fireplace in the public bar. 'I had a student from Dartmoor once. He insisted that Dartmoor had the worst weather in the world. When I asked him to describe the climate he said that in Dartmoor they had eleven months of winter—followed by one month of bad weather.'

Warnie chuckled then went to fetch three pints of bitter from the bar.

Flummoxed and frustrated by all this talk of impossible murder, I decided to seize upon Warnie's absence to throw the switch back to philosophy.

'What you were saying earlier, Jack, about having an encounter with God . . .'

'Yes?'

'You see, that's the sort of claim I have great difficulty with. Imagine for a moment—and I don't admit this—but imagine that God exists, that there's a Mind behind the universe, a Big Brain that began it. Imagining that is true, why would such a Being be interested in us?'

Warnie returned and placed the three pints on the table between us. Then he sank back into an armchair and pulled a book out of his coat pocket. It was, I saw, the detective novel he'd mentioned to us: *It Walks by Night*. He was soon engrossed in his mystery.

'The boot,' said Jack, 'is on the other foot. Why wouldn't the Supreme Being be interested in us? What makes you think he wouldn't be?'

I shook my head. 'Come on, Jack—face reality. We live on one tiny planet in a vast universe which contains countless millions of stars and no one knows how many planets. And on this one small, obscure, remote planet we are just one species out of thousands. Surely it's egomania of the worst sort to claim that any Supreme Being could possibly have any interest in us.'

'Let me answer you with a little story, or fable, or parable.' Jack stopped to light his pipe and then resumed, 'You regaled me with the four blind men and the elephant story earlier, so let me try this one on you.'

He puffed in silence for a moment and then said, 'The scene is a scientific research laboratory. Swimming around in fluid in some laboratory glassware are a number of bacteria. These bacteria have the power of thought and speech—well, I did warn you this is a fable—and they have a debate among themselves. These are microscopic bacteria and they are debating whether or not the vast creatures in white coats that loom over them have any interest in them. The negative case is that those creatures in white coats are so unbelievably huge (to tiny bacteria) and clearly so clever and so busy and so important that they could never be interested in anything so small, so tiny, so insignificant as a few bacteria swimming around in nutrient fluid.'

He puffed in silence for a moment, Warnie grunted and turned over a page of his book, and then Jack resumed, 'The truth is that those bacteria are in a medical research laboratory looking for a cure to a serious disease. And the total attention of that whole laboratory is focused on those few bacteria. All the experimentation and activity, all the thought, all the planning—everything centres on those bacteria. It is all about them.'

'The point being?' I asked, wiping beer foam from my upper lip.

'That size is no indicator of significance. A mountain is not more important than a baby just because the mountain is bigger than the baby. What's important is important, regardless of how remote it is or how small it is.'

I thought about this for a moment and then said, 'Well, I still can't see why God would be interested in us. I still can't understand why the Supreme Being of the entire universe should care about us insignificant little creatures.'

'In saying that you are telling me something about Tom Morris, but nothing at all about God,' Jack said with a cheerful grin. 'You're telling me that if you were that big, that powerful, that important you would take no interest in the small, the remote or the (seemingly) insignificant. But what on earth makes you imagine that God's mind works like Tom Morris's mind? If God is far above and beyond us, then his interests and concerns are far above and beyond what we can imagine.'

Jack finished the last of his beer and added, 'It's certainly staggering and beyond our grasp that God should care for us. But the intricate, interlocking design of the world, perfectly fitted to be inhabited by thinking, upright bipeds—by us—tells us that he does. Even more, the coming of Jesus tells us that he does. It's certainly uncomfortable to feel that we're under some sort of divine microscope, but I'm not interested in what's comfortable—only what's true.'

At that moment Annie Jones walked in wearing an apron and wiping her hands on a tea towel to announce that dinner was served. Five minutes later we were digging into a delicious steak and kidney pie.

'Let's hope this rain clears up,' said Warnie as he swallowed a mouthful of pastry. 'We need a fine day for our investigation. What's on the agenda for tomorrow, Jack?'

Before his brother could reply, a large figure in a blue uniform loomed in the doorway.

'I must say that steak and kidney pie looks delicious,' said Constable Dixon.

'Are you here to investigate the food?' I asked.

'Ah, no, sir. At least, not until I'm off duty. Inspector Crispin sent me to tell you that the inquest into the death of Franklin Grimm will be held tomorrow afternoon at two o'clock in the church hall—and to request you gentlemen to be in attendance as your testimony will almost certainly be required.'

Having delivered his message, and spent some more time admiring Annie Jones's cooking, the constable left.

'Well, that's tomorrow afternoon taken care of,' said Jack, pushing away his empty plate. 'So I suggest we spend tomorrow morning tracking down Ted Proudfoot, the angry chap Amelia Proudfoot told us about—and then have another chat with Amelia herself. She might be more forthcoming on a second visit.'

SEVENTEEN

~

The morning dawned bright and sunny with no sign of rain. After a breakfast of bacon and eggs and thick slices of hot buttered toast and marmalade, I was dispatched to purchase a map. I located what I wanted—a road map of the district—in a small shop on the high street that sold stationery amongst a wide and eclectic range of items.

The elderly proprietor found what I was looking for on a high shelf between a container of tooth powder and a jar of gentlemen's relish. I took the map back to *The Boar's Head* and, to avoid a repeat of the navigating fiasco of the day before, had our publican, Frank Jones, mark in pen on the map the route to the farm that Mrs Proudfoot had called 'the Farnon place'.

After a second cup of tea, and a careful reconnoitre of the map by Warnie, the three of us set off. We were travelling in the opposite direction to the day before and soon found ourselves walking down a narrow lane with high hedges on both sides.

There was almost no traffic on this small back road. The road itself meandered back and forth, as if following a track first made by a wandering cow that had either a hangover or serious concussion.

We were passed by a horse-drawn wagon, rattling with empty milk cans on the back, and later by a farm worker on foot. He tugged his cap politely in our direction as he gave us a sullen scowl.

We reached our destination after some three-quarters of an hour of brisk walking. Entering through the farm gate we walked up the muddy driveway to the farmhouse that stood on a small rise. Flanking the house on one side was a machinery shed and on the other a row of stables.

We stopped a boy carrying a bucket towards the stables. Like many small boys who live on farms, he looked as if, after carefully washing and dressing in the morning, he had then rolled in mud and leaped into a hay bale. We asked this walking collection of soil samples if Mr Ted Proudfoot was about. He said nothing, but pointed towards the machinery shed, then resumed his errand.

We stood in the wide open doorway to the shed and looked around. It had only one occupant: a tall thin man with his back towards us.

'Mr Ted Proudfoot?' Jack said.

Without turning around the man growled in an unpleasant voice that seemed to be missing a tonsil, 'Who wants to know?'

Jack didn't reply, but waited in silence until curiosity got the better of the farm worker. When he finally turned around to squint at us, I saw that his dark face had the surly, sullen expression of a dyspeptic bulldog on a bad day—a bulldog that had just received bad news. And his voice suggested a bulldog that had tried to swallow a bone that had got stuck halfway down.

He put down the tools in his hands, straightened up from the unidentifiable piece of farm machinery he'd been tinkering with and walked towards us, wiping his hands on a piece of oily rag.

'Well? Who are you three then?' he growled. He looked no more likable up close than he had when observed across the distance of the shed.

'My name is Lewis,' Jack replied. 'This is my brother, and our friend Mr Morris. Are you Mr Ted Proudfoot?'

'What of it?' He made it sound as if we were accusing him of being an anarchist bomb thrower, and he was going to wear the accusation as a proud badge.

'We were in the bank this week when Mr Franklin Grimm died.'

'Yeah, I heard about that.' Then a slow smile spread across his face that somehow contrived to make him look even more sinister. 'And some people say there's no justice in the world.'

'I gather you were not a friend of Mr Grimm?' Jack asked.

'Grimm had no friends—only enemies.'

When he stopped on this word, Jack prompted him, 'Enemies? What sort of enemies?'

'Two sorts: women he exploited and men he belittled. Other people were only there to serve the nasty, selfish ends of Frank Grimm.' This explanation was followed by a chain of so many expletives that even I, who had just spent three years among the colourfully spoken undergraduates of Oxford University, did not recognise all of them. If a new edition of the English Dialect Dictionary was being planned, I would advise the editors to consult Mr Ted Proudfoot.

'Anyone who hated him enough to kill him?' Jack persisted.

'Hundreds of them,' replied Ted Proudfoot with a humourless laugh. 'But why are you three asking? You're not from the police, are you?'

'Certainly not!' said Warnie indignantly. 'Rather the other way round, old chap. Because we were there at the time, the police rather suspect us of having something to do with it. Ridiculous I know, but there you are.'

The young farm worker took some time to process this information. His eyes glazed over and it was almost possible to hear the gearwheels turning inside his head. The effort of his cogitation suggested that some of those gearwheels were rusted and broken from lack of use. But they did eventually produce a result.

'So you think you can get yourselves out from under by pointing the finger at someone else, is that it?'

'Well, I suppose if you put it like that . . .' Warnie began, looking down at his boots and shuffling his feet.

'We're just trying to "assist the police in their inquiries", I think is the expression,' said Jack soothingly, 'so that they'll release us to be on our way.'

'I'm not gonna help you,' said Proudfoot with finality. 'I hope whoever killed Grimm gets away with it forever. I hope he gets a medal. I hope the killer lives a long happy life. If you find out who it is, let me know and I'll send him a pound note as a token my gratitude.'

'But we'd all like to see justice done—' I began. I got no further because at this point Ted Proudfoot stuck two greasy fingers in his mouth and whistled loudly. He followed the whistle with a shout of 'Lightning! Come here, boy!'

In response a large dog came bounding across the farm yard—an enormous black dog that ran to Proudfoot's side and looked up at him as if waiting for the command to kill something. Its lip curled up exposing its razor sharp canines, and it began to salivate at the exciting prospect of having live prey to pursue.

Proudfoot stroked the dog's head as he said to us, 'You three'll be leaving now.' It was clearly not intended as a polite request. 'And be sure to close the gate as you go,' he added.

We went.

Standing in the lane in front of the farm gate Warnie grunted, 'Didn't accomplish much there, I'm afraid.'

'I'm not so sure,' I said. 'We saw the man. We formed some estimate of his character. And I for one believe him quite capable of murder.'

'Suppose so,' Warnie muttered. 'Well, where to now?'

'We pay a second visit to young Mrs Amelia Proudfoot, widow of the second murder victim,' Jack said.

'Are you so certain that Nicholas Proudfoot was murdered then?' I asked.

'Do you really have any doubts?' Jack asked.

We walked back to the nearest crossroads and stopped while Warnie examined the map and then pointed us down a leafy laneway. The day was rapidly heating up. It looked like turning into one of those steamy days when butterflies look for a shady leaf to land on and let their wings droop. Out in the fields even the most energetic rabbit would lie down in the long grass, rest its chin on its front paws and decide to take it easy for the rest of the day.

But in the shade, out of the direct sunlight, it was a pleasant day for walking.

'It's supposed to be a walking holiday,' I said cheerfully, 'and at least we're walking today.'

'Only around in circles,' Warnie grumbled. 'Why are we going to see young Mrs Proudfoot again?'

Jack said that it was obvious that the day before she was not telling us everything she could. Perhaps today she would be calmer—more giving, more informative. She might, Jack suggested, have had time to think things through and have decided to tell us what she knew.

It took us the better the part of an hour to circle the town and find ourselves back on the stone bridge over the stream, close to where we had found the body of Nicholas Proudfoot. Here Jack stopped to light his pipe and look slowly around. Once again he seemed fascinated by the powerful branches of the old willow tree that hung over the bridge.

'Is that a bit of rope caught up in that branch?' he asked, pointing with the stem of his pipe.

'It might be,' I said, shading my eyes and squinting into the sunlight.

Then he transferred his attention to the deep scratch marks on the stone at the centre of the arch.

'What are you doing?' I asked.

Jack said he was trying to imagine the sequence of events as they might have unfolded at the moment when Nicholas Proudfoot died. Warnie quickly lost interest and leaned over the stone parapet of the bridge, staring at the bubbling, fast-flowing water beneath.

'Might be trout in that stream,' he said. 'Sort of place trout tend to like.'

'We should ask our friendly publican, Frank Jones,' I suggested, 'if he ever serves fresh trout.'

'Jolly good idea,' said Warnie with a laugh. 'I love a meal of fresh trout. Preferably pan fried in butter. Have you finished, Jack? Are you ready to move on?'

Jack said he was, tapped out the ashes from his pipe on the stonework of the bridge, and we resumed our walk.

Perhaps a quarter of an hour later we were at the front gate to the Proudfoot farm. Surprisingly it was swinging open.

'Careless of them,' muttered Warnie.

We walked up the gravel driveway into the farmyard and were struck once again by the oppressive silence.

'It's odd,' said Jack. 'There's not a farmhand around the place—nor an animal.'

'Well, if they've been struggling for money,' I suggested, 'perhaps they had to lay off anyone they'd employed, and perhaps even had to sell their stock.'

Jack knocked on the front door. There was no reply, and he knocked again. As on our previous visit, the sound seemed to reverberate through the small stone farmhouse.

'I'll scout around,' Warnie volunteered, and he took off around the corner of the house as Jack knocked again. I wandered across the farmyard and checked the outbuildings. There was no sign of life, and the only piece of machinery I found in the shed was an ancient disc plough designed to be pulled by draught horses.

Warnie returned to report that he'd peered in through the windows and seen no one. 'It's deserted all right,' he concluded.

After a final loud rap on the front door we gave up and made our way back to the road. Here we found a small Morris car had just drawn up and a bulky man in tweeds was squeezing himself out of the driver's seat.

'Morning, gents,' he said in a cheerful greeting. While we watched he opened the boot of the car, pulled out a 'For Sale' sign attached to a wooden stake, and drove this into the ground beside the entrance to the Proudfoot farm.

'Sad business,' he said as we watched this happening. 'It's going on the market to repay a bank mortgage—a foreclosure sale. You gentlemen wouldn't be interested, would you? Only needs a little hard work to build it up into a going concern again.'

Warnie quickly dismissed any possibility that we were potential buyers.

'All of this is rather sudden,' said Jack suspiciously.

The man in tweeds shrugged his shoulders and replied, 'I'm just the estate agent. If the bank manager tells me the place is to go on the market as a mortgagee sale, I just nod my head and pocket my commission. Good day to you.'

With those words he squeezed himself back into his small car and roared up the country lane in a cloud of blue exhaust smoke.

EIGHTEEN

~

We walked slowly back towards the town wrapped in thought, trying to make sense of these rapidly moving events.

'It's all very strange—selling the farm out from underneath the young widow like this. But does it tell us anything about the murder?' I asked.

Warnie chewed his moustache in silence for a minute and then said, 'What if there's embezzlement involved?'

'Explain yourself, old chap,' Jack said.

'Well, suppose the Proudfoots thought they were keeping up with their payments—struggling, but managing to keep their heads above water—and suddenly they're told they're in arrears and the bank is about to foreclose. Now, if the situation was something along those lines, I wonder if Franklin Grimm was siphoning their mortgage payments into his own pocket? From what we've heard about Grimm's character I wouldn't put it past him. And it would certainly give Nicholas Proudfoot a powerful motive to murder Grimm.'

'But when we saw Proudfoot at the bank,' I protested, 'it was the manager, Edmund Ravenswood, he was angry with, not Grimm.'

'Well . . . if he got a demand notice from the bank, the first person he'd blame would be the manager,' Warnie extemporised.

'But perhaps when he thought about it he realised that the shark in the water was Grimm.'

'No, no.' Jack shook his head. 'It won't wash, old chap. Not enough time. We saw Proudfoot furious with Ravenswood, and just minutes later it was Grimm who was murdered. How can he have switched the focus of his fury so quickly?'

'Quite apart from the question,' I added, 'of how he got into the sealed cellar of the bank to commit the murder.'

'Hmm, all a bit difficult,' Warnie muttered, and we walked for some minutes in silence as we each chewed over this intractable problem.

'It's very odd,' I exclaimed a few minutes later, returning to the question that still troubled me. 'Foreclosing on the farm so soon after the farmer's death—it strikes me as very odd, or heavy handed, or something.'

'Very well then,' said Jack with a broad grin. 'Let's go and ask Ravenswood why he's done it.'

'Chap'll probably throw us out!' protested Warnie. 'No reason he should tell us anything.'

'And there's no reason why we shouldn't ask,' said Jack cheerfully. 'Come on.' And with those words he quickened his pace.

When we stood in front of the bank, half an hour later, wilting from the heat and looking to get out of the sun, we found the door closed and the notice tacked up by the police still in place. This, however, did not stop Jack from knocking on the door. When there was no reply, he looked around and found a bell pull to one side.

'Probably rings in the manager's flat upstairs,' he said as he gave it a hefty tug.

We waited patiently and a few minutes later footsteps could be heard on the other side of the door. It opened slightly and Ravenswood's face appeared.

'The police have ordered the bank cl—' he began, then he recognised us. 'Oh, it's you three.'

'We wondered if we could have a chat,' said Jack, smiling encouragingly, 'about this whole awful business.'

'I don't see why I should talk to you three,' growled Ravenswood.

'Is there any reason why you shouldn't?' Jack asked pleasantly.

In the long, hot silence that followed, the bank manager's face resembled one of those books where the images change if you rapidly flick over the pages. His initial irritation and annoyance was replaced by curiosity—with just a hint of cunning.

'No, I suppose you're right,' Ravenswood agreed. 'We're all in this together. Come in out of the heat—Edith has just put the kettle on.'

We followed him into the bank and found the thick stone walls were keeping it pleasantly cool. This time he didn't lead us into the offices and public area on the ground floor, but up the stairs to his flat. At the head of the stairs was a short hallway. Ravenswood opened the first door on the left and showed us into a small but comfortably furnished sitting room.

'I'll just go and tell Edith we have guests,' he said as he hurried away. 'Make yourselves at home.'

Warnie and I looked at each other and then at Jack. We had no idea what he thought this conversation might achieve or what he wanted to ask the Ravenswoods about. I took an armchair under a window and Warnie followed my example. A warm breeze came through the open window in lazy puffs, as if the door of a baker's oven was being opened and closed.

Jack paced around the room looking at the pictures on the walls, mostly cheap prints of Landseer paintings. The *Monarch of the Glen* was at one end of the mantelpiece and a portrait of a Newfoundland dog was at the other.

Edmund Ravenswood bustled back into the room followed by his wife Edith, who was carrying a tea tray. He waved Jack to take a seat, and sat down himself at the end of a settee.

'How do you like your tea, gentlemen?' he asked as if this was just a social call from old business acquaintances.

As we gave our orders and Mrs Ravenswood took up the teapot to pour our cups, the bank manager continued, 'I'm sorry, but all I can remember from our last meeting is that two of you are named Lewis and one Morris. Is that correct?'

'I'm Major Lewis,' said Warnie, 'British Army. This is my brother Jack—he's an Oxford don—and this is our friend, young Tom Morris. We only got tangled up in this infernal business because we're on a walking tour in the district and I (rather carelessly, I'm afraid) dropped Jack's wallet into a fireplace so he needed some cash.'

'It's an awful business, as you say,' Ravenswood agreed. 'But I don't quite understand why you've called in to see us—unless it's to commiserate over this whole dark cloud of tragedy.'

He shook his head sadly, looking, I thought, rather like a second-rate actor in a small provincial company trying to give the socially appropriate response to bad news.

'The police won't let us leave the district,' Jack explained, 'but we've been walking this morning in the country lanes around the town—and we came across the Proudfoot's farm.'

A silence followed Jack's announcement as he paused to sip his tea. Then he resumed, 'We were rather surprised to see it's already for sale.'

Edith Ravenswood dropped her teaspoon into her saucer with a loud clatter.

'Oh, Edmund!' she exclaimed, 'You haven't? Not already? Poor Amelia Proudfoot . . .'

'Bank business is none of your business, Edith,' Ravenswood snapped. 'I've told you that before.'

'But surely you could have waited,' she protested feebly. A furious glance from her husband silenced her. Edith Ravenswood struck me as an excessively timid and nervous woman.

'It does seem all very swift,' said Jack gently, smiling over the top of his tea cup.

'The bank makes the rules, not me,' replied Ravenswood in a voice that was a sullen grumble.

There was a still, and rather tense, silence following this remark—a silence that lingered on. Finally Ravenswood broke it by saying, 'Anyway, I spoke to Amelia Proudfoot myself. She was quite happy for the farm to be sold. With young Nicholas dead it holds too many memories for her. She was happy to get rid of the farm and get away from the place.'

'When did you speak to her, Edmund?' his wife asked. 'I didn't know you'd been out to their farm.'

'I don't report my movements to you, Edith,' he replied in a way that suggested he was struggling to suppress his anger. In fact, this whole conversation seemed to be provoking him until he looked like a small volcano in a bad mood that was trying hard not to explode while there was company in the house. 'You knew I was out in the car late yesterday,' he said, 'and I don't have to report to you on where I go or who I see.'

'No, Edmund,' she said meekly, turning her head away.

Finding ourselves in the middle of a stormy low pressure system on the domestic front, I looked for something else to talk about.

'You don't happen to know where she's gone to, do you?' I asked. 'Mrs Proudfoot, I mean. It's just that when we were out there the place seemed to be deserted—already completely empty.'

'How should I know?' barked Ravenswood abruptly. 'I'm not her keeper. She wanted to get out of the place, that's all I know.'

He took a sip of his tea and then seemed to pull himself together. 'Sorry if I snapped at you then, Mr Morris,' he said. 'This whole awful business is getting to me. Getting to all of us, I suppose. Nerves on edge—that sort of thing.'

I told him to think nothing of it, but then I repeated my question, adding that she must have packed and left in an awful hurry.

'All I know is that she wanted to get away from the memories the place held for her,' Ravenswood said. 'I believe she has relatives up north somewhere. I can only assume she caught an early train and is on her way to them even as we speak.'

Jack raised one eyebrow and asked quietly, 'Even before her husband's funeral?'

'Well . . . she'll . . . obviously come back for that,' Ravenswood blustered.

'But who'll make the arrangements?' asked Warnie.

'Not our concern!' snapped the bank manager. 'Anyway, nothing can happen until the police release the body and that won't happen until after the inquest.'

'And she'll have to come back for that,' I speculated.

Edith Ravenswood opened her mouth as if to make a comment, but catching her husband's eye she thought better of it and said nothing.

We finished our tea making awkward small talk, thanked Mrs Ravenswood and made our departure.

We were still talking about the swift sale of the farm and the immediate departure of Amelia Proudfoot as we walked back into the bar parlour of *The Boar's Head.*

Frank Jones was behind the bar and he heard our conversation as he pulled three pints of bitter.

'If it's Amelia Proudfoot you're asking about,' he said, handing us our beers, 'you should ask Ettie, our parlour maid. She's Amelia's cousin. She might know something.'

When we asked where we might find Ettie, the publican told us to go into the front parlour and he'd send her in to us.

Five minutes later a plump fifteen-year-old came into the parlour looking terrified.

'Mr Jones said you gentlemen wanted to talk to me,' she said in a voice just above a whisper.

'Just about your cousin, m'dear,' said Warnie in his hearty manner, trying to put her at ease. 'Amelia Proudfoot—she is your cousin, I take it?'

The girl nodded.

'We were out at the Proudfoot farm this morning,' Jack explained, 'and found the place deserted. We wondered where she might have gone. Mr Ravenswood said he thought she might have gone back to her relatives somewhere up north.'

'Oh no, sir,' said Ettie. 'She called in here this morning, first thing. She had her suitcase with her. Poor thing . . . it were clear she'd been crying. She wanted to borrow a few bob off me, but I didn't have any money so I couldn't help.'

'That must have disappointed her,' said Jack, with a puzzled expression on his face. 'Did she say what she wanted the money for?'

'She said she wanted to get further away,' replied Ettie in her quiet, nervous voice.

'Further away than where? Where was she going to?' Jack persisted.

'She's gone to the coast. She's at Plumpton-on-Sea. That's where she's gone. She said if she had a few more bob she could get further away. But like I say, I couldn't help. She took it bad, did poor Amelia. She said she had no choice then, and walked off to the railway station. If you want to talk to her, that's where you'll find her, sir—she's in Plumpton-on-Sea.'

Jack looked more puzzled than ever as Ettie resumed her

story. 'Maybe she'll have a bit of money after the sale of the farm goes through. Unless the mortgage swallows up the whole of the sale price, that is. But I assumed she just wanted to get away from her sad memories and anything that reminded her of Nicholas. Poor thing. When she left here she were as limp as a rag and looked fit to collapse.'

NINETEEN

~

When Ettie left us, we drank our beer in silence for some minutes. Then Jack said, 'We have to interview Amelia Proudfoot. Behaviour as odd as this must be connected to the two murders.'

'Whose behaviour is odd?' I asked. 'The bank's in foreclosing so quickly, or Amelia Proudfoot's?'

'It was Mrs Proudfoot I was thinking of,' Jack said. 'The day we spoke to her she was clearly hiding something. And then the moment the sale of the property is announced she leaves. Perhaps it's not too much to say she flees. From the bank's point of view surely she could have stayed at the farm until the sale went through.'

'But—but—you can't imagine she might be the murderer?' spluttered Warnie. 'We've both seen her. She's just a slip of a thing.'

Jack shrugged his shoulders and said, 'Women have killed before—remember Constance Kent and the Road Hill House murder?'

'Well, it's possible, I suppose,' Warnie mumbled. 'It might explain why she's fled from the district in such haste.'

'That's a thought,' I added. 'I wonder if Inspector Crispin knows she's gone. Surely he ordered her to stay around the district, just as he did us. Should we tell him?'

'No,' said Jack, thoughtfully and carefully. 'Let's follow this up ourselves. If Amelia Proudfoot really is the killer, or knows the killer, then both murders would have been intensely personal. She's no threat to the wider community. We need to get down to Plumpton-on-Sea and have a chat to her.'

'But there's a problem,' I said. 'According to Inspector Crispin we're not to leave the district. So how can we get down to the coast to interview Amelia Proudfoot?'

'I'm sure there's a way,' Jack said with his conspirator's smile, 'if we just apply our minds to it.'

'Sneak off? That sort of thing?' chuckled Warnie.

Jack nodded, but then said we could do nothing today because of the inquest into the death of Franklin Grimm, which we'd be expected to attend. But later—tonight perhaps—well, he said, let's see what was possible.

We went out to the beer garden—the lawn behind the pub—and took our places at a table in the sunshine where we could watch the River Plum sparkle and gurgle just a few yards away. It looked like a ribbon of rippling silk—like a dress-maker's finishing touch at the foot of a gown.

Mrs Jones brought us out a tray of bread and cheese with a jar of pickles and we ate a leisurely lunch. The bread was still warm from the bakers, and exactly the way I like it—soft and fresh on the inside, crusty and golden on the outside.

Jack, who always ate faster than Warnie and I, gulped down a cheese and pickle sandwich and disappeared into the pub. He returned a moment later carrying a local railway timetable.

Spreading this out on the table, he said, 'There's a milk train that leaves Market Plumpton just before midnight tonight. One of us might be on it while the other two stay here in plain sight of Constable Dixon or whoever's keeping watch on us.'

'Is he?' asked Warnie. 'Keeping watch, that is? I didn't see him in the street. Do you think the police might have put a plain clothes spy in the pub to watch us?'

'I don't think we're quite that important,' said Jack. 'I suspect our friendly publican has taken over as the eyes and ears of the police for the moment. Perhaps a police officer will take over from him after dark. But my point stands. As long as two of us remain here—as long as there is no mass exodus—I'm sure one of us could slip away quietly late tonight and be on that milk train when it leaves.'

'Where does it go?' I asked.

'The village of Plumpton is the first stop,' replied Jack, consulting the timetable, 'then Plumpton-on-Sea, then it goes on to Tadminister.'

'Which of us should go?' I asked.

'Well, as the youngest of us, Tom,' replied Jack with a broad grin, 'I thought this is something that calls for your youthful energy and spirit of adventure. Besides which, both Warnie and I need a good night's sleep.'

The last thing I felt like volunteering for was a late night trip on a slow train, but I could hardly say no. Instead I asked, 'What's the plan then?'

'There'll be a back door to this pub. We need to find it without appearing to be too inquisitive. Then tonight we all retire to our rooms. When it's late enough for the pub to have closed and Frank Jones and his wife to have retired for the night, you slip out quietly—Warnie and I will keep watch. Keep to the shadows and the back streets and make your way to the railway station. Make sure there are no policemen on the platform watching for absconding suspects, board the train and get off at Plumpton-on-Sea. You'll be there very early, probably well before sunrise, so you'll need to find a comfortable spot to spend an hour of two, and then begin your investigation.'

'Yes, that's the tricky bit. What am I supposed to do?'

'Go to the boarding houses, guesthouses and pubs—ask for Amelia Proudfoot. In case she's not using that name, describe her to them. Ask if anyone matching her description has arrived in the last day or so. I'll tell you what you need to ask her when you find her.'

I nodded glumly. It sounded like an uncomfortable night ahead with very little sleep for Tom Morris. As a result I ate the rest of my meal in silence while Warnie told a story about what had happened in the officers' mess the week before last.

Just as we were finishing the last of the bread and cheese, the large, plump shadow of Constable Dixon once again floated between us and the sunlight, looming over us like a threatening zeppelin—a zeppelin with a large moustache and an officious attitude—telling us that the inquest was about to start and Inspector Crispin had sent him to 'ensure our attendance at same'.

The inquest into the death of Franklin Grimm was held in the church hall, which stood behind the old stone church through which we had earlier escaped the watchful eye of Constable Dixon. Seated at the front of the hall, behind a table, was an officious-looking little man sorting out his papers as we entered. He had a face as wizened as a prune and a pair of gold-rimmed pince-nez clipped to his nose. We took our seats on the hard wooden chairs among (or so it seemed) most of the town's population.

'Who's that chap?' I asked Dixon as we squeezed into some of the few remaining chairs.

'That's Mr Brewer,' the policeman explained. 'Mr Harvey Brewer. He's a local solicitor and he usually acts as district coroner at these hearings.'

At that moment Mr Brewer called us all to order by tapping the table impatiently with the blunt end of his fountain pen. It was only a quiet sound, not the banging of a gavel, but it appeared that this was what everyone was waiting for, and silence fell almost immediately.

'This is a coronial inquiry,' he announced in a thin, fluting, self-important voice, 'into the death of Mr Franklin Grimm of the town of Market Plumpton.'

He proceeded to empanel a jury of twelve local citizens and instruct them in their duties. Then he called the police surgeon to give evidence as to the cause of death.

Dr Haydock explained to the court what we already knew: that the deceased had died as a result of a single knife blow to the throat. 'This blow,' he added, 'severed the carotid artery and punctured the larynx.'

'Would death have been rapid?' asked Mr Brewer.

'Almost instantaneous,' Dr Haydock replied.

'Were there any defensive wounds or signs of a struggle?'

'None.'

'Would the blow have required considerable force?'

'That would depend on the sharpness of the blade—which the police have, thus far, not recovered. A very sharp blade would not have required very much strength to inflict the fatal injury.'

'Could the injury have been self-inflicted?'

'It would be difficult to strike such a blow against oneself—difficult but not entirely impossible for a determined person. However, in the absence of a weapon at the scene—'

The coroner cut off Dr Haydock's speculations at this point and excused him from giving further evidence. Then Inspector Hyde was called to give an account of the finding of the body.

This was all so familiar to us that I found my attention

wandering. I leaned back and looked up at the hammer-beam ceiling of the church hall and found myself speculating about the building's history. Perhaps, I thought, this might once have been a medieval banqueting hall attached to a great house. And perhaps the little Norman church beside it had been the chapel for the noble family that owned the house. I could picture the sort of people Chaucer described living in such a setting. Then in my imagination I could hear Lewis proclaiming once again, in his impeccable Middle English: 'Whan that Aprill with his shoures soote, The droghte of March hath perced to the roote . . .'

I was woken from my Chaucerian daydream by the sound of my old tutor's name being called. He went to the witness stand and was sworn in.

'Your name is Clive Staples Lewis?' asked the coroner.

Jack admitted to these, his birth names, although he detested them, and went on, in response to questions, to tell the whole story of that morning when we wanted nothing more than to withdraw cash from the bank and became embroiled in a series of dramatic and tragic events.

'At any time during these events,' asked the coroner, 'did you see a knife or weapon of any sort in the hands of the deceased?'

'Never,' said Jack, and Ruth Jarvis, who was seated only a few rows in front of me, began to sob.

'Or, in fact, did you see such a weapon anywhere in the bank at all at this time?'

'No, there was no sign of whatever weapon was used. Or, indeed, of any weapon at all.'

'Not so much as a letter opener?'

'As you say—not so much as a letter opener.'

A sceptical cloud passed over the coroner's face, as if he found it impossible to believe that a bank office would not have at least one letter opener somewhere. He paused to scribble down a note, then resumed his questioning.

'What frame of mind would you describe the deceased as being in, the last time you saw him?'

'He was focused entirely on the problem of getting Mr Ravenswood, the bank manager, out of the strongroom in which he had been locked.'

'Did he appear alarmed or distressed at all?'

'Those are not the words I would use. He was busy. Active. Seeking a remedy for the situation. He was not focused upon himself at all.'

Jack was excused. Next the coroner briefly questioned Warnie and me along similar lines but we had nothing substantial to add to Jack's answers.

Inspector Hyde was then recalled to give an account of the search for the murder weapon. This was more interesting so I paid close attention, but it was entirely unenlightening. Hyde's statement was as slow and meticulous as the search had evidently been—and with the same results.

'You recovered no weapon at all? You saw no evidence of the hiding or destruction of a weapon?'

'None at all.'

The destruction of a weapon? That was a thought that had not occurred to me. Might Grimm have been killed with some sort of weapon that could be destroyed or made unrecognisable in some way? But in what way? I was still completely baffled.

'Could an ordinary object have been used as a weapon? Perhaps the blade of a pair of scissors?'

'We tested all such objects in the bank for traces of blood and found none. As you know, it is virtually impossible to remove all traces of blood from a weapon. Minute traces are sure to remain. Based on our tests I am certain we have not yet seen the weapon. The search continues.'

Then Inspector Crispin was called and asked to give an account of the current state of the police investigation. In as few words as possible he explained that inquiries were continuing and that several lines of investigation were being pursued. He was asked if he believed the death could have been self-inflicted.

'Out of the question,' he said firmly, and went through the medical and scene of crime evidence to explain why.

The coroner gave his final directions to the jury, who immediately returned a verdict of 'murder by person or persons unknown'. This being what the coroner wanted, he tapped the table with his pen once more and declared the hearing closed.

TWENTY

~

We found ourselves being jostled out of the church hall and into the town square by the crowd that had filled the public gallery. As we walked back towards *The Boar's Head*, I noticed Constable Dixon keeping a discreet eye on us from a distance—proof that we were still under official observation. Warnie and I chatted about what had happened at the inquest, but Jack, I noticed, seemed to be lost in silent thought.

When the crowd had thinned out, and as we were drawing nearer to the pub, I said, 'Well, now—about tonight. I have two questions. First, how do I get out? And second, what do I ask Amelia Proudfoot if I manage to find her?'

'Taking them in reverse order,' said Jack, 'I want you to ask Mrs Proudfoot about her personal relationship with each of the people at the bank: Franklin Grimm, Ruth Jarvis, Edmund Ravenswood and Edith Ravenswood.'

'Just that?' I was surprised. 'No more?'

'Just that,' Jack said firmly. 'That will give me the missing final piece of the puzzle. As to how you get out, well, I think we might assign Warnie the task of scouting around the pub and finding a back way out. That should be right up your street, old chap.'

Warnie chuckled and said, 'I'm good at talking to folk in

pubs—and getting them talking. Leave it to me. I'll have the information before we've finished eating our tea.'

And Warnie was as good as his word. At some point he disappeared into the bowels of the pub, only to reappear fifteen minutes later just as a roast dinner was being served for us in the snug.

'Well?' asked Jack through a mouthful of roast duck.

'I played my usual role,' chuckled Warnie, 'of the old bumbler who has no idea of where he's got to. And I found out exactly what we need to know.'

He paused to chew and swallow and then resumed, 'There's a back door that opens out of the kitchen. It gives on to a narrow alley behind the pub. At night it's latched and bolted from the inside. If you slip out that way, young Morris, leaving the door closed and bolted behind you, no one will know you've gone. I'll lock up behind you as you leave.'

'But once the pub's locked up I won't be able to get back in,' I protested.

'You won't need to, remember?' said Jack. 'You'll be catching the milk train to the coast and you won't be back here until well after the pub has opened tomorrow morning.'

This loomed before me as a most unattractive prospect. I drowned my sorrows in roast duck and potatoes swimming in thick gravy.

After dinner Warnie drifted into the public bar where I could see, through the open doorway, that he was roped into a game of darts with the locals. Jack and I lingered in the snug over a glass of brandy.

'"Person or persons unknown",' I said. 'That was the best verdict that was possible at today's inquest. And sometimes that's the best, the most intelligent, verdict that's available to us in these big questions we've been discussing.'

'Ah, we're back to the God question,' Jack said, with the gleam of eager combat in his eye. 'And has your thinking progressed any further?'

'I've decided that the best verdict it's possible to bring in is an open one.'

'Meaning agnosticism?'

'Meaning that we admit when there's not enough evidence to decide one way or the other. That's when we bring in a verdict that is the philosophical equivalent of "person or persons unknown". It's the only honest thing to do.'

'But the point of today's verdict was to continue the inquiry. It was an interim verdict, not a final one. Inspector Crispin is not about to say, "Well, there you are then: persons or persons unknown. That settles the matter, so I can now move on to another case." Rather the point of an open verdict is to say: gather more evidence, do more thinking.'

'I still think I'd like to keep an open mind.'

'Forever?'

To avoid replying I took a sip of brandy and Jack responded by continuing, 'G. K. Chesterton is a very dangerous writer for a young atheist or agnostic to read; he keeps planting explosive ideas in the mind. When I was still an atheist I read his remark that the purpose of having an open mind is rather like having an open mouth—in order to close it on something solid. So would you admit, young Tom, that an "open verdict" can only ever be an interim position?'

'And I've decided there's another problem,' I responded, rapidly changing the subject to avoid answering this challenge, 'another problem with this whole field of thinking.'

'Meaning?'

'With this whole category of religion.'

'The problem being . . .?'

'What religion has brought to our world. It's religion that gave us the Spanish Inquisition and the Crusades and persecutions in which so-called "heretics" were burned at the stake. Religion has divided families and divided nations. Europe was torn apart by the Hundred Years' War—and that was over religion. Galileo was persecuted by religion for his science. Religious superstition stood in the way of the birth of modern science until it was pushed aside by the weight of the evidence.'

'And the other side of the ledger?'

'I can't see that there is one. I mean to say, what good has religion ever done anyone? I can't see that there's any answer to that charge. So let's hear how you get out of that one, Jack.' I sat back in my seat, rather pleased with myself, mopping up the last of the gravy with a piece of bread.

'My first objection would be that your label—your whole category of "religion"—is so wide and so vague that it's not possible to make the huge sweeping statements about it that you do.'

'I don't understand.'

'Well, you speak of "religion" as if it were one thing. That's like treating a subject such as—well, sport, let's say, as if it were one thing. Now I'm no sportsman, but even I know that it would be possible to build a case for saying that all sport is evil and all sport should be banned based on the worse examples.'

'I don't follow you.'

'Well, think for a moment. If I talked about sports such as dog fighting and cock fighting; if I talked about brutal bare-knuckle boxing; if I talked about the totally unnecessary risks and dangers that people expose themselves to in some sports—I could start to build up a case that whatever this thing called "sport" is, it must be something evil. I could talk about how the supporters of different football teams so easily seem to fall from jeering at each other to fighting each other. I could talk about international competition as evidence that sports divide nations and divide communities. I could cite examples of cheating in sport to show that sport brings out the worst in people. It would be an unfair and unbalanced catalogue, of course, but it wouldn't be hard to make some sort of case against this whole vague category of "sport". And that's exactly what you've done in the case of your very large, vague category of "religion".'

I was still thinking about how to reply to this when Jack went on, 'Instead of making a case against a category as vague as "religion", you'd be much more persuasive if you made your case against Buddhism, and against Hinduism, and then against Islam, and then against Christianity . . . and so on. And I think you'd find that your case would be quite different in each example.'

'Such as?' I challenged.

'Well, I doubt that you could make a case that Buddhism was war-like, for instance. As far as I know, and I admit my knowledge is limited, Buddhism is an almost entirely pacific belief system. However, on the other side of the ledger you could argue that the Buddhist belief in reincarnation has had the effect of discouraging the foundation of charities for the disabled. Apparently Buddhists believe that if you're born with a disability you're being punished for the sins—the "bad karma", I think they'd call it—of a previous life. Given that belief, you can readily see why there were few charities in most Buddhist countries until the arrival of Christian missionaries.'

'But—' I began. However, Jack had up a head of steam and kept going.

'The Hindu practice of *sati*, the burning of a widow on her husband's funeral pyre, was stopped by the arrival of Christianity in India.'

'Let's see if I've got this right—you're arguing that every time I use the word "religion", I'm pointing at such a wide range of things I'm not hitting my target, and what I should be doing is investigating, and criticising, specific religions for their specific faults.'

'Exactly. Picking out the worst examples and claiming that you've wiped out the whole category of "religion" is like quoting the worst greeting card verse and using that to attack the whole category of "poetry", or focusing on frankly awful popular tunes and claiming this shows that "music" is all awful.'

'Actually, you're beginning to make sense,' I admitted as I poured another glass of brandy. 'All this talk about "religion" is now looking intellectually lazy. The thing to do would be to focus on a particular, specific religion.'

'That would certainly be the intelligent and well-informed thing to do. But I think I'd go even further than that, since your real target is not "religion" at all, but Christianity. I got the impression when you were rattling off your charges against what you called "religion" it was really Christianity that you were taking aim at. If that's so, it's better to say so. Don't disguise your attack on Christianity by woolly thinking about "religion". Be specific, and try to land some knock-out blows on the reasonableness of Christianity.'

'Then let's agree that our debate is not about "religion" but about the reasonableness of Christianity. That said, it's still the case that the catalogue of evils I rattled off can be laid at the door of Christianity.'

'I'm not sure it can,' said Jack. 'Even you must admit that your list is highly selective and carefully omits the rest of the story.'

'In what sense?'

'Well, Christianity invented the concept of the hospital. It was Christianity that invented the university. Christianity both provided and encouraged education. It's simply a fact of history that it was Christianity—the ideas contained in the Bible—that gave rise to charities. And your argument about science, it seems to me, is simply wrong as a matter of history. The people who argued against Galileo didn't do so because they were Christians but because they were, philosophically, Aristotelians, and Galileo's science disproved Aristotle. The relationship between science and Christianity is the exact opposite of what you claimed. In reality, it was Christianity that gave rise to modern science. The founders of modern science, Newton, Boyle, Copernicus, Galileo himself and countless others, were devout Christian believers. They pursued their science *because* they believed the world to be intelligently designed; hence there was a design to be discovered.'

'I'll need to look into the history of that,' I muttered over the top my brandy glass. 'But—but—can Christianity be reasonable if wars have been fought in its name?'

'It depends what you mean by Christianity.'

'I don't follow.'

'If a medieval prince wants to expand his territory and declares war on a neighbour claiming that he is doing so in the name of Christianity, would such an action be consistent with the Christian faith that he claims to be waging war in the name of, or wouldn't it?'

'That . . . I think . . . would depend on what counts as genuine Christian faith.'

'And surely the way to establish that would be to go back to the teachings of Jesus. If you're trying to weigh up whether genuine Christian belief is reasonable or not you need to look at the founder of the faith, and not at some medieval prince—who may, or may not, have been well taught in Christian things, and who may, or may not, have been abiding by what he was taught.'

'But surely if the Church, or one of the major denominations, acts in a certain way . . .'

'Don't try that argument on me because I won't respond to it. I'm not interested in defending, or attacking, any of the major denominations or churches. It's the core, the common faith, the historical faith taught by the Founder that I believe can be shown to be entirely reasonable.'

'And in the case of wars and torture?'

'Jesus told Peter to put away his sword, and he told Pontius Pilate, "My kingdom is not of this world." Let's examine critically, and intelligently, the reasonableness of the Christianity of Jesus. Surely that gets us to the heart of the matter.'

TWENTY-ONE

~

Shortly after eleven o'clock that night I crept out of my room, carrying my boots in my hand, and began my slow and silent departure. As I tiptoed down the darkened corridor, a narrow finger of light appeared beside me as the door to Warnie's room was opened an inch. An eye appeared in the gap. Seeing me, Warnie pushed the door wider and put his finger to his lips to signal silence. Did he really think I was about to slap him on the back and shout, 'Warnie, what are you doing up at this time of night?'

But Warnie was clearly enjoying his plunge into this cloak and dagger stuff, and, fuelled by his endless reading of thrillers, he was playing his role with all the relish of an old ham actor in a juicy melodrama.

Warnie stepped out into the corridor, taking the lead and beckoning me to follow. He had also removed his boots and was treading carefully down the stairs in his woollen socks. About six steps from the bottom he put his weight on one step that creaked loudly. In that silent pub it sounded like the explosion of Krakatoa. We both froze, waiting to hear if anyone had been roused. After a lengthy silence Warnie resumed his cat-like tread to the foot of the stairs. I followed, being careful to step over, and not on, the sixth step from the bottom.

Warnie then led the way behind the bar and through the door into the kitchen. Here he struck a match, and it's a good thing he did: around us were kitchen benches stacked high with pots and pans. If we had bumped those over we would have had a crash to wake the dead, the entire pub, most of the town and all the closer farms. Then, of course, we would have had a lot of inventive explaining to do, and my overnight adventure would have been cancelled.

As it was, we negotiated our way between the benches and the piles of cookware, then down a shorter hallway. This was clearly used as storage space by the publican, with boxes piled upon boxes. We had to turn sideways and inch past these. Then we were at the solid wooden door at the back of the pub.

Warnie slowly eased back the latch and bolt and slid the door open. I squatted down on the floor to pull on my boots and lace them up. As I was doing this the flickering match burned down to Warnie's fingers. He blew it out and lit another.

I stepped outside. Warnie shook my hand, wished me luck in a whisper, and gave me the thumbs up sign as a gesture of encouragement. Then he gently closed the door behind me. I heard him slowly ease the latch and then the lock securely into place. A second later I heard the bolt on the door slide home.

Now I had no way back.

A crescent moon came out briefly from behind a cloud and cast a pale blue light over my surroundings. I was standing in a narrow alley that ran behind the back wall of the pub. Treading as lightly as I could on the old cobblestones of Market Plumpton, I made my way to the corner of the building and peered around. I was looking down another alleyway that ran between the pub and the building next door, past the side windows of the pub. The moonlight clearly revealed the rubbish bins that lined this passage. I carefully squeezed past these potential hazards. My aim was to get to the front of the pub because that was a street I had come to know well, and I thought from there I could easily find my way to the railway station.

At the end of the second alley I cautiously peered around the corner. The street in front of the pub was a river of darkness dotted with small splashes of dim, yellow light beneath the street lamps. I looked up and down the street. It appeared to be completely deserted.

I was about to step out from behind the corner of the pub when I heard a sound from the opposite side of the street. Quickly I stepped back, quietened my breathing and tried to peer into the deep shadows opposite the front door of the pub. The sound came again—the scraping of a boot on the footpath. This was followed by the striking of a match, and a moment later I saw a young uniformed policeman lighting a cigarette. The flame of the match died and all I could see was the dull red glow of the end of the cigarette.

He didn't move. I waited and waited, and still he didn't move on. I decided he was not a bobby on his beat but was stationed in front of the pub to make sure we didn't do a midnight flit. But flitting was what I had in mind. Making a midnight flit was essential to our plans. So I retreated down the alleyway, past the rubbish bins and along the first alley that followed the back wall of the pub.

I passed the now-locked back door and kept going. Once again the clouds broke long enough to give me a few moments of dim, silvery moonlight. By this I found another narrow laneway leading off to my left. On one side were the back walls of terrace houses and shops, each with its back door opening into the lane, and on the other a long, high, unbroken brick wall. I guided myself by running my fingers lightly along this wall, moving forward slowly and cautiously. I didn't want to kick over a rubbish bin and attract attention.

The lane widened out as it led downhill. Downhill, I knew, was the general direction in which the railway station lay, so I pushed on. Eventually the lane opened into a slightly wider street. This sloped up to my left and down to my right. I turned right.

A few minutes later I stepped into a small square, and from here I could see down to the railway station itself—the platform dimly lit with a warm, buttery-yellow light. I hurried through the darkened town towards my destination. I quickly lost sight of the station behind the buildings, but I was now confident that I was heading in the right direction.

I walked down the middle of this wider street to avoid colliding with rubbish bins or stray cats. Somewhere in the distance a dog barked. A congregation of dogs in nearby backyards yapped their liturgical responses. The street reminded me of some lines by Alfred Noyes I had learned as a child: 'The wind was a torrent of darkness among the gusty trees, The moon was a ghostly galleon tossed upon cloudy seas, The road was a ribbon of moonlight . . .' And so it was, as the clouds broke into feathery traces and a crescent moon appeared, painting the street in pale light alternating with solid, black shadows—looking rather like an old woodblock print.

The street I was hurrying down ended in a yard behind the railway station. At this time of night the area was empty, except for a single truck parked next to the back wall of the station. Two men were struggling to slide large, heavy milk cans off the back of the truck onto the ground.

I skirted around the edge of this goods yard, keeping away from the lights and sticking to the pools of inky black shadow, until I reached the back wall of the station building. At this point I had no choice but to step out into the light. A steady nerve was what was needed here, I decided, so I squared my shoulders and with a confident swagger walked the length of the building to the ticket office.

I looked in through the small window to see a young man putting a kettle on a gas ring. I took some coins out of my pocket and tapped them on the counter to attract his attention.

'Sorry, sir,' he said, 'didn't see you there.'

As he walked across to the counter I said, 'A return ticket to Plumpton-on-Sea please.'

He turned to a rack of tickets beside him, selected the right one and said, 'One and sixpence please, sir.'

I counted out the money and exchanged it for the ticket. The young man explained that the train was departing from platform one in ten minutes. I breathed a heavy sigh—I had only just got there in time.

'Looks like rain,' said the ticket seller in a bored voice.

'I hope not,' I replied, pocketing the ticket and hurrying through an archway towards the platform. At the corner of the building I paused and glanced up and down. At the far end of the platform, facing away from me, with his hands clasped behind his back, was a uniformed policeman. Clearly, Inspector Crispin was determined that none of his suspects would slip away and none of his witnesses would go wandering.

I drew back into the shadows of the archway. The next time I cautiously glanced out, the policeman was slowly turning around, and I quickly withdrew my head behind the edge of the brickwork.

'So what do I do now?' I asked myself. I walked slowly back through the archway to the yard behind the station. The two men had finished unloading their milk cans from the back of the truck. One of them climbed into the driver's seat and drove off with a roaring rattle that seemed to echo around the silent town. The noise slowly died away in the distance. The other man looked gloomily at the milk cans, then began dragging them, one at a time, around the end of the station building onto platform one.

Boldness, I thought—this calls for boldness. I strolled up to the chap struggling with the heavy cans and said, 'Like a hand?'

At first he was surprised. Then he looked at my clothes. I was wearing my old hiking gear, not a suit, and I think that convinced him I was making a genuine offer.

'Thanks, mate,' he said. 'Just grab that handle on the other side.'

I'd won a blue for rugby at Oxford so I could match this labourer muscle for muscle. Between the two of us we soon had the dozen or so large milk cans half-dragged, half-slid around the corner of the building, across platform one, and in through the open door of the goods van at the back of the train.

The police constable glanced up once then turned away, taking no interest in what two labourers were doing.

When the last of the milk cans was on board the workman I'd assisted touched his cap and said, 'Thanks, guv.'

I just nodded, and seeing the policeman was at the far end of the platform and looking in the opposite direction, I hurried down the length of the train and clambered aboard a second-class carriage.

This turned out to be empty except for one other passenger: a middle-aged man dressed as a farmer with a cage balanced on his knees. Inside the cage was a fat white hen. The man himself had his head tilted backwards and was sound asleep, snoring loudly. The hen, whose eyes had also been closed, was the only one of the two to take any interest in my arrival. She half opened one eye, gave me a cold stare for disturbing her sleep, then closed her eyelid again. The farmer didn't stir.

I took a seat in the farthest corner, away from the platform, and turned to look out of the window into the darkness beyond so that I wasn't showing my face to the carriage or the platform. A few minutes later there was a loud hiss of steam followed by the clanking of carriage couplings taking strain. Then came the slow, powerful chugging sound of large locomotive cylinders starting to work. With a jerk the train started moving, accompanied by that glorious locomotive smell of steam, coal smoke and hot oil.

Soon there was a rhythmic rattle of rails underneath us, a steady chuffing from the locomotive ahead, and we were on our way to Plumpton-on-Sea.

TWENTY-TWO

~

We rattled noisily over the iron bridge across the Plum River and chugged steadily over the dark countryside. In the early hours of the morning we stopped in the village of Plumwood where the only other passenger in my carriage got off, taking his hen with him. The hen once again opened one eye but took no serious interest in the proceedings (clearly a seasoned traveller to whom one railway station was much the same as any other). Further down the platform I could hear some of the milk cans being unloaded.

Then we were off again. Now I was the only occupant of the carriage, so I stretched out my legs and rested my feet on the seat facing me. Not, I grant you, the behaviour of a gentleman, but perhaps understandable in a gentleman who would much rather have been tucked up in a nice warm bed.

We passed through a tunnel where both the sound of the locomotive and the smell of coal smoke became more noticeable. Back out in the open air, spots of rain began to splash against the windows of the carriage. Steadily the rain got heavier, and within ten minutes it was a torrential downpour that drummed on the roof of the carriage and thundered like a waterfall down the windows.

Half an hour later the rain eased off again to occasional drops, but it was replaced by wind. Mixing with the sound of the clacking rails and the chuffing engine I could hear the wind howling softly, like a distant banshee or a rather gloomy ghost complaining about its lot in the afterlife: 'My colleagues get to haunt castles and here I am stuck with haunting a railway line. There's no justice!' As my eyelids closed and these thoughts drifted through my tired brain, I cursed my overactive imagination—and told myself to think logically, like the detective I was trying to be.

Then faintly, beneath the rail noises and the wind, I could also hear crashing waves.

The window beside me had become misted by my breath. I wiped it clear with a gloved hand and pressed my face to the glass. As I watched there was another brief appearance of the crescent moon. This time it was reflected by an inky black sea, and it was clear that we were running down the coast with farmland on one side and waves and rocks on the other.

It was half past three in the morning when the train pulled into the platform at Plumpton-on-Sea. Once it had jolted and clanked to a complete halt, I left the comfort of the carriage for the damp, windy dimness of the platform. Light misty rain was still falling so I turned up the collar of my coat and pulled down the brim of my hat. There was only one railwayman on the platform. He was picking up bundles of newspapers and loading them onto a trolley. He stopped as I approached and collected my ticket.

I asked for directions and was told there was only one road leading from here into the town. I stepped out of the oasis of dim light that was the railway station and there it was—a steep road leading down the hillside to the harbour and the town. I wrapped my scarf more snugly around my neck, pushed my hands into my coat pockets, and, with my head lowered into the oncoming breeze, set off for the town of Plumpton-on-Sea.

On a hot summer's day it was probably a delightful spot. But none of its attractions were obvious in the dark and damp of that night. The brisk walk, however, kept me warm. The only illumination came from the pinpricks of street lights at wide intervals.

The road leading down from the railway station became the high street of the town and led me to the seafront. It was four in the morning by the time I found myself staring at the sleeping faces of a row of buildings that looked across the high street to a stretch of grass and a pebble beach beyond. Dark, lethargic waves were rolling up the beach and breaking in limp, frothy surges on the pebbles, as if they found the effort exhausting.

It was at least an hour to sunrise, and I needed to find somewhere to wait for the town to wake up. I tried a bus shelter on the high street, but it was exposed to the wind. So I walked onto the pier that jutted out above the beach. Here I found another shelter, and a bench—presumably for sightseers who wanted to rest while enjoying the view. This was much better, for the back of this little refuge was to the driving wind and I could sit out of the misty rain. I slid to one end of the bench, rested my head against the side of the shelter and closed my eyes.

I must have fallen asleep because when I opened them again it was broad daylight and I could hear the cry of the gulls circling above the beach. I woke up feeling stiff in the joints and uncomfortable—perhaps a little like the poet Shelley after a night on the tiles with Lord Byron.

I looked at my watch: it was almost half past six. There must, I thought, be somewhere open at that hour that would serve me breakfast. In my imagination I could already hear the sizzling bacon—and smell it. Half the pleasure of bacon is the wonderful, inviting aroma it gives off when it's frying. Yes, breakfast, I told myself, must be my first priority.

I stood up and stretched my arms and legs. I pulled off my scarf and stuffed it into a coat pocket. Sleeping in my clothes, I decided, had left me feeling as ragged as a badly tied up brown paper parcel.

The wind had dropped and the clouds were breaking up, promising a warm and sunny day. Here in England, I thought to myself, we don't have climate, only weather—ever changeable, never-quite-what-you-expect weather.

Most of the shops and guesthouses on the seafront still had their shutters up, but several were starting to open. The newsagent's was open and its lights were on. The teashop next door was also taking its shutters down, even as I looked.

I walked across the deserted road and pushed open the front door of the teashop. This caused a small bell on the top of the door to tinkle.

'Good morning,' I said. The young girl behind the counter looked at me blankly. She was, clearly, not quite awake: the shutters were still closed behind her eyes.

'Too early for breakfast?' I asked. She looked at me blankly, as I if had spoken in Lithuanian and she was struggling to translate.

'How about a cup of tea, love? You can manage that, can't you?'

'Yes, sir,' she murmured, recovering from the shock of having a customer so early in the morning. 'Take a seat and I'll bring it to your table.'

I took a window seat and stared across the road at the almost dead flat sea that was washing against the pebbles. A few minutes later the girl turned up with a cup and saucer, a small teapot and a small jug of milk.

'Sugar's on the table,' she said, waving vaguely in the direction of a bowl of sugar cubes.

'Thank you,' I said. 'Now, would a hot breakfast be possible, do you think?'

She nodded and pulled a tiny notebook out of the pocket of her apron.

'Would bacon and eggs be on the menu?'

She said nothing, but scribbled in her notebook and walked away.

Ten minutes later the bacon and eggs arrived. Twenty minutes later, having wrapped myself around hot food and two cups of tea, I was feeling human again.

I walked up to the counter to pay, but held my money tightly in my right hand while I asked a question: 'I'm looking for a Mrs Proudfoot—Mrs Amelia Proudfoot. She would have arrived in the last day or two. Probably staying at one the guest-houses or boarding houses. Young woman—in her twenties I would guess. Quite good looking. Dark hair. Have you seen her around?'

The girl's face went as blank as a whitewashed wall. This appeared to be the expression she adopted when she was thinking intensely.

Finally she replied, 'No, I don't think so. Not in the last day or two.'

'Is there anyone else here who might have seen her, or might know if she's in town?'

The girl yelled over her shoulder to the open doorway leading to the kitchen, 'Mrs Henson! Man here's got a question for you.'

Mrs Henson waddled out of the kitchen wiping her hands on a tea cloth. 'How can I help you, sir?'

I repeated what I'd said to the girl. Then Mrs Henson and the girl went into conference. 'I don't think there's been anyone like that, do you, Rosie? Can't say I've seen anyone like that around the place. And the name doesn't ring a bell at all. I've never heard of this Amelia Proudfoot. Have you, Rosie? So there you are, sir—Rosie hasn't heard of her neither. I suppose she might be around somewhere, but keeping herself to herself, so to speak.'

And this turned out to be the pattern for all the replies I received at every possible place in Plumpton-on-Sea. At boarding houses, guesthouses, shops, pubs, homes that took in lodgers—everywhere except the bus depot and the post office—I asked my set questions. Over the course of the morning I worked my way along the length of the seafront stopping at every building that had a sign up saying 'room available' or that might do business with a visitor. They all gave the same answer: the name Amelia Proudfoot meant nothing to them. As I described her to them I realised that my description was rather vague and it would have helped if I'd had a photograph. But I didn't. And my description awoke no sign of recognition for anyone.

Then I left the seafront and checked out the few guesthouses higher up the hill, behind the high street—but with the same result.

I also found two shops with signs indicating that they were 'Estate Agents and Letting Agents'. I tried both of them in the hope that Mrs Proudfoot might have rented a flat, but once again with entirely negative results.

By mid-morning I was back where I'd started, staring at the pebble beach and the lifeless waves with no more information than when I'd begun. Disappointed, I decided it was time to take the train back to Market Plumpton and report my failure.

I walked into the newsagent's to buy a copy of the *Times* to read on the return journey. I paid for the newspaper and then, on a whim, said to the man behind the counter, 'There's a young woman I'm trying to find. She may have arrived here in the last day or two.'

His face lit up at the possibility that there was a colourful story behind my words. I went through the routine of name and description with exactly the same result as before. But then he said, 'Of course, you're asking the wrong person. It's my wife who knows everything that's going on in this town.'

He turned towards the back room and shouted, 'Hey, Dolly—come out here a minute, love.'

A moment later his wife appeared, running her fingers through her tousled hair. He repeated my question. His wife shook her head slowly from side to side, but even as she did so she was thinking. After a moment's more thought she said, 'I ran into old Mrs Dawson yesterday. She said she's got a new paying guest.'

'Could it be the woman I'm looking for?' I asked eagerly.

'Well, I don't know what her name is,' said the newsagent's wife. 'And I don't know what she looks like. All I know is that Mrs Dawson said she was a painted tart. Some rich man's kept woman.'

I felt deflated. That didn't sound like Amelia Proudfoot at all. We'd met her. We knew that she was a heart-broken young woman whose husband had only just died. There was no way she could be a 'kept woman' or a 'painted tart'. But then I thought that my investigation should be thorough, so I asked for Mrs Dawson's address, thanked the couple at the newsagent's, and set out to make what I told myself would be the last investigation on my trip to Plumpton-on-Sea.

TWENTY-THREE

~

Mrs Dawson lived in an isolated house on Cliff Road, at the edge of town. At the end of the high street I climbed the hill until I came to the address the newsagent had given me. It was a two-storey terrace of grey stone.

In response to my knock, the front door was opened by a plump middle-aged woman.

At that moment I realised that I hadn't worked out what I was going to say. If my quarry was, by any chance, staying here, she was keeping out of sight, in which case a clever piece of deception might be needed to discover the truth. But I could think of none. Being entirely unprepared with an appropriate and convincing story, out of sheer desperation I stuck to the truth.

'Mrs Dawson?' I asked.

She nodded.

'I'm looking for a woman named Mrs Amelia Proudfoot.'

'No one of that name here,' she replied, and began to close the door.

'She might be using another name,' I said hastily.

'And why would she be doing that?'

'She's just been through a rather unhappy time. She might be trying to put it behind her.'

'What sort of unhappy time?'

'Her husband has just died, and the farm they lived on has been repossessed by the bank.'

'I'm sorry to hear that. But my paying guest, and I only have the one, is not a married woman. So she can't be the person you're looking for.'

'The lady I'm looking for would be in her twenties, dark haired, quite good looking.'

Mrs Dawson's brow clouded with suspicion. 'And who might you be anyway? Are you a debt collector?'

'Nothing of that sort. I just wanted to ask her a few questions.'

'Well, my paying guest has given me strict instructions that she's not to be disturbed. She keeps to her room, she does—and she sees no one except her gentleman friend.'

'Her gentleman friend?'

Mrs Dawson looked uncomfortable and shuffled her feet. 'A widow woman in my position can't afford to be too choosy. I need the rent so I take whoever comes.'

With those words she began to shut the door.

'But does she match the description?' I asked hurried.

'That she does—but then so do hundreds of others. Now if you don't mind, I have a kitchen floor to mop.' And with that the door was closed firmly in my face.

My train journey back to Market Plumpton was uneventful. I read my newspaper and tried not to feel too depressed by my total failure to uncover the missing woman in Plumpton-on-Sea. She might be Mrs Dawson's paying guest—in which case, who was her 'gentleman caller'? Or she might be staying with a friend and that's why I was unable to discover her whereabouts. Or Mr Ravenswood might have been right when he suggested she had returned to her 'relatives up north'.

In the end I threw my newspaper to one side and stared glumly at the sunny landscape sliding past the windows of the railway carriage. It does a chap no good at all to be staring at bright sunshine and cheerful fields filled with contented cows when his mind is full of fog—and damp, dark fog at that.

Back in Market Plumpton I walked back to our pub with my hands in my pockets and my head down, like a student who's just got a bad exam result. As I reached the front door of *The Boar's Head*, a large figure came charging out and almost knocked me over.

I grabbed the doorpost to steady myself while Edmund Ravenswood swayed unsteadily and complained, 'Watch where you're going!' His voice was a full volume bellow, as if he was calling the cattle home across the sands of Dee.

Then he recognised me and seemed to pull himself together. 'Oh, it's you. Young Morris. Sorry about that—in rather a hurry.' With those words he charged up the street continuing his bull-in-a-china-shop impersonation.

I stepped inside the dim coolness of the pub and said to Frank Jones behind the bar, 'Did you see that?'

The publican looked up from the glass he was wiping with a tea towel and replied with a grin, 'He's not a happy man is our bank manager.'

I asked what the problem was and the publican replied, 'It seems there's been some sort of falling out between Mr Ravenswood and his wife. He came here asking if we'd seen her—or if she was staying here.'

'That sounds like more than a falling out,' I commented. 'It sounds rather more like she's left him.'

Jones grinned salaciously but said nothing. Then I asked him where the Lewis brothers were, and following his directions found them seated in cane chairs in the sunshine on the lawn behind the pub. Both were reading books. Jack had a pocket edition of Spenser while Warnie was turning the pages of *It Walks by Night*.

'Ah, the traveller returns,' grunted Warnie.

'Was my absence noticed?' I asked. 'Was I missed?'

'I'm afraid so,' said Jack. 'In fact, the good Inspector Crispin was rather miffed to discover you'd slipped the net. He calmed down a little when I promised that you'd return shortly. He left here only ten minutes ago, muttering darkly about the calamities that might fall upon your head.'

'Should I go and see him at the police station?' I asked nervously. I didn't fancy the idea of upsetting policemen—especially senior policemen from Scotland Yard.

'We all have to, old chap,' said Warnie, putting down his book and levering his bulk out of the low-slung cane chair. 'We three are under instructions to present ourselves at the police station the moment you return.'

'And we shall,' said Jack, 'but first I'd like to hear your report, Tom.'

So I narrated my adventures, providing a complete and unabridged edition. I have the ability to recall and report conversations verbatim, and this is what I did. When I finished, I apologised for my total and abject failure.

'Not at all, old chap,' said Jack heartily, 'not at all. In fact, I think you did very well—and I believe you discovered enough for me to slide another probable piece into place in the jigsaw puzzle. Now, off to confront our unhappy inspector.'

'And have you heard the news?' I said as Jack rose from his chair. I told them about Mrs Ravenswood apparently leaving her husband. In response Jack shook his head sadly and Warnie muttered something about Ravenswood being 'a pompous, unpleasant man'.

Before we left the pub I went upstairs to shed my now unnecessary coat. As I did so, I caught a glimpse of myself in the mirror and decided that I looked like a corpse that had just been fished out of a river—or, more alarmingly, like someone whose face belonged on a 'Most Wanted' poster on the walls of a Chicago police station. Not wanting to create a bad impression at my interview with the inspector, I had a quick wash and brushed my hair. Checking the results in the mirror, I decided I still looked like a corpse—but a neater, more cheerful corpse.

As we left the pub I felt like a Christian in ancient Rome about to shake hands with one of the lions.

At the Market Plumpton police station, the sergeant on the desk kept us waiting in the lobby for almost twenty minutes. Then our old friend Constable Dixon emerged from somewhere deep within the bowels of the station and said, 'Detective Inspector Crispin will see you now—if you'll just follow me, gentlemen.'

He lifted the flap on the front desk and we filed through. Dixon led us to a small room towards the back of the building with the words 'Interview Room' painted on the door. It was bare and had a single high window. It was furnished with a plain deal table and half a dozen straight-backed chairs. Dixon left us there and closed the door.

'Now I really feel like a suspect,' grumbled Warnie. 'No doubt we're about to be interrogated. We'll be given what the American detective novels I read call a "grilling". They also refer to this process as the "third degree"—which I've never understood. They never seem to give anyone the "first degree" or the "second degree". Puzzling.'

Jack and I took our seats and waited patiently, but Warnie paced around the small space muttering, 'This is not an interview room, it's an interrogation chamber!'

Warnie continued grumbling in this gloomy fashion until the door opened to admit Detective Inspector Crispin and his faithful assistant, Sergeant Merrivale.

At the inspector's insistence Warnie took a seat beside Jack and me on one side of the table while Crispin and Merrivale sat on the other.

'By rights,' said Crispin in a quiet but grim voice, 'I should interview each of you three separately—but time is pressing and we need to get on, so we'll do it this way. And we'll begin with you, young Morris. What did you mean by fleeing the district when I explicitly told you not to leave without informing us?'

'I didn't flee,' I protested. 'I paid a brief visit to Plumpton-on-Sea, that's all. I was only gone one night—less than twenty-four hours in all. And I came back. That hardly qualifies as "fleeing".'

'I take it you didn't go to paddle in the waves, so why did you go?'

On our walk to the police station we'd agreed that we'd be completely frank with the inspector, so I told him about my attempts to locate Amelia Proudfoot.

'Mr Ravenswood,' responded Crispin, 'who dealt with the foreclosure, told us that she's returned to her relatives up north. I've asked the Yorkshire constabulary to try to locate her.'

'They won't,' said Jack confidently.

'Explain,' snapped the Scotland Yard man.

'She's down on the coast.'

'But your friend here looked and failed to find her!'

Inspector Crispin leaned back in his chair and stared at Jack for the better part of a minute, trying to make him out. I could almost hear the thoughts running through his head: is this just an Oxford don playing clever games? Or does he really know something? Or does he have a theory of the crime that would make sense of all the puzzles?

In the absence of a question Jack said, 'Mr Ravenswood seemed most unhappy when he visited *The Boar's Head* this morning.'

'Mr Ravenswood's marital difficulties have no bearing on this investigation,' Crispin responded.

'She's left her husband then?' I asked.

Sergeant Merrivale broke his silence to say, 'We knew before he did.' He said this with a rather smarmy smile on his face, so I asked him how he knew.

'Well, sir,' he replied, with the smile still firmly in place, 'we do keep an eye on the key witnesses in a case like this, and our man saw her leave their flat above the bank before dawn this morning. She was carrying a suitcase. He followed her to a boarding house on the other side of town. It seems that now she's in line to inherit the money that was coming to her late brother, so she's decided she no longer needs to put up with that unpleasant man.'

Inspector Crispin expressed his displeasure at this revelation by saying 'Thank you, sergeant' through gritted teeth. 'Now,' he continued, 'we'll go back over your evidence. I want a moment-by-moment account of what happened, and what you observed and what you heard, on the day of the murder.'

And that's what he got. It took us until lunch time and consisted of treading and re-treading over highly familiar territory.

When he was finally satisfied that there was no new information to be squeezed out of us, Inspector Crispin told us we could leave. As we rose to go he added, 'And don't forget you'll be required at this afternoon's inquest.' I must have looked puzzled because he explained, 'Into the death of Nicholas Proudfoot. You three discovered the body—your evidence may be required.'

On that coldly formal note we left.

TWENTY-FOUR

~

Lunch was once again served in the sunshine on the lawn behind the pub. Mrs Jones had made us a large plate of generous sandwiches filled with slices of cold roast beef and lashings of hot English mustard.

'Now that's what I call real mustard,' said Warnie with a satisfied snort. The mustard that so delighted him seemed to be clearing my sinuses, turning my tear ducts into flowing cisterns and burning a large hole in the roof of my mouth. I went into the bar and returned with a tray bearing three pints of ale.

As the beer extinguished the fire and I leaned back in my comfortable cane chair, I decided that I wanted to think, and talk, about anything other than baffling murder mysteries and investigations that led to dead ends. So I turned to Jack and said, 'I wonder if, in the end, this Christian religion that you keep going on about is really part of a greater crossword puzzle—the crossword puzzle of life.'

He told me that was a comparison he'd never heard before and invited me to explain.

'Perhaps what it gives us are clues to what is hidden in the human heart, and to whatever it is that lies at the heart of the universe. You keep talking about how satisfying you found Christianity, how it answered all your questions. Well, perhaps

I've been too harsh. Perhaps Christianity *does* contain some useful clues—but they are buried underneath a lot of supernatural mumbo jumbo.'

I thought for a moment Jack was going to let my 'mumbo jumbo' crack go through to the keeper. But looking at me kindly, and using the gentle words that turneth away wrath, he said, 'Perhaps when all the other clues are understood, the supernatural element ceases to be mumbo jumbo and emerges of part of the larger, more complex picture.'

I wasn't going to let him off the hook that easily. 'You're missing my point,' I insisted.

'Which is?'

'That all we should expect from your Christianity is a few clues to the crossword puzzle of life. That's all the Christian belief system in the end delivers—a few clues.'

'Quite possibly every world view and every belief system attempts to do that,' Jack suggested. 'They all point to a hunger of the human heart—a hunger we have for meaning and a need to understand our purpose in life. There was certainly a deep longing in my heart when I was an atheist, and I was startled to discover that Christianity satisfied that longing.'

'So you were looking for something and you didn't know what it was that you were looking for?'

'It was as though,' said Jack thoughtfully, 'I kept catching fragments of music, or a haunting melody, heard only faintly when the wind was blowing in the right direction. In Christianity I discovered the entire satisfying symphony.'

'But my point is a bit different,' I protested. 'I admit there are some clues around to the universe we live in—more than there used to be—but still not enough. The puzzle is not complete. Perhaps one day modern science will discover enough to tell how the world works and why.'

'Science will never answer why,' Jack said confidently.

'That's a bold claim,' I laughed.

'No, it's just a logical one. You stop and think about what science is and how it functions. What, for example, does science study?'

'Well, the universe around us. From the largest component to the smallest, from the stars to the molecules.'

'All of which are . . . ?'

'I don't understand.'

'Physical. Science studies the physical universe—it's make-up and its machinery. To understand the mechanisms of the universe we turn to science. But science only studies matter, and the universe is more than matter.'

'I'm not sure you can say that so confidently. Philosophers have been debating that for centuries, and the more modern science discovers, the more is explicable in terms of matter.'

'If you don't believe me,' said Jack confidently, 'then explain poetry in purely material terms.'

I opened my mouth and quickly shut it again. I wasn't sure what to say.

'Poetry,' continued Jack, 'is more than matter; it's more than black marks on white paper. Music is more than matter; it's more than vibrations in the air. And the whole of philosophy from Plato onwards has acknowledged that.'

'So what *can* science do?'

'It can explain the material universe, what it's made of and how it works. And it does so brilliantly. But beyond the physical universe is the metaphysical. Beyond the black marks on paper is the poem itself.'

I stopped to drink my beer and think about what Jack was saying. After a lengthy silence I said slowly, 'But there must be more to it than that. Surely science is the peak of the hill the human race has been climbing for centuries. In *The Golden Bough* Frazer shows that ancient humans lived in what he calls the "age of magic", which evolved into the "age of religion", and that in turn has developed into the "age of science". That's progress, isn't it? Isn't science the knowledge the human race has been seeking for and aiming at for millennia?'

Lewis threw back his head and laughed heartily.

'You certainly know how to ask a big question,' he said, still chuckling. 'You are walking in my footsteps, young Morris—you are standing where I once stood. As a young atheist I proudly waved my copy of Frazer's big book as proof that all religions and all mythologies were just human inventions—the products of human imagination.'

'Well, perhaps they—' But I didn't finish the sentence for Lewis was ploughing on.

'But Frazer's great weakness is that he is writing anthropology. That is to say, he's writing about human beings and the ideas inside their heads. He gives us a vivid description of how he thinks human heads have changed over the years, but he never examines the truth of the ideas inside those heads. The *history* of an idea and the *truth* of an idea are two separate things.'

'Another beer?' asked Warnie.

'Not for me thanks,' said Jack, and then he turned his attention back to me. 'My atheistic foundations were shaken to the core by a friend of mine—a fellow atheist, I should add—who remarked to me in passing how much good evidence there is for the historicity of the gospels.'

'The point being?'

'That if the gospels *really happened*—if they are not just some human invention, not the product of human imagination, but something real in our world—that tells us something about our world. Or, as my old atheist friend said, surprisingly it looks as if Frazer's stuff about a "dying god" actually happened once. And if it actually happened it's more than one small clue to your "crossword"—it's the one vital clue.'

Lewis leaned back in the cane chair he was sitting in and smiled benignly at me as he lit his pipe.

I bit into the last of my sandwich. The mustard brought tears to my eyes and I reached for my pint as I swallowed hard.

'It's certainly true,' Lewis continued, his head now surrounded by a cloud of blue smoke, 'that from the dawn of history human beings have been trying to make sense of the world—asking questions about how it works and why. And the answers to the "how" questions have moved over the millennia from guesswork to science. That's certainly progress. But the "why" questions are beyond the scope of science to tackle.'

Warnie returned with another pint. He resumed his seat, took a sip, wiped the foam off his moustache, then tilted his head back to enjoy the sun—studiously avoiding our debate.

'If you asked me how a fountain pen works,' Lewis resumed, 'I could give you a scientific answer about nibs and ink reserves and the capillary action of liquids that propels the ink to the point of the nib and so on. But if instead of asking *how* you asked *why*—for example, if you asked why this man is writing with this pen on this piece of paper at this time—I would have to talk about intentions. Perhaps he's sitting for an exam, or perhaps he's writing to his fiancé—but the answer is about a mind and its intentions, not about matter and the mechanisms of matter. Do you see the point?'

'I think I do,' I said. Now this was, I can say looking back on it, a turning point in the whole debate for me. I could see the sense of what Jack was saying and I had to grant him a small victory, so I continued, 'Science gives us useful and measured, tested information about the material world, but when science has answered every possible question about the material world there's still an unexplained residue left over.'

'Well put! And that "unexplained residue" beyond the reach of science is the most important thing of all. It's what Plato called the "realm of ideas", what Aristotle called the "metaphysical". It's what you might call the realm of pure intelligence—where all intention and purpose is formed. Plato was convinced that there is Mind independent of matter, and no philosopher and no scientist has ever demonstrated that he was wrong.'

'So how does this tie in with your atheist friend's casual remark that there's historical evidence for the gospels? Even if there is, what difference does it make?'

'If the gospels are history, then our world is more than the natural, material, physical stuff around us. If the gospels are history, then Mind and matter can mesh in ways that we could never have guessed. If the gospels are history, then our world has been invaded. We live on a visited planet: the metaphysical has invaded the physical. The Mind behind the universe has stepped into human history.'

Lewis paused to puff on his pipe, then resumed, 'This visitation didn't come in the form of one of those great interplanetary spaceships we read about in Mr Wells's scientific romances. It came in the form of a baby, born to a specific young woman at a specific time in a specific place. That's what Saint Luke demonstrates in his record, by nailing it to history: "And it came to pass in those days, that there went out a decree from Caesar Augustus that all the world should be taxed. (And this taxing was first made when Cyrenius was governor of Syria.)" How remarkable: the Emperor's accountants in Rome want a census so they can impose a taxation levy, and that is used to mark the moment in time when God steps into human history.'

Warnie had finished his pint and dropped off to sleep. A few moments later we heard a sound that might have been a pig drowning in glue. Warnie was snoring.

Jack smiled indulgently and continued making his point. 'As well as the time being nailed down, so is the place. The town of Bethlehem is not some imaginary spot out of myth and legend; it's not Camelot. It's a dusty little town in Palestine. If you visited the place today you could walk down its streets. Real time, real place, really happened.'

'And that's the big clue to my crossword puzzle of life?' I asked.

'It certainly reveals the vital bit science can never discover—the intention, the purpose, behind this world and behind our lives.'

In the silence that followed we were startled to hear the sound of weeping. I looked up towards the window of the pub's kitchen just behind us and saw Ruth Jarvis, the young woman who worked at the bank. She had her head on the shoulder of the publican's wife and was sobbing her heart out.

I turned back towards Jack and saw that he too was looking at what was happening in the kitchen with close interest. I drained the last of my pint and remarked, 'Emotional moments make me feel uncomfortable.'

'Nevertheless,' said Jack rising from his chair, 'I think we should investigate.'

TWENTY-FIVE

Jack made his way into the pub and around towards the kitchen. I stayed on the back lawn, but I strolled slowly closer to the open kitchen window so that I could overhear what went on.

Ruth Jarvis was speaking softly to Annie Jones, and her words were broken up by repeated sobs so that at first I couldn't hear her voice at all clearly. Then I heard a door open and Jack's voice say, 'I'm sorry. Is this a private conversation?'

'Yes, Mr Lewis,' replied Mrs Jones sternly. 'And you really shouldn't just walk into the kitchens.'

'It's all right, Annie,' interrupted Ruth. 'He knows. He was there when I told the police about . . . about . . .'

'Here, borrow my handkerchief,' said Jack, his voice, usually booming and hearty, sounding soft and sympathetic.

'Thank you, Mr Lewis,' sobbed Ruth. 'I'm afraid I'm not coping with this very well.'

'I doubt that anyone would,' said Jack. The sound carrying through the kitchen window suggested that he'd stepped closer. 'Finding yourself pregnant and unmarried and the baby's father suddenly dead is more than most people could bear.'

'I'm going to put the kettle on,' said Annie Jones. 'I know it's silly, but I always feel a good cup of tea will fix almost anything. Will you have a cup of tea with us, Mr Lewis?'

'That's very kind of you. I'd be delighted. Now, Ruth. Do you mind if I ask you a few questions? About this awful business?'

'If I can help. But I don't think I can . . .'

'Well, let's see, shall we? So, what kind of a man was Franklin Grimm? The Scotland Yard man, Inspector Crispin, says we're most likely to catch his killer by understanding the victim, so what was he like?'

There was a loud sniff and then Ruth began to speak, slowly and haltingly. 'He was funny. That was the first thing I noticed about him. He made me laugh. And he was a dreamer; he had great plans for getting to London and making his fortune. But if I was honest I'd have to say he couldn't always be trusted. He let people down.'

'In what ways?' Jack asked.

'Often in little, unimportant ways. He'd tell me he'd meet me somewhere and then either arrive an hour late or not turn up at all. The next time I saw him he'd be full of apologies, and very persuasive reasons why this time, just this once, he wasn't able to keep his word. And I wanted to believe him, and so I did. But looking back now I see that it kept on happening, again and again. I must have been a fool.'

'Did he make enemies in the town?'

'The other young men couldn't stand him,' Ruth replied with a touch of anger in her voice. 'They were so dull and slow. It's like they're carved out of a lump of wood. But Franklin was alive, always moving, always dreaming, always catching another gleam of light . . . like a . . . like a blob of mercury sliding across a table. Never still, always changing shape.'

'Did anyone feel strongly enough to kill him?' Jack probed gently.

'I don't really know, Mr Lewis,' said Ruth with sound of real puzzlement and uncertainty in her voice. 'He made some of them jealous, and made some of them feel second-rate. But people don't commit murder for those reasons.'

I heard the sound of a tray being placed on a bench. 'Here's the tea,' said the publican's wife. 'But if you're looking at the young men of this town to find your murderer, Mr Lewis, you're looking in entirely the wrong direction.'

'Where should I be looking?'

There was a pause before she replied, 'If I tell you, you'll only laugh at me.'

As cups and saucers clinked Jack replied, 'I promise to take whatever you tell me entirely seriously.'

Annie Jones seemed to think about this, and then she said, 'Some of us know of the dangers that lurk in the darkness. Some of us have second sight.'

Ruth Jarvis interrupted to say, 'Annie's wonderful, Mr Lewis. The things she sees, the things she can tell us from the cards. I wouldn't have believed it myself, but she's done the cards for me, and what she told me was so right it sent a shiver down my spine.'

'Carry on, Mrs Jones,' Jack encouraged.

'Well—I'll tell you then. Some eighty years ago there was a murder in that building, the one the bank's in now. A horrible murder it was, more like butchery than plain killing. Then the victim was buried in a shallow grave in the cellar of the house. That sort of violence and horror creates psychic shock waves that imprint themselves on their surroundings. That's why houses, and other places, are haunted. The murdered man was a footman named Boris.'

She paused for dramatic effect then went on, 'He's been seen in that cellar repeatedly these eighty or more years. Now that he's finally killed a man, his own spirit may be freed from the place where he was doomed. Violence begets violence, Mr Lewis.'

'I'm sure it often does. But why do you evoke the spirit of this distant murder in this case?'

'Because it explains everything. Oh, I know the details of what happened that day. Everyone in town does. In a town as small as this, a police constable tells a friend and before you can say Jack Robinson everyone knows. Franklin Grimm was alone in that cellar. You and your friends and Ruth were in the bank, watching the cellar door—and no one went in or out. Mr Ravenswood was locked in the vault behind six inches of steel. He was trapped. And there's no other way in or out—'

'And Franklin wouldn't take his own life, Mr Lewis, truly he wouldn't,' Ruth Jarvis interrupted.

'Ruth's quite right,' agreed Annie Jones. 'Franklin was the last sort of young man to take his own life. Trust me, Mr Lewis, it was a phantom hand and a spectral blade that took his life that day.'

At that moment the loud clump of size twelve boots on the pub floor announced the arrival of Constable Dixon. His face looked more than ever like a lump of puffy dough waiting to go into the oven. The addition of his moustache made him look like a lump of dough with a black caterpillar crawling across it. He informed us that our presence was required at a coronial inquest due to begin in ten minutes.

Then, with a loud wheeze that sounded like air slowly escaping from a deflating balloon, he complained, 'You gentlemen knew the time of the inquest—you could have gone on your own, you know. Instead I've had two different inspectors barking at me to run and fetch you.'

'Just relax, old chap,' chuckled Warnie, slapping him on the shoulder. 'We're obeying orders and quite prepared to be marched under your eagle eye to the scene of the inquest.'

Five minutes later we were back in the church hall for the second inquest in Market Plumpton in two days. The excitement was almost too much for the inhabitants of the town, who once again packed the hall. And once again Harvey Brewer was sitting at a table at the front, shuffling papers, making notes and looking important.

All the seats in the hall were taken and we had to stand halfway down on one side. We chose a spot near an open window because the combination of the warm weather and the sardine-squeeze of human bodies made the atmosphere in the hall stifling. And with all those neighbours loudly gossiping and speculating to each other, the noise was deafening. Until, that is, Mr Harvey Brewer, annoyed that his polite pen tapping for attention was going unheard, rose to his feet and called for silence.

A slightly embarrassed hush settled over the crowd as the coroner resumed his seat.

'This is a coronial inquiry,' he announced after a suitable delay to re-establish his dignity and his command of the situation, 'into the death of Mr Nicholas Proudfoot of this parish.'

Then he went through the process of empanelling a coronial jury, but this time the process was swift, and the assembled jury was almost identical to the one of the day before.

The first witness to be called was our old friend Constable William Dixon, who gave an account of the finding of the body. I rather expected one of us to be called to verify his narrative, but it seemed that this time our testimony was not going to be required.

Inspector Gideon Crispin of Scotland Yard was called next to give evidence of the recovery of the body from the river, and the state of the body when found. He also gave evidence concerning the discovery of a suitcase filled with stones in, as he put it, 'close proximity to the deceased'. This caused a rumble of low murmurs amongst the crowd, although it can hardly have been news to them, given the efficient gossip mechanism of small towns.

Harvey Brewer rapped the table sharply with this pen and the murmurs settled into silence. Inspector Crispin completed his evidence and was excused.

The next witness called was the police surgeon, Dr Stanley Haydock. He gave the cause of death as drowning, explaining the quantity of water found in the lungs, but went on to describe the signs of a blow to the back of the head.

'Would the blow have been sufficient to render the victim unconscious?'

'Almost certainly.'

'So if the victim entered the water in an unconscious state . . .'

'. . . that would certainly be sufficient to explain the drowning.'

The doctor was excused and the coroner called loudly for Mrs Amelia Proudfoot. His voice echoed around the hall and died away in silence. Inspector Crispin rose to his feet to explain that Mrs Proudfoot appeared to no longer be in the district and that police had been unable to find her. I felt like raising my hand to say, 'We also went looking for her, and we couldn't find her either.' But I was not foolish enough to actually do it.

Crispin remained on his feet to ask the coroner to adjourn the inquest while 'police pursue several lines of inquiry'.

Mr Brewer rapped the table sharply and announced that the inquest was adjourned *sine die*. Then he gathered up his papers and left. The crowd exploded in speculative conversation as they slowly rose and made their way out of the hall. We trailed along behind them. Like dolphins plunging through the wake of a large ship, we were carried along by the human waves of the town's population.

We left the church hall and entered the town square in silence. Jack appeared to be buried deep in thought. I was wondering what it was he was wondering about when I felt a sharp jab in the ribs from Warnie.

'I say, old chap,' he said, 'take a look at that.'

Following his pointing finger, I saw Edmund Ravenswood on the far side of the square, dragging his clearly unwilling wife in the direction of the bank.

He had a firm grip on her arm and, being a small woman, she was finding it impossible to resist.

'Ugly scene,' muttered Warnie. 'I don't like the look of that.'

'I quite agree with you, sir,' said Constable Dixon who had, by this time, caught up with us. 'But my instructions are never to interfere with a domestic unless specifically summoned to do so.'

Edmund Ravenswood fumbled with his keys, got the bank door open, dragged his wife inside and slammed the door closed behind them.

'What was going on there?' I asked.

'He was taking her back home,' replied the policeman.

'Back home from where?'

Constable Dixon repeated the information Merrivale had given us the day before—namely, that they, meaning the police, had been keeping an eye on 'everyone involved in this case' and so they were aware that Mrs Ravenswood had fled from the marital home and from her unhappy marriage.

'Fled?' I asked. 'Where to?'

'The constable keeping an eye on her said she went to Mrs Brompton's boarding house.'

'And now she's been dragged back home again,' said Jack. 'So how did that happen?'

'I have no idea, gentlemen,' said the beefy constable at our side. 'No idea at all.'

'Well, let's find out,' said Jack decisively as if he had suddenly been seized by an idea. 'Where is this Mrs Brompton's boarding house?'

Dixon pointed to the far side of the square. 'Just up Holland Lane,' he said. 'The first corner on the right.'

'That's where we're going then,' said Jack. 'Are you coming with us, constable?'

The question brought a doubtful expression to Dixon's face. 'I think I should go back to the station and report in.'

So he left us, and we headed off in the opposite direction—across the square and down the narrow thoroughfare signposted as Holland Lane. We found the boarding house without difficulty, entered the small hallway and rang the bell.

A few moments later a tall, broad-shouldered, stern-faced woman appeared.

In response to Jack's question she identified herself as the Mrs Brompton who ran the boarding house. When Jack said we'd come because we were concerned for Mrs Edith Ravenswood, she responded warmly, 'I'm glad someone is. I'm afraid I did the wrong thing by that poor woman.'

'In what way?' Jack asked.

'She came here, with a suitcase, late yesterday. She told me the sad story of her unhappy marriage breaking down and asked to stay here for the time being. Well, of course I said yes at once. This morning she broke the news to me that she hadn't actually got any money at the moment—any money at all. She said she was expecting an inheritance, but for the time being could I be patient and wait for payment? Well, that bothered me. I run a business here. I can't afford to keep non-paying guests. So I decided to telephone her husband. I thought he'd have the decency to pay her bills until her inheritance came through.'

'But it didn't work out that way?'

'The man's a brute. He came charging into this house demanding to know where his wife's room was. I found him very threatening so I had to tell him which room she was in. Then there was a lot of shouting upstairs. Then he was dragging her downstairs and out the front door. He shouted as he left that I should pack her suitcase and send it across to the bank. I've done the wrong thing, haven't I?'

TWENTY-SIX

~

Dinner that night was roast beef with Yorkshire pudding. After the table had been cleared we three sat around the fire in the snug, each nursing a glass of port and each puzzling over a solution to what Warnie was now calling 'the mystery of the corpse in the cellar'. Clearly he has read too many of those yellow-jacketed detective novels.

'The only question that matters in the end,' Warnie was saying as his conclusion to a long summary of the case, 'is how the blighter got in.'

'What blighter? Got in where?' I asked, not having paid very close attention to his monologue.

'The murderer, you chump,' replied Warnie with a grunt. Jack passed me a bowl of nuts, and as I chose a few Warnie rose and wandered over to the window of the pub. He was clearly restless tonight. He flicked open the curtains and looked out into the street.

'Is there a uniformed watchman on duty, keeping an eye on us?' asked Jack.

Warnie looked up and down the street. 'Not yet. Perhaps he's on a late shift.'

He came back to the fire, took a fistful of nuts and finished his port. 'We shouldn't be sitting here,' he complained. 'We should be up and doing. We should be conducting our own investigation the way we'd planned. In those books I read, it's never the Scotland Yard man who solves the case, it's always the amateur.'

'Unless it's Inspector French,' chuckled Jack.

'Ah, yes, of course,' said Warnie. 'I'd forgotten that you read one of my Freeman Wills Crofts novels a few months ago. Yes, of course, French always solves the most baffling mysteries and gets his man. Usually involves breaking alibis: looking at train timetables and how long it takes to bicycle from point A to point B—that sort of thing. But in most of these detective novels it's the amateurs, Lord Peter Wimsey or Albert Campion, who solve the thing while the police are still scratching their heads.'

'Who do you want us to be, Wimsey or Campion?' Jack asked with a smile.

'I want you to be Jack Lewis, the man with a brain the size of Scotland, who solves the case and gets us back to our walking holiday.'

'Very well,' said Jack as he cracked an almond shell, 'what do you have in mind?'

'It's a fine night out there. The clouds have broken up, the moonlight is flooding the streets, let's get out and snoop around that bank building. There must be some other way into that cellar—there's no other possible explanation.'

'Why not?' said Jack with a cheerful grin on his ruddy face.

'Why not indeed!' I added. Now that I'd recovered from my bootless investigations in Plumpton-on-Sea, I was ready to play the bloodhound once more.

Warnie grinned widely at our enthusiastic response to his plan and led the way to the front door of the pub. The locals in the front bar parlour paid us little attention. By now they were used to us and we'd become part of the scenery. Out in the street I found the wind a little chilly. Fortunately I still had my scarf in my coat pocket, so I pulled it out and wound it warmly around my throat. Jack buttoned up his tweed jacket. Warnie never seemed to feel the cold.

With hands thrust into pockets we walked briskly down the street. The pale moonlight made the black shadows and the edges of the buildings stand out sharply and clearly. The town square was a pool of moonlight, dotted at sparse intervals with street lamps that gave out only a pale yellow glow, creating dim splashes of buttery light in the moon-blue landscape.

Somewhere in the distance an owl hooted. Looking up I saw a black shape flit across the night stars—a shape that I was certain was a bat.

On the edge of the town square we stood in the shadow of a shopfront and surveyed the scene. It was silent and deserted. A few dead leaves were picked up by the night breeze and pushed over the cobblestones in limp, lazy swirls. A black cat leaped silently from the top of a brick wall and then walked across the centre of the square, tail held high, the lordly owner of all it surveyed. A moment later it vanished silently into the inky blackness of a moon shadow.

The ground floor of the bank building was plunged in darkness. On the floor above only a single light showed through drawn curtains.

'That'll be the bedroom,' muttered Warnie, 'where poor Mrs Ravenswood is trapped with that brute of a husband of hers.'

'Presumably that means,' added Jack, 'that they are too preoccupied to notice visitors snooping around their building.'

We didn't go directly across the square but walked around the edges, keeping mostly to the shadows of the buildings and avoiding the pools of dim light surrounding the street lamps.

Soon we were standing in front of the bank in a shadow blacker than ink.

'This is where we start,' said Jack in a whisper. 'What do we look for, Warnie old chap? You're the expert on amateur detectives—point us in the right direction.'

'We need to look for some way into the basement,' he replied in a murmur so low it was little more than a soft growl. 'There just has to be a way in that we don't know about, or that the police haven't found.'

That seemed highly unlikely to me, but this was Warnie's expedition and I was happy to follow his lead.

'The bank's basement used to be a coal cellar,' said Warnie, 'years ago, when it was a residence. At least, I'm sure someone told us that—when we were told the story of that old murder from years ago. Well, if it was a coal cellar there must have been some sort of opening onto the street for the coal man to make his delivery.' With these words Warnie dug into one of the inside pockets of his coat and, after fishing around for a long time, produced a small electric torch. I never ceased to be amazed at the cornucopia of rubbish that Warnie kept in his bulging coat pockets.

When Warnie turned on the torch it gave a feeble light. Clearly the batteries were on the verge of giving up the ghost.

'At least,' I whispered, 'that light won't give away our presence. Now, where do you suggest we start looking?'

'The footpath,' Warnie hissed back. 'And in the walls. Low down, where the walls meet the ground.'

We searched in silence for the next ten minutes. Jack gently tapped at each paving stone with his walking stick, listening for one that might ring hollow. I crouched down and ran my fingers over the lower bricks of the bank wall and the adjoining paving stones, feeling for some sort of join. Warnie bent close to the ground and ran the pale beam of his torch over every surface. If Constable Dixon or one of his colleagues had come upon us at that moment, they would most probably have found our behaviour highly suspicious.

'Hang on,' I said. 'Didn't one of the police officers tell us that they'd investigated the old coal chute?'

'Just keep looking,' growled Warnie like a bear whose cave was being disturbed. 'I keep telling you—in all those detective novels the police always miss the obvious. It's up to us to find the way into the bank cellar the killer used.' So the search continued.

We eventually decided that the front of the bank was entirely innocent of surreptitious entry points. On one side the bank was attached to the building next to it, but on the other there was a narrow alleyway. We made our way slowly down this passage, continuing our stone-by-stone, surface-by-surface search. Again to no avail.

And that brought us to the back of the bank, which was on a narrow lane. Here, after only a few minutes, our search turned up some results.

Jack's tapping with his walking stick produced a metallic ring rather than the usual concrete thud. Warnie and I hurried to his side.

'It's a metal plate or trap door,' I whispered, 'set into the footpath hard against the back wall of the bank.'

'That's the old coal chute for sure,' hissed Warnie. 'Let me have a closer look.'

But his closer look proved to be deeply disappointing. The door to the old coal chute was bolted closed. Furthermore, the bolts all had layers of rust on them. There was no movement in them at all, and it was clear they had not been unfastened for many years.

'But there must be another way into the bank cellar,' Warnie insisted in a whisper, 'there must be.'

'You may be right,' said Jack quietly, 'but this is not it.'

I stood up to get the cramps out of my thigh muscles and decided I was just about ready to return to the light and the warmth of our pub. In straightening up I bumped against some kind of large metal can, which rocked and rattled and sent a clattering noise echoing down the street and back again. In the hushed night it sounded like a chimneypot crashing through the roof of a glass house.

We all froze where we were, waiting for a light to go on or a window or shutter to open. There was a long silence during which absolutely nothing happened. Eventually we began to breathe a little easier.

'Perhaps they think it's a cat jumping around the rubbish bins,' I whispered hopefully.

'What is it you bumped into?' asked Warnie.

'Actually, it *is* a rubbish bin,' I replied, 'and keep your voice down. They won't think it's a cat if they can hear a conversation.'

'Sorry,' said Warnie, dropping his voice back to a whisper. 'Is it the bank's bin?'

'I think it must be,' I hissed. 'There are two bins here, both next to the back door of the bank, so they must both belong to the bank.'

'That's gives me an idea,' said Warnie, a gleeful note in his hushed voice. My heart sank as he continued, 'In an American detective story I read recently, by that Erle Stanley Gardner chappie, he was saying that good detectives always search through rubbish bins. There can be important clues in rubbish bins. Or trash cans as they call them in America.'

'All right then, Warnie,' said Jack good-naturedly, 'ease the lids off quietly and shine your torch inside.'

I did the easing and Warnie did the shining. The first bin was full of kitchen scraps, and the second was filled with paper—the contents, it seemed to me, of the bank's waste paper baskets.

'Anything of interest?' I asked.

Warnie ignored the kitchen scraps and rummaged around in the bin full of paper.

'Can't see anything,' he grumbled. 'Mind you, banks never throw out important papers. They either burn them or store them for years and years. Hello—what's this then?'

From under several layers of paper Warnie fished out an oily rag. It didn't look very exciting to me. He unwrapped the rag to reveal an oil-covered screwdriver. He studied it closely by the dim light of his torch.

'Perfectly good screwdriver,' he said. 'Nothing wrong with it. Just needs cleaning up a bit, that's all. Hate seeing things wasted like that.' He wrapped the screwdriver back into its oily rag and thrust it deep into one of his capacious coat pockets.

'Now,' I insisted, 'let's get back to a nice warm room at the pub.'

TWENTY-SEVEN

~

Later that night we were gathered again around the blazing fire in the snug at *The Boar's Head.*

As Warnie walked in from the bar carrying a tray containing a brandy and soda for each of us, he said, 'Bit of a blow that, eh? I was just wasting your time. Sorry about that—I thought we might find something that had been overlooked.'

'My dear chap,' Jack exclaimed, 'that was well worthwhile. Viewing the scene and exploring the possibilities is always worthwhile.'

'Oh, really?' grunted Warnie, looking quite chuffed. 'Well, that's all right then.' He sipped his brandy and soda and then said, 'And I know what you two are about to do: start that argument of yours all over again. So if you don't mind I think I'll join those jolly chaps in the front bar parlour. Might have a game of darts while I'm at it. I'll leave you two to argue about the meaning of life in peace.'

'It's a discussion, not an argument,' I started to say, but by then Warnie's back was disappearing through the doorway.

'Well now, young Morris—where were we up to?' asked Jack with relish, clearly savouring the prospect of another battle of wits.

'Actually, since our last discussion I've come to the conclusion that this debate can't possibly ever get us anywhere.'

Disappointment showed on the face of the happy warrior as he asked me why.

'What I've realised, more clearly and firmly than ever before,' I replied, 'is that I'm just not religious. I don't have a religious bone in my body.'

At these words he brightened up again and with a broad smile said, 'Is that all? Because I'd have to say that on the whole that's a good thing.'

'Now you've got me confused. I thought you were trying to persuade me to be religious.'

'Well, of course, that all depends on what you mean by the word "religion",' said Jack with a sly grin, and I knew I was in for one of his famous word games.

'Go on,' I said like a chess player tentatively moving his knight into a possibly exposed position.

'In one sense of the word everyone is religious—even the most chest-beating atheist.'

'Even Bertrand Russell?'

'Even Russell.'

This was a bold attack on my flank that I hadn't expected and didn't understand.

'Since what you say seems to be patently absurd, I'm sure you'll have a good explanation.'

Jack's smile widened as he said, 'There is some dispute over the origin of the English word "religion", but nowadays most philologists suggest that it comes from the Latin *religare*—which you'll remember means "to bind". Our word "ligature" comes from a related source word, and, of course, a ligature is a binding. So if, as it seems, "religion" means "that which binds" then everyone is religious, because everyone has something that they are bound to—or something which binds them.'

'What's Bertrand Russell's religion then?'

'That I couldn't possibly answer. For a start he belongs to the other university, so I don't know the man personally. And I haven't read enough of his writings to know what opinions he feels tied to—feels bound to defend no matter what. Of course, for some people their "religion" (that to which they are bound hand and foot) is their own pleasure, or their career, or some particular task. But feeling bound and committed to something is part of human nature. So in that "binding" sense, everyone has something that could be called their "religion".'

I leaned forward and said, 'You'll notice that I'm squinting here, trying to get a good look at these fine philosophical hairs you're splitting.'

Jack laughed heartily. 'And if you're telling me that etymology is not meaning you're quite right. So looking at the word "religion" as it's most commonly used in our world today, it seems to me that God is not religious.'

This was another bold move, as if he was trying to leap across the board and capture my queen. 'Hold on, that's a step too far for me. Back up several paces and explain that one.'

'You'll understand that since, reluctantly, abandoning my atheistic dogmas and becoming a Christian I've been reading my Bible assiduously. And from my reading it seems to me that what God cares about is not religion—if by religion we mean things like membership of this or that body, attendance at services, rituals and routines and the like. It strikes me that much of what we label "religion" these days consists of things the Bible would have called "idolatry". Again and again God seems to tell his people that an empty show of ritual is not what pleases him. It's matters of the heart that please him, not belonging to the "religious club" or taking part in this or that service or act of worship or ritual.'

'Well, if God's not religious, what is he? What is it he really wants from us?'

'It seems to me that what God cares about is relationship, not religion. His goal is not that you become religious, but that you have a personal relationship with him. Remember when Jesus was asked to summarise God's requirements of us he said they could be boiled down to just two commandments. The first was to love God with all our heart and mind and soul and strength, and the second was to love our neighbour as ourselves. Now, what are those two commandments about? Surely both are about relationships. The first says: here's how to relate to God. And the second says: here's how to relate to each other.'

'So if I am sincere in pursuing an appropriate relationship with God, that will put me right—even if I dodge all the hymn singing and organ music and lighting candles and stained-glass windows?'

'There is, in a sense, only one requirement, young Morris: that you pursue a relationship with God in the way that God requires and the way that God makes possible.'

At that moment Warnie sailed back in through the door carefully balancing a fresh brandy and soda in his hand. He saw our heads together and Jack's eyes sparkling with battle and said, 'Ah, you're still at it, I see. Then it's another game of darts for me.' And with those words he disappeared again.

'But what if,' I said, 'I have no interest in pursuing God? What then? It seems to me that I am a strictly secular person. Is there no place for secular folk like me?'

'The notion of being secular doesn't bother me at all,' Jack replied. 'We are all secular, since the word "secular" just means pertaining to this mundane, everyday world around us. My problem is with your expression "strictly secular". That sounds as though you have ruled out a whole region of thought—a whole realm of life. We human beings are made to be amphibians.'

'Amphibians?'

'We have two modes of existence. Just as those creatures we commonly call amphibian can thrive both on land and in the water, so we are designed to thrive in dual environments—both in the secular and the sacred, both in the material and the spiritual. Once you label yourself as "strictly secular" you are narrowing your life down to half of its potential.'

'But if I'm only ever aware of the secular, of the material, what then?'

'Ah, but you see, young Morris, I don't believe that you are. There are those things that lift your heart, that make your spirit soar, that fill you with hope or with longing. In those moments you catch a glimpse of that realm that is beyond the strictly secular and material.'

'Such as?' I asked, not denying his observation because I knew it had a kernel of truth in it.

'When, after a day's hard walking, you get to the peak of a high bluff and look out on beautiful countryside, rolling away to a distant horizon, lit up in brilliant red and gold by a setting sun—the stirring in your spirit cannot be explained as the product merely of photons of light striking the retina at the back of your eye and nothing more. Something else is going on. You should investigate what that something is.'

I sipped my brandy and soda in silence for a moment, then said, 'And if I investigate, what do you imagine I'll discover?'

'Any thoroughgoing and honest investigation will turn up the key that opens this particular door. Namely that Jesus founded a universal faith—not a regional religion.'

This seemed to me to be switching the discussion onto an entirely different track, but I didn't interrupt. I wanted to see where this line of thought was leading.

'There are parts of the world,' Jack said, 'defined both

geographically and ethnically, in which cultural systems are based on Hinduism or Buddhism or Confucianism or what have you. But everywhere the message of Jesus arrives it takes root and flourishes and finds appropriate local cultural expression.'

'And this is because . . .?'

'It's because Christianity doesn't belong to the East, its birthplace, or to Europe, its current stronghold, but to the world. The "coming down" (and I don't mean spatially, of course) of God into human history, into time and space, takes Christianity from the realm of spiritual speculation into the realm of facts and events. It takes it into the realm of reality—and of a reality that is eternally true.'

'Now there I have to challenge you. Truth is more flexible and personal than that. The notion that this or that truth is absolute and eternal is surely nonsensical. There are no such truths.'

'There are, young Morris, truths that are universal. The six times table was true a thousand years ago and it's true today. It's true in England and it's true in Japan—and if we were on the surface of the moon it would be true there. The message about Jesus is like mathematics—universal, eternal truth.'

'A truth that explains what exactly?'

'It explains the other half of existence—the half not covered by words such as "secular" and "material". The parallel here is modern science, in that Christianity exposes the basic principles the world works on. Not, of course, the material and physical principles; rather the metaphysical, supernatural principles. By way of illustration: the formula for water is H_2O in every country, in every culture, in every century. Modern science is a universally true explanation of the material world, as far as it goes. It still has much to discover, and still undoubtedly contains some errors that will one day be corrected. Nonetheless, it serves as a parallel or illustration for the way Christianity is the universal truth about that part of Tom Morris that is more than physical—that part of every human being that is more than physical. It is the necessary explanation, the necessary guide, we all need—and without which we are all lost.'

Just then we heard the sound of raised voices in the front bar and went to investigate. We found an angry, red-faced Edmund Ravenswood leaning over the bar and shouting at our publican, Frank Jones.

'Is she here, Jones?' he demanded. 'Just tell me that. Is she here?'

As he spoke Ravenswood reached out to grab Jones by the shirt collar. The publican stepped back from the grasping hand and bumped heavily against the dark, wooden panelling behind the bar.

'Now just calm down, Mr Ravenswood. There's no call for you to be upset with me.'

'Just answer my question, damn you! Is she here?'

As Jack and I walked into the bar from the snug, Warnie strolled across to the angry bank manager, still clutching several darts, and in his briskest military manner said, 'I take it your wife has left you again, Mr Ravenswood?'

The bank manager spun around on his heels and spluttered, 'What? Well—what has that got to do with you?'

This did not disconcert Warnie, who responded, 'It's a free country, you know. If she's over twenty-one she can do what she likes.'

'Oh no she can't,' growled Ravenswood. 'Not this time she can't. This time she's made herself into a thief. This time she's stolen my wallet.'

Jack actually laughed at this revelation. 'Well, if she has

cash, Ravenswood, I think you'll find she's gone—and this time she'll be out of your reach.'

'She's probably gone back to Mrs What's-her-name's boarding house,' said Warnie, who by now was looming over the fuming bank manager.

'She's not there,' Ravenswood snarled as he lowered his eyes and managed, for a moment at least, to look a little embarrassed. 'I've already looked there.'

'Well, she's not here, sir,' said Frank Jones from behind the bar. 'We only have three guests staying here at the moment—these three gentlemen here.'

Ravenswood looked around, hesitated, then strode angrily out into the night.

'Unpleasant gentleman,' said Warnie mildly. 'I'll have another brandy and soda, please. Anything for you two?'

Jack and I declined a drink. Warnie told the locals in the bar to carry on the darts game without him and walked with us back into the snug.

Seated around the fire I turned to Jack and said, 'Well, what do you make of that?'

'Events seem to be coming to a climax,' said Jack. 'I think perhaps tomorrow morning I should have a talk to our friend Inspector Crispin.'

TWENTY-EIGHT

~

The next morning Jack didn't have to go looking for Inspector Crispin; he came to us. He arrived just as we three were getting stuck into a hearty breakfast, with the bacon and eggs sitting on slabs of hot buttered toast as thick as doorsteps.

'Good morning, gentlemen,' said Crispin. 'I've come to tell you that you're free to leave. We'll detain you in Market Plumpton no longer. Of course, when this matter finally comes to trial, we'll be in touch with you again—I believe we have the contact details for each of you. And you may be called to give evidence at the trial, either by the prosecution or the defence. But that, of course, is still some way off.'

'So you've solved the baffling mystery of the corpse in the cellar?' Warnie said, chuckling with surprise. 'Jolly good for you. I must admit I didn't think you boys from Scotland Yard were up to it. It just shows that the detective novels don't always get it right. So you've solved it, eh? How about that.' Warnie raised his eyebrows and returned to giving his breakfast the serious attention it deserved.

'Are you free to tell us the name of the culprit, inspector?' Jack asked.

'There's no harm in telling you, sir, that we've issued an arrest warrant for Mrs Edith Ravenswood. She being the one who benefits from the death of Franklin Grimm as his next of kin.'

'But she's missing,' I said. 'At least I take it from what Mr Ravenswood said last night that she's missing.'

'Flight is itself often an admission of guilt, sir.'

'Mrs Ravenswood . . . who would have thought?' I gulped, half choking on a mouthful of bacon. 'But I don't understand. She's the last person I would have suspected.'

'It's always the least likely person who turns out to be guilty,' mumbled Warnie. 'Happens all the time in those Agatha Christie books.' Then he paused, a puzzled expression passing over his face, and asked, 'But how on earth did she commit the murder? I mean, how did she get into the cellar unseen to do the killing—and then get out again, still unseen?'

'I'm sure that in due course she'll explain that to us when she's interviewed under caution,' replied the policeman.

By now Jack had finished his breakfast and he rose from his seat. 'Inspector,' he said, 'could you and I have a chat in private please?'

Crispin seemed surprised by this unexpected request, but he replied, amiably enough, 'Certainly, sir, if you wish.'

Jack led him outside to the lawn behind the pub running down to the river. There I could see them through the window, pacing back and forth in the golden morning sunshine. As they walked Jack was speaking, gesturing emphatically with his hands. The inspector was listening politely but seemed to be unpersuaded by whatever it was Jack was saying. Jack would make a point emphatically and Crispin would shake his head slowly. Then Jack left him and dashed back inside.

Coming back to the breakfast table he said, 'Warnie, old chap, do you still have that whatsit that we found in the rubbish bin at the bank last night?'

'The old screwdriver? Safely stowed in my pocket, old chap.'

'May I have it please? I want to show it to the inspector.'

'Certainly,' mumbled Warnie, withdrawing the oily rag from some recess deep within his coat. Jack grabbed it and rushed back outside to continue his conference with the Scotland Yard man.

I resumed my spot at the window, watching the silent pantomime, trying to work out what was going on. First Jack handed over the grimy package to Crispin, then he began making those methodical gestures I've seen him make in a lecture hall at Oxford often enough—the gestures that marked out the stages of a tight, logical argument. Crispin continued to look sceptical.

But after a while there seemed to be a change in the tone of the conversation. Crispin began asking questions, pointing first in one direction and then in the opposite one. Whatever Jack's answers were they must have been satisfactory because before too long the inspector was nodding his head, and the two of them looked more like conspirators than debaters.

The conference drew to a close. Inspector Crispin left through the front door of the pub, and Jack returned to our breakfast table to pour himself another cup of tea and spread another slice of toast with marmalade.

'Well?' I said. 'Are you going to tell us what all that was about?'

'I've managed to get our good friend Crispin thinking down fresh channels,' Jack replied with a sly grin.

'Got him using his little grey cells,' Warnie chuckled, 'as Mrs Christie's little French detective calls them.'

'Belgian,' I said pedantically.

'Who? What?' asked Warnie through a mouthful of toast.

'Hercule Poirot is Belgian, not French,' I explained.

Warnie blinked at me and then said, 'Ah yes, of course.

You're quite right, old chap. Foolish of me.'

Jack swallowed the last of his toast and gulped down the last of his tea. As he rose from the table he said, 'There's something else I've just remembered that I need to explain to the inspector. I'm off to the police station.'

Jack took three steps towards the door with Warnie saying to his retreating figure, 'Are we still free to leave, then?'

'I'm afraid not, old chap,' said Jack turning around. 'And Morris—I have a job for you.'

I nodded, raised my eyebrows and waited for him to explain.

'I want you to find Ruth Jarvis. You'll remember we were told she's staying with her mother. Find the address. Our publican's wife, Annie Jones, should be able to tell you since she and Ruth are cousins.'

'And when I have the address?'

'I want you to pay a call on Ruth Jarvis. See what you can find out about the mortgage taken out by Nicholas Proudfoot. She might have keys and be able to let you into the bank to look at the books. She might even remember something. But ask her—see what you can find out.'

With that he turned on his heels and disappeared rapidly.

I found Annie Jones tidying up behind the bar. In reply to my question she explained that Ruth's mother lived in a cottage on the riverbank, and gave me directions to find it.

I went back to the snug to find that Warnie had spread out *The Times* over the breakfast crumbs and was engrossed in its pages.

'I'm off to carry out Jack's assignment,' I said. 'You coming with me?'

Warnie emerged from his reading to a sufficient level of consciousness to decline the invitation. In fact, he said, he might take his newspaper out into the sunshine for a leisurely read. He toddled off to do this while I headed out of the pub in the direction of the river.

The River Plum wound around half the town. Not far from the railway bridge that connected Market Plumpton with the wider world, I found the towpath and followed it in the direction indicated by Annie Jones's instructions. For the first part of my walk I had the river on my left and the high brick walls of the backs of houses on my right. Steadily the ground on my right, sloping down to the river, got steeper, and instead of houses I was soon brushing past willows and heavy undergrowth. Then I rounded a bend and saw the cottage, sitting almost on its own peninsular with the river waters swirling around.

'That must be very damp,' I thought to myself. 'Can't be at all healthy.'

I knocked on the front door and it was opened by Ruth Jarvis herself.

'Good morning, Ruth,' I said. 'You remember me? Tom Morris.'

She nodded.

'May I come in?'

She was clearly surprised by my visit, but she stood to one side and ushered me into the small, low-beamed thatched cottage. The front door opened into a narrow whitewashed hallway. Ruth led me down this and showed me into a small parlour. It had the air of being a rarely used 'best room'—not used by family but reserved for visitors.

She waved me into an overstuffed armchair and sat down facing me.

'I can't imagine what you want to talk to me about, Mr Morris,' she said.

'I don't know whether you've heard or not,' I began, 'but we three Oxford gentlemen have been making some inquiries of our own into the mysterious and tragic death that we were witnesses to.'

'I've heard,' she said. 'So has everyone in town. You can't keep secrets in Market Plumpton.'

'Well, my friend Mr Lewis is, at this very moment, conferring with Inspector Crispin from Scotland Yard. From that I take it that our private inquiries have become a bit more official. At any rate, Jack—Mr Lewis—has sent me here to ask you some questions.'

'What about?'

'The mortgage held by the bank over Nicholas Proudfoot's farm.'

'I'm not sure I can talk about that, Mr Morris,' said Ruth, looking nervous and chewing her bottom lip. 'After all, it's bank business, and bank business is terribly confidential.'

'But in this case, Ruth,' I persevered, 'there's been a murder. A particularly horrible murder of someone who was dear to you. Surely in this instance . . .'

She still looked doubtful, so I continued, 'And at any rate, the mortgage is now over—Nicholas Proudfoot is also dead and the property has been resumed by the bank. Surely that means that the file is now closed and you're free to talk about it.'

'Yes, I suppose you're right,' she said slowly. 'What do you want to know?'

'Well, Jack wanted to know if you have a key to the bank—if you can let me in to have a look at the books. I assume he wants to know the pattern of payments.'

'We don't need to go to the bank for that, Mr Morris,' she replied. 'It was so unusual I remember quite well.'

I sat back in the big old armchair and rested my head on the antimacassar while Ruth told her story.

'Nicholas was about my age—we were in school together—so

even though the bank's accounts are confidential, and I would never have told anyone, I couldn't help noticing when the mortgage was taken out, and when the payments were made.'

'And was there a pattern to those payments?' I asked.

'At first Nicholas came in once a month, regular as clockwork, and made his payments. He'd spent the money he raised with the mortgage to improve the property—buy new farm machinery and fix the fences. He was pleased as Punch. He seemed to think he'd made a really good investment and the mortgage would be paid off in no time.'

'But this changed?'

'There was a long dry spell, and a very cold winter, so the crops were poor. Everyone in the district was saying that. Then stock prices fell and the farmers were getting less at the farm gate. For those who had no debt it didn't matter much—they just tightened their belts and waited for it to pass. But it was cruel for those who had payments to make.'

'Like Nicholas Proudfoot?'

'Poor Nick. Every time he came into the bank he looked more worried. Then he missed a payment. Then made a late payment. Then missed another one. So Mr Ravenswood summoned him in to call him to account. Everyone in town will tell you how strict Mr Ravenswood is over bank business. He never gives an inch of slack. Not that I can blame him for that. I suppose he has no choice really—he has to answer to the bank's head office.'

'So he made demands on Nicholas Proudfoot?'

'Yes. I remember the day Nick and Amelia came in. They were in Mr Ravenswood's office for such a long time. In the end there were raised voices and a lot of shouting. When they came out, Amelia was in tears and Nick was looking like thunder.'

'So why wasn't the mortgage called in immediately after that meeting?'

'I think Nick must have found another source of income.' Ruth was looking into the distance, as if seeing those past events again.

'What makes you say that?'

'Well, a few days after that awful row, Mr Ravenswood drove out to the farm and spoke to them again. A little while later I noticed in the book that payments were being entered against their mortgage.'

Again Ruth was staring dreamily. Then I realised that she was looking at something over my shoulder. I turned around and the door of the parlour, which had been open a few inches, closed silently as I watched. Someone had been at the door, listening to our conversation. But who? Ruth Jarvis's elderly mother? Perhaps—some old women are inveterate gossips. And if not her, then who?

I tried to muster my thoughts and bring them back to the issue of the Proudfoot mortgage that Jack wanted me to investigate.

'So if the payments were being made,' I said, trying to focus, 'why was Nicholas Proudfoot so angry on that morning when Jack and Warnie and I were in the bank?'

'I don't know,' said Ruth, shaking her head and looking genuinely puzzled. 'Perhaps Nick felt that the bank was bleeding him dry—taking every last penny. I really don't know. But I've never seen him look that furious, not even on the day he had that awful meeting with Mr Ravenswood.'

'Yes, he certainly looked volcanic when we saw him,' I agreed.

I took Ruth over the same ground several times but she was able to add nothing to it. And she kept looking nervously over my shoulder, as if she expected someone to appear in the doorway to the front parlour—someone she'd prefer me not to see.

When she showed me out into the narrow hallway and led me to the front door, I had that uncanny feeling of eyes staring at the back of my neck. I quickly turned around, quickly enough to see a door swinging closed, but not quickly enough to see whoever was behind it.

Well, I thought as I walked back down the towpath, I have some information for Jack—and another little mystery to share with him.

TWENTY-NINE

~

As I may have mentioned before, I have the ability to report conversations verbatim, and this is what I did when I returned to the pub. Jack was already there, having completed his second consultation with Inspector Crispin, and he drank in every word I said eagerly.

We were sitting in the front parlour of *The Boar's Head*. Warnie was smoking a cigarette, Jack was puffing on his pipe and all three of us had a pint of bitter in front of us.

'So how close are you to solving the whole thing?' I asked. 'The puzzle of how Franklin Grimm was killed when he was in the cellar alone, and by whom, and why?'

'I have almost all the pieces in my hand,' said Jack. 'The one missing piece I can guess at—and Inspector Crispin is currently searching for that piece to turn the guess into reality.'

'There you are!' chortled Warnie. 'I knew you'd solve the mystery before the lads from Scotland Yard.'

'Let's not be too hasty, old chap,' Jack said with a hearty laugh. 'I'm sure I have all the pieces; what I have to do now is put them together so they make a complete picture.'

'Oh, I see,' said Warnie, looking a little deflated as he wiped froth off his moustache. 'Rather like a jigsaw puzzle then?'

'Something like that,' Jack agreed.

'And what about us being allowed to leave and get on with our holiday?' I asked.

'Very soon,' said Jack, relighting his pipe, which had gone out. 'In fact, I propose that we take a walk in the countryside now.'

'Anywhere in particular?' Warnie asked.

'Nowhere special,' said Jack. 'I just need fresh air and open countryside to clear out my head and help me see the picture of the crime come together and make a complete pattern.'

'I agree,' I said, rising from my seat. 'We've been sitting around for too long. 'I'll go up to my room and collect my mac and we can get out in the fresh air among the trees and the meadows.'

As I headed for the stairs I was instructed to collect various other items while I was up there. I returned shortly loaded down with coats for Jack and Warnie, along with Jack's hat and walking stick as well as my mac.

Ten minutes later we were heading north out of Market Plumpton, looking for a walking path our friendly publican, Frank Jones, had told us about that would take us to a lookout point above the town. 'You can see the whole district from up there,' he had said. 'It's a real panorama, as pretty as a picture.'

The breeze was gentle and the sun warm, so we carried our coats over our arms. For some considerable distance we walked in silence, both Warnie and I reluctant to interrupt Jack's thinking processes.

At last, I thought, this is what we are supposed to be doing on this holiday—walking through the countryside. In fact, the scenery and the weather were so idyllic that I expected a pneumatic drill to start hammering loudly nearby at any moment. This did not feel like a holiday that had ever been destined to go well.

We left the road and headed across a farmer's field to where a well-worn walking track bordering a dry stone wall led up a gentle slope.

We stopped while Jack turned his back to the breeze to relight his pipe, then said, 'Now we really must reach some sort of conclusion in this debate of ours, young Morris.'

Warnie instantly lost interest and walked on ahead of us. 'We began,' I said, 'with me accusing you of being narrow-minded in claiming not only that Christianity is reasonable, but more than that—that it's the only view of the world that conveys the truth and reality of the cosmos.'

We stopped talking while we clambered over a stile, and then I resumed, 'Well, I still think that. My mind has not been changed by this whole debate. Even if you are right that there is a Mind behind the universe—that is to say, that God exists—how on earth can you claim that Jesus is the only way to know God?'

'Oh, I don't,' said Jack. 'Not for a minute.'

'But . . .'

'I don't make that claim—Jesus does.'

'It doesn't matter who makes the claim,' I protested, 'it's still outrageous.'

'But it does matter,' Jack replied, grinning broadly. 'It makes all the difference in the world. If I'm making that claim then it's my credibility you have to weigh up. But if it's Jesus himself who makes that claim then it's his credibility that's at issue. And that's what the whole question is about: the credibility of Jesus.'

'Does he really make that claim?'

'There is no getting around the fact that Jesus repeatedly, and often, claimed to be the one and only unique way back to God. In various ways, and in different words, Jesus in effect said, "If you know me, you know God." So the question is not what he said but whether you believe what he said. So—do you hold Jesus in that sort of regard? Do you take what he said seriously?'

'Of course,' I said hastily. 'I would never deny that Jesus is one of the great teachers of humanity. He is one of those figures that dominate the landscape of civilisation—along with Socrates, Aristotle, Confucius, Buddha, Shakespeare, Milton, Sir Isaac Newton . . . and countless other important names that don't leap immediately into my head.'

'Ah ha,' said Jack, almost rubbing his hands together with glee—well he would have, had his hands not been wrapped around his walking stick. The path we were on was becoming steeper, and we had to watch where we put our feet. 'So, young Morris, you hold Jesus in that sort of high regard, do you?'

'Most certainly. It's not possible to look at the history of civilisation and not regard Jesus in that way. As you pointed out earlier, and I now agree, it was followers of Jesus who founded hospitals, universities and charities. When they did so they were being faithful to the profoundly civilising influence of his teaching. His great teaching story about the Good Samaritan alone has had an immeasurable influence for good. And, on the other hand, when other people have fought wars in his name, I think it's possible to show that they were departing from his teachings. So I have no hesitation in putting Jesus in that exalted category.'

'Which means you take what he said and what he taught with absolute seriousness?'

'To be consistent, I must,' I admitted.

'Including,' said Jack, grinning at me around the stem of his pipe, 'what he taught about himself?'

'Why not?'

'Well, let me give some words verbatim as spoken by Jesus

about himself: "I am the way, the truth, and the life: no man cometh unto the Father, but by me." And he said: "He that hath seen me hath seen the Father." What do you make of those claims, young Morris?'

I wanted a chance to think about my response, so I shouted out ahead, 'Hey, Warnie—slow down a bit, old chap. Wait for us. Come on, Jack, we should make up a bit of ground.'

With me leading the way we scrambled up a steep incline to find ourselves on the summit of a high, flat-topped hill. All three of us turned around slowly, catching our breath and taking in the magnificent scene. We had a 360-degree view of rolling farm lands, patches of woodland, winding roads, a meandering river glittering in the sun, the arrow-straight iron of the railway tracks, and, in the distance, a glimpse of the sea.

'That must be Plumpton-on-Sea,' I said, 'where I was yesterday.'

'Well,' puffed Warnie, 'Frank Jones promised us what he called a "panorama" and this place certainly delivers.'

'We should have brought a packet of sandwiches and a flask of tea,' I said, 'and we could have sat here and enjoyed the view for hours.'

'I doubt it,' said Jack. 'Look to the north. Those clouds are purple thunderheads, and unless I'm much mistaken the mist below them indicates that they're already breaking into rain.'

'Hmm . . . think you're right, old chap,' grunted Warnie.

'I would guess the rain will be here in perhaps half an hour, so we should start making our way back.'

We all saw the good sense of this remark and set off at once to retrace our steps. This time I was leading the way, followed by Jack with Warnie bringing up the rear.

'Well, come along, Morris,' said Jack good naturedly over my shoulder, 'stop dodging the question and tell what you think about what Jesus—this great moral teacher, as you call him—says about himself.'

'Perhaps he said that sort of thing,' I said hesitantly, 'to impress his first followers. They were primitive people; perhaps he had to say that to hold their attention and get them to remember all he was teaching.'

'In other words, you're calling him a liar. More than that, a deliberate and manipulative liar.'

'Well . . .'

'You see, you can't have it both ways. Jesus can't be both a great moral teacher *and* a deceptive and manipulative liar.'

'Well then,' I mumbled, groping for some other explanation, 'perhaps he was confused about himself. Perhaps, coming from that primitive society, he somehow saw himself as God . . .'

'At any time in history any person who has claimed to be God has been either an arrogant egomaniac—in the vein of the Roman emperors—or a lunatic, someone completely out of touch with reality.'

'Yes, I suppose so,' I admitted reluctantly.

'And the one thing that is clear in reading the contemporary accounts of Jesus is that he was the sanest man who ever lived. No other historical figure was as clear-headed as Jesus.'

'And yet he made the claim?'

'And yet, as you say, he made the claim to be God come among us to restore our broken relationship.'

'Which broken relationship? With who?' I asked, and then quickly corrected myself, 'With whom?'

'Principally with himself—and flowing from that, ultimately, with his creation around us and with each other. Jesus himself summed it up by saying that he "came not to be ministered unto, but to minister, and to give his life a ransom for many". That's the claim Jesus made, and he made it repeatedly.'

'So why did he make it then?'

'Consider this possibility, Morris: he said it because it is true. Everything about his life, his behaviour and his teaching supports his extraordinary claim to be the Mind behind the universe come to this world as a human being. That would put him in a class of his own, quite unlike Socrates, Aristotle, Confucius, Buddha, Shakespeare and all the rest.'

I said nothing in response. My mind was busy chewing over this very different way of looking at Jesus.

Jack continued, 'And he gave a reason for this. He said that he was the only way back to God because he was the only one who would die for us. That, of course, is perfectly true in the sense that Buddha didn't die for you, nor did Confucius, nor did Mohammad, nor did Brahma, nor did anyone—other than Jesus. It was Jesus who died your death, and suffered your punishment and purchased your forgiveness and conquered death on your behalf. That's what Jesus did.'

The conversation stopped while we scrambled over a stile and onto the road leading back into town.

'Let me give you another verbatim quote,' said Jack. 'This one comes from Saint Peter, the fisherman who followed Jesus from the beginning and knew him well. He said, "Christ also hath once suffered for sins, the just for the unjust, that he might bring us to God." '

Jack paused to let this sink in, then resumed, 'This road we're on leads back to Market Plumpton. We know where it goes. I venture to suggest that it's the only road leading from where we are right now into the town we want to get to. There is such a thing as the right road to be on.'

'And we'd better hurry along this one before the rain catches us,' said Warnie.

As we stepped up our walking pace, Jack continued, 'It was once said that all roads lead to Rome. But all roads don't lead back to God. Every road back to God is blocked by human imperfections, by human failures and failings. The only way through, the only road that is open to us, is the way that Jesus cleared the blockages away from by dying. His death opened up that one way back to God. All the roads may lead up the mountainside, but only one of them gets to the top. Jesus is what he claimed to be: the only way back to God.'

The first few spots of rain began to fall, so we pulled on our coats and increased our pace still further.

'So there you are, young Morris,' Jack concluded. 'I've talked for a long time, and I'm keen to hear what you have to say. To borrow an image from Jesus: would you prefer to follow the crowds heading down the broad road, or follow Jesus down the narrow way? Can you look at Jesus and reject him?'

The spots of rain were getting heavier, so I turned up the collar of my mac as I replied, 'No, I can't reject Jesus out of hand. I'll have to think about it. You've given me much to mull over.'

'Come along, you two,' bellowed Warnie, 'this is turning into a real downpour. We need to get a move on.'

We almost ran the last few yards until we reach the Market Plumpton town square and took shelter under a shop awning.

THIRTY

~

We had to wait for the rain to ease before we could make our way back to *The Boar's Head*. For a while it teemed down by the bucket load, and water tumbled in streams over the edge of the shop awning protecting us. But after ten minutes the heavy rain stopped just as abruptly as it had started, so we left our shelter and headed for the pub.

Walking across the town square, Warnie pointed up at the sky and grunted with surprise: the clouds were starting to drift apart and gleams of golden sunlight were breaking through, lighting up the wet world around us and making it shine as if it had recently been spray painted with lacquer, perhaps by a careless painter with excess supplies left over from a recent job.

As we approached the pub we saw Inspector Crispin emerge from the front door and hurry up the street in the direction of the police station. He looked like a man on a mission, and he strode rapidly away before we could get near enough to ask him what could possibly be of such urgent concern.

We carefully wiped our muddy boots on the mud scraper outside the pub, then pushed open the front door and took off our coats.

Frank Jones was behind the bar so Warnie asked him, 'What was our Scotland Yard friend after? Was he looking for us again?'

'Not this time,' replied the publican without looking up from his task of wiping glasses. 'He was asking about Mr Ravenswood from the bank. Apparently that's who he's looking for. He wanted to know if he'd been in again.'

'And had he?' asked Jack. 'Have you seen Ravenswood today?'

'As a matter of fact, I have,' replied Jones. 'The inspector only just missed him. Mr Ravenswood was in here asking about his wife again—had I seen her? That kind of thing.'

'Was he as angry as the last time we saw him?' I asked.

'Not at all. Quite different this time. More worried than angry I'd say. And when I told him his wife wasn't here and we hadn't seen her, he asked for the address of Ruth Jarvis's mother. Apparently he also wants to find Ruth. Perhaps they're about to let him reopen the bank and he needs her back at work.'

'And did you tell him the address of the girl's mother?' asked Jack, an anxious look clouding his face.

'I didn't, but my wife did.'

'How did Ravenswood react?'

'He rushed out. And two minutes later your police inspector friend arrived.'

Jack turned to Warnie and me and said in a quiet, intense voice, 'That stupid girl. If she's done what I think she's done—' He paused and then said, 'No, that's not fair. She's not stupid; she was just trying to help a friend. But they're both in deadly danger. Come along, you two: we have to get there as quickly as we can. Morris, you know the way—you take the lead.'

Urged on by the concern and urgency in Jack's voice, I grabbed my mac from the hook by the door where I'd left it and hurried out into the street. Jack and Warnie were close behind me as I half walked, half ran towards the river.

I heard Warnie ask, 'You said they're both in danger. Who's the "both"? Who's the other person beside Ruth Jarvis?'

Breathlessly Jack replied, 'Young Morris was right when he thought there was someone else staying in the house with Ruth Jarvis—someone other than her old mother, that is. The person who listened to his conversation from behind a half-closed door was Edith Ravenswood.'

'So that's where she's been hiding out all this time?' I puffed over my shoulder. 'And why would either of them—or both of them—be in danger?'

'Less talk and more action, Morris. We need to get there quickly,' said Jack.

Soon we were on the towpath and trotting rapidly in the direction of the white-washed thatched cottage that sat right on the water's edge.

We arrived out of breath and I knocked at the front door. It seemed an eternity before the door was opened and an old lady with a face as crumpled as a crab apple was standing there looking up at me.

'Mrs Jarvis?' I puffed, still trying to catch my breath.

She nodded.

'Is Ruth here?' I asked. Jack stepped onto the doormat beside me and added, 'Ruth and her friend?'

'No, they're not here, dearie. When the rain stopped, the two of them went out for a walk together. Well, they've been stuck indoors for such a long time they needed a breath of fresh air I expect.'

'Which way?' Jack asked.

She nodded with her head as she said, 'That way. Down the towpath.'

We didn't stand on ceremony but hurried off in the direction she'd indicated.

'I just hope we're not too late,' grunted Jack.

We ran in silence for the next few minutes following the

narrow towpath, with the rushing water of the rain-filled Plum River on one side and dripping wet bushes on the other. I had no idea what danger Jack was dreading, but I'd known him long enough to trust his judgement.

After a few breathless minutes we rounded a bend and saw in the distance, two hundred yards ahead of us, a strange spectacle. Edmund Ravenswood was standing on the towpath barring Ruth Jarvis's way. They seemed to be arguing—at least Ravenswood was waving his arms around angrily. Ruth Jarvis was standing her ground and refusing whatever he was demanding.

Then Ravenswood snapped. He grabbed Ruth Jarvis by the throat and started to choke her. Her knees crumpled under the pressure of his strong hands around her neck.

'Hey! Hey!' I yelled. 'Stop! Stop, I say!' Ravenswood appeared not to hear me. I broke into a sprint and ran towards him as fast as I could. As I took off, another figure appeared out of the bushes beside the towpath. It was Edith Ravenswood. She grabbed her husband's arm and tried to pull him away from the girl he was strangling. He turned and struck her a powerful blow across the side of the head. She fell to the path, apparently unconscious.

Ruth Jarvis had sagged into a collapsed heap when Ravenswood had released his grip on her. I was now close enough to make myself heard.

'Stand back!' I yelled angrily. 'Get away from those women!'

Ravenswood looked up, surprised to discover he was no longer alone. But he didn't turn and flee. Instead, his face flushed with blood, he reached into his coat pocket and pulled out a revolver—and pointed it at me.

I threw on the brakes and stopped suddenly in my tracks. But by now I was only a few yards from him, and Jack and Warnie had caught up with me.

'Don't be stupid, Ravenswood,' I said, gasping for breath. 'There are three of us to one of you.'

'But I'm the one with the gun,' he growled.

'I recognise the weapon,' said Warnie quietly over my shoulder in a breathless wheeze. 'Military issue Webley. Must be a souvenir from the war. They do a lot of damage those things. Be careful, young fellow.'

He added those last words because I had started to inch forward towards Ravenswood.

'That's close enough,' snapped Ravenswood, raising the revolver to point at my head.

'It's a Mark IV,' gasped Warnie in a hushed voice, 'a .38 calibre. I wouldn't take him on if I were you, old chap.'

At that moment Ruth Jarvis started to stir and Ravenswood lowered his gun to point it at her. At the same moment he cocked the hammer of the revolver. I seized the chance and lunged forward. Just as quickly Ravenswood raised the gun and fired off a shot that whistled past me. But I had lowered my shoulder into a rugby tackle, and I struck him hard a fraction of a second later.

Then we were on the ground struggling. The revolver had fallen from his fingers and he was scrabbling to reach it while I was trying to pin him down. In a moment I had Warnie on one side and Jack on the other. Jack clamped a firm boot on Ravenswood's shoulder while Warnie stooped and picked up the gun. He carefully released the cocked hammer and put the weapon in his pocket.

'Thank you, gentlemen,' came a shouted voice from somewhere just ahead of us. 'We can take it from here.'

I looked up to see Inspector Crispin and Sergeant Merrivale approaching at a run. Soon the burly Merrivale had pulled Ravenswood to his feet and clapped handcuffs on him.

This done, Inspector Crispin, who was still catching his breath, said, 'Edmund Ravenswood, I arrest you for the murders of Franklin Grimm and Nicholas Proudfoot, and for the attempted murders of Tom Morris . . . and Ruth Jarvis . . . and probably everyone else here at the moment too.'

Then Crispin turned to Warnie and said, 'And I think I'd better take charge of that gun, sir.'

'Huh? Oh, yes, of course. Much better in your hands,' mumbled Warnie, handing over the weapon.

'How are the two women?' asked Jack. But as he spoke he was finding the answer to his own question. He was down on one knee looking at the red marks on the throat of the dazed Ruth Jarvis, then turning to look at Edith Ravenswood beside him, who was groaning and slowly returning to consciousness.

'Why don't we take these two women back to the cottage,' Jack said to Crispin, 'and call for Dr Haydock to take a look at them?'

'That would be for the best, Mr Lewis,' the Scotland Yard man replied. 'If you don't mind looking after that while we take this specimen back to a cell at the police station. Oh, and I'd ask Dr Haydock to take a look at your young friend too.'

Puzzled by this remark, I looked down to the place where the inspector was pointing and saw there was blood on my sleeve, just below the shoulder.

'I don't feel anything,' I said. 'It can't be serious.'

'But you must have it looked at, old chap,' said Warnie as he and I helped Mrs Ravenswood to her feet. She was very unsteady, so we walked on either side of her while Jack helped the badly shaken Ruth Jarvis.

We were a slow procession and it took us a while to get back to their cottage. Once there, old Mrs Jarvis fussed over the two girls while Jack used the telephone and asked the exchange to connect him with Dr Haydock.

Fifteen minutes later the young women were both much recovered and were sipping the hot tea that Ruth's mother insisted we all needed. And she was quite right. I have never felt the benefit of a cup of hot, sweet tea as much as I felt the benefit of that cup at that moment.

I had taken off my coat and Warnie had expertly tied a clean handkerchief around my wound. After Dr Haydock had taken care of the two girls, he examined it, pronounced it superficial, cleaned it with antiseptic and bandaged it properly.

'How are the two young women?' Jack asked.

'Suffering from shock more than anything else,' said the doctor. 'Ruth's throat will be sore for a day or two, but there seems to be no serious damage. Edith will have a massive bruise for a while, but nothing's been broken. What I prescribe for both of them is bed rest, and time for their shattered nerves to recover. I'll leave a sleeping draft with Mrs Jarvis to ensure both girls get a good night's sleep.'

We left the doctor and the old lady fussing over the young women and made our way slowly back to *The Boar's Head*.

'Well,' said Warnie over and over again, shaking his head in disbelief. 'Well, well, who would have thought? The local bank manager, a homicidal maniac.'

'There was no mania in what he did, old chap,' said Jack. 'It was all very calculated and coldly planned. As his plans came unstuck, he obviously lost his grip and began to panic. But from the beginning it was very cold blooded.'

'I don't understand,' I said. 'None of it makes sense to me. Why did he do these things? And how did he do them?'

'We'll get you back to the pub,' Jack said, 'and get a brandy inside you, and I'll explain everything.'

We walked a moment in silence, and then Jack patted me on my uninjured shoulder and said, 'By the way, young Morris—you did very well back there.'

THIRTY-ONE

~

As it turned out, Jack refused to explain anything until we all had a brandy in our hands and were gathered around the fire in the bar parlour at *The Boar's Head*. Warnie and I had gone straight back to the pub, but Jack had called into the police station to have a long chat with Inspector Crispin. Then he joined us and we settled into comfortable chairs in the parlour.

'Come along, old chap,' said Warnie after taking a sip of brandy and licking his lips with a satisfied smile. 'Time for you to reveal all. Start with the clues. That's what that Poirot chappie always does in Mrs Christie's stories—he starts by explaining the clues.'

Jack grinned indulgently at this brother and then said, 'The first real clue that pointed me in the right direction was that suitcase filled with rocks found in the riverbed at the place where Nicholas Proudfoot died.'

'That's right! That's the way it's done,' grunted Warnie with satisfaction, 'surprise us with unlikely clues before you dazzle us with your logical thinking.'

'I promise you I'm attempting nothing of the sort,' Jack insisted. 'I'm just taking you through the chain of reasoning that I followed.'

'So what did a suitcase filled with rocks tell you?' I asked, anxious to start seeing some light in the darkness.

'Who would fill a suitcase with rocks and throw it into a river? By itself it's a nonsense. But then we found the remains of a piece of rope tied to the tree that overhangs the bridge at that place. Now suppose the two were connected. As soon as you start imagining that, you'll find yourself picturing a weapon.'

'Got it!' I said. 'A suitcase filled with rocks swung from a rope to knock Nicholas Proudfoot off his farm cart and into that swift-flowing river.'

'Exactly,' said Jack. 'And remember two other things. First, that everyone around here seems to have known that Proudfoot couldn't swim, and second, that our murderer is a middle-aged bank manager who would undoubtedly have come off second best in any direct physical confrontation with a strong, fit young farmer.'

'But why would Ravenswood want to murder young Proudfoot?' asked Warnie.

'We'll get to that in a moment,' said Jack. 'The question of motive had me baffled for a good while, but I eventually put the pieces together and guessed at the solution. At the police station a moment ago Inspector Crispin was kind enough to tell me that he now has the necessary testimony to show that my guess was correct.'

'But the killing of Proudfoot was the second murder,' I interrupted. 'It's the first one that makes no sense: Franklin Grimm, alone in the cellar of the bank. And we know from our own observations that no one went in and no one came out.'

'Warnie found me the weapon—and when he did that it confirmed everything I'd been thinking up until that point. Once I held that weapon in my hand, I saw that there was only one way that murder could have been committed and, in consequence, only one person who could have committed it.'

'What weapon?' I asked.

'The oily screwdriver Warnie found in the rubbish bin at the back of the bank.'

'That was the murder weapon?' I mumbled. 'I still don't understand who or how.'

'Well, we know *who* now that Ravenswood has been charged with that murder,' said Warnie. 'But it still beats me. In fact, it's more like a story by that John Dickson Carr chappie. You know the sort of thing: locked room, no way in, no way out, impossible crime.'

'You're quite right,' Jack agreed. 'It does look like that. It fact, it looks rather like a magic trick. And that's because there is a trick to it. What all magicians do is distract our attention. Circumstances conspired to do that in this case. We were looking at the wrong thing and thinking the wrong way.'

'Ravenswood,' I protested, 'was behind a locked vault door—a heavy steel door with a double combination lock and two big locking levers—when the murder was committed. An expert had to come from the bank head office to get that vault door open.'

'Exactly!' said Jack triumphantly. 'That's the illusion.'

'It's not an illusion,' I complained. 'That vault door was really locked. Franklin Grimm himself checked and doubled checked it. When the head office man arrived he checked it. It was securely locked, with the locking mechanism firmly in place, and the combination was needed to open it. We couldn't get it open without the combination—which none of us had.'

'Exactly!' Jack repeated. 'That's the circumstance that created the illusion. Tell me, young Morris: what are vault doors, or safe doors, designed to do?'

'To keep things safe,' I suggested warily, suspecting I was walking into a trap. 'To stop thieves breaking in and taking the valuables in the vault.'

'In other words, vaults doors are designed to be impossible to break into—not break out of. The door was sealed to us because we were on the outside. But Ravenswood was on the inside, and that's a different proposition altogether. Those combination locks are complicated mechanisms. They must need to be oiled from time to time. They must need to be serviced and checked from time to time. For such purposes there must be a service panel on the *back* of the locking mechanism. And Ravenswood was on the inside looking at the back of the door.'

'Ah, I'm starting to see,' I gasped.

'I'm not,' grumbled Warnie. 'It's still as thick as a pea-soup fog to me.'

'Recall what we were told Ravenswood was doing in the bank. Do you remember?' Jack asked.

'I'm afraid not,' murmured Warnie.

'We were told,' Jack continued, 'that Ravenswood was inside the vault carrying out the regular maintenance. We saw for ourselves that there was an electric light inside the vault, and a box of tools. He was there to oil and check the mechanism that worked the combination lock. When he was locked in, all he needed to do was switch on the light in the vault, open up the service panel on the back of the locking mechanism and operate the combination lock from the inside. Remember he was the one man in the Market Plumpton bank who knew the combination.

'The door was impossible to unlock for us on the outside, but for Ravenswood on the inside it was simplicity itself. And that's what he did: he operated that locking mechanism, swung the door open, stepped out into the bank cellar and murdered Franklin Grimm. Then to give himself an alibi he stepped back inside the vault, pulled the door closed, operated the mechanism, again from inside, and waited for the man to come from head office with the combination to “let him out”. We were fooled as if by a magician’s trick: we were looking at a solid steel vault door that was impossible to break into. But Ravenswood was on the inside “breaking out”, as it were—a different story entirely.’

‘Well, blow me down,’ puffed Warnie. ‘How very ingenious. Do you think he planned it like that?’

‘No, but I think he seized an opportunity that presented itself to him.’

‘Why?’ I asked. ‘I still don’t understand why Ravenswood would want to murder Franklin Grimm. Did it have something to do with money?’

‘No. It had something to do with darkness.’

I took another sip of my brandy and soda and waited for Jack to continue. Having left a moment for his mysterious words to hang in the air, he went on.

‘When Ravenswood let himself out of that vault, I believe that was all he thought he was doing—getting out of the vault. Then he saw a heavily built young man sitting in the shadows in the cellar. Remember how dimly lit that cellar was? In the darkness he didn’t recognise Franklin Grimm. He took that shadowy figure to be the young man he *really* wanted to kill. He seized the moment. He seized the opportunity. Using the oily screwdriver in his hand as a blade, he stepped up quickly and quietly from behind the young man and thrust that narrow blade into his victim’s neck. Death, as we know, was almost instantaneous. It was when he saw the victim lying on the cellar floor, in the dim light, that he realised he’d killed the wrong man.’

Jack paused to sip his brandy and then continued, ‘I’ll give him this much: he kept his head and acted swiftly, and cleverly, and decisively. He knew that he had no motive for killing

Grimm so he was unlikely to be a suspect on those grounds. And he could make his appearance of innocence complete by stepping back inside the vault, pulling the door closed, operating the mechanism from within and waiting to be "released". It left us with what looked like an impossible murder—and Ravenswood with what looked like a steel-strong alibi.'

'So who was he trying to kill then?' asked Warnie.

'The man he did kill just a short time later: Nicholas Proudfoot.'

'With the weighted suitcase swung on a length of rope?' I said.

'Exactly,' Jack agreed. 'But all this talking is making me very dry.'

'I'll get another round of drinks,' said Warnie. 'What'll it be?'

'I'll have a pint this time,' said Jack. I asked for the same. Warnie departed and returned a moment later with three pints of bitter. Settled back into our chairs, Jack resumed, 'It was vital to Ravenswood's future that young Proudfoot died.'

Warnie looked at me and I looked at him. 'Now we're both baffled,' I said.

'It all revolved around the mortgage on the Proudfoot farm. That and the character of Edmund Ravenswood are what set this crime in motion,' said Jack.

He paused to sip from his pint and wipe the froth from his upper lip. 'Think about the sequence of events as they were told to us. The first step was Nicholas Proudfoot defaulting on his mortgage payments. Next came the confrontation we've heard about. Proudfoot, and his beautiful young wife Amelia, call to see the bank manager—who refuses to allow them any leeway and warns of impending foreclosure. A short time after that, Ruth Jarvis told us, Ravenswood went out to the farm.

Following that visit she saw in the books that payments had been resumed.'

'We know all this,' mumbled Warnie. 'What I can't see is how it connects to the murder.'

'Just be patient, old chap,' Jack cautioned. 'All will become clear. What I don't know, but the police are currently investigating with the aid of an auditor, is whether those mortgage payments really resumed, or whether Ravenswood only wrote them up is if they had. If it's the second, as I suspect, he was in serious trouble with the law as well as the bank when Nicholas Proudfoot discovered what was going on.'

'What *was* going on?' I asked. 'I'm with Warnie—I still can't see a motive.'

'Besides the mortgage,' Jack continued calmly, 'the other ingredient in this crime was the character of Edmund Ravenswood. He was known as a hard, mean-spirited bank manager, and as a man who made his wife desperately unhappy. When I considered the course of events, I asked myself this: what if the day Ravenswood visited the Proudfoot farm it was not to see Nicholas but to see his beautiful young wife—and to see her alone without her husband being present? What if, at that meeting, he offered to take care of the mortgage if she would make payment "in kind"—if she would give him her favours in return for his making the mortgage problems go away? We now know from Amelia Proudfoot's tearful testimony to the police that this is exactly what happened.'

'The filthy swine,' growled Warnie.

'Indeed,' Jack agreed. 'Ravenswood turns out to be a thoroughly odious man. And once that situation had come into being, all that followed makes sense. Somehow Nicholas Proudfoot became aware of what was happening between his wife and the bank manager. Perhaps he arrived one day in time to see Ravenswood's car driving away. Perhaps his distressed wife broke down and confessed. You can well imagine his anger. In fact, we saw that anger on the morning he burst into the bank and confronted Ravenswood. He also showed astonishing self-control, determined as he was to keep himself out of a police cell and see Ravenswood behind bars. But his self-control broke down at the end of that confrontation and he pushed Ravenswood into the vault and locked the door behind him.'

'Which is where we came in,' said Warnie.

'And I think I understand now,' I said. 'When Ravenswood released himself from the vault, in the way that you explained, he thought he saw Nicholas Proudfoot sitting in the dim light and seized the opportunity to kill him.'

'Precisely—to keep himself out of prison and to keep his career with the bank.'

'Which is why, as soon as possible after this incident, he had to ambush young Proudfoot and kill him by knocking him into the river.'

'Right again.'

'But what happened to Amelia after that?' asked Warnie.

'Somehow Ravenswood persuaded her that the farm would have to be sold to redeem the mortgage immediately, leaving her homeless and penniless. Then he offered to set her up as his "kept woman" nearby on the coast. Terrified, and unable to think clearly, she agreed.'

'She's told the police all this?' I asked.

'She has,' said Jack.

'And she was the woman boarder I failed to see on my visit to Plumpton-on-Sea?'

'I'm afraid she was. But her very insistence, through her landlady, on privacy that amounted to secrecy made me certain it was her.'

'Horrible business,' growled Warnie. 'Indecent business.'

'Tragic,' Jack agreed, 'but the consequence of corrupt human nature unrestrained by Christian civilisation.'

Then Warnie grinned hugely and said, 'At least all the puzzles have been solved. I knew you'd beat the Scotland Yard boys at their own game. I had every confidence in you, Jack.' Warnie turned to me and with a wink said, 'Brain the size of the Albert Hall—you know that, don't you? Now, Jack: I take it we are free to resume our walking holiday?'

'First thing tomorrow morning. We've had enough excitement for one day, and we all need a good night's sleep before we go back on the road.'

I'd been thinking about Warnie's words and said, 'I am impressed. That puzzle looked complicated and impossible to solve, and yet you wrestled with it, Jack, until you found the solution.'

'It's worth wrestling with the big questions of life, young Morris,' said Jack with a cheerful grin. 'And to keep on wrestling until you come to the solution.'

AUTHOR'S NOTE

This adventure in which C. S. Lewis helps to investigate a grisly murder is entirely fictitious. However, Lewis, his brother Warnie and various friends often went on walking holidays of the kind described. A few of those real-life friends are mentioned in the text: J. R. R. Tolkien ('Tollers'), Hugo Dyson and Owen Barfield.

The story is set in 1933, just after the publication of Lewis's first book, *The Pilgrim's Regress*. This was slap bang in the middle of what is often called the Golden Age of Detective Fiction, when great writers such as Agatha Christie, Dorothy L. Sayers, Freeman Wills Crofts, Erle Stanley Gardner and Margery Allingham were plying their trade. Several famous fictional detectives created by these writers are mentioned in the text: Hercule Poirot (Christie), Lord Peter Wimsey (Sayers), Inspector Joseph French (Crofts) and Albert Campion (Allingham). Also mentioned is the American writer John Dickson Carr, whose 1930 book *It Walks by Night* was his first featuring a kind of problem for which he became famous: the locked-room mystery.

There are a handful of other period references in the book:

- Ben Travers (1886–1980) was an English playwright best known for a series of popular farces staged in London in the 1920s and '30s.
- An Aga cooker was a popular brand of stove heated by wood or coal.
- 'Constance Kent and the Road Hill House murder' refers to a notorious 1860s case in Wiltshire, UK, in which a three-year-old boy, Francis Kent, was murdered by his sixteen-year-old half-sister, Constance.
- *The Golden Bough* by Scottish anthropologist James Frazer was a twelve-volume history of human beliefs from primitive magic to modern science. It was highly influential in the early twentieth century.
- The 'interplanetary books' of early British science fiction writer H.G. Wells included *The War of the Worlds* and *The First Men in the Moon*.